The Unfinished Symphony of Love

Liz van Santen

Liz van Santen

This book is a work of fiction. Names, characters,
businesses, organizations, places and events are the
product of the author's imagination. Any resemblance to
actual persons, living or dead, events or locales is entirely
coincidental.

www.BurtonMayersBooks.com

For troubled children, their families, and all who help and support them.

Liz van Santen

ACKNOWLEDGMENTS

Writing the story of *The Unfinished Symphony of Love* has been a long journey, with many ups and downs, and a few twists and turns along the way. It has been one of the most rewarding ventures I have ever undertaken. And I got there! But I could not have done it without the help and support of the following important and wonderful people:

My publisher, Richard Mayers: thank you for believing in me and my story. Working with you has been a rich learning experience, reminding me once again of the true power of words, and the complex challenges of English grammar.

Jo Daley, my dear friend and music buddy: thank you for devoting your time so generously, for challenging me to dig deep into Annie's world, and for your unique creative brilliance. You shine like the brightest star in the sky.

Wendy Spray, my friend and life coach: thank you for your wisdom, empathy and compassion. Your life coaching has been instrumental in encouraging and supporting me through the twists of turns of my story. Without you this book might never have been finished!

Chris Malone, a terrific author in her own right: thank you for your time, boundless energy, expertise and humour. You are an inspiration to me.

My heartfelt thanks to Dave Glanville for your love, patient support, listening ear, and for the copious amounts of coffee you have provided during the writing of this book. You are my life partner and best friend.

My children - Jenny, Joey and Jamie - and my amazing grandchildren. I am very proud of you all. Thank you for encouraging and supporting my creative juices to flow, and for enriching my life in so many ways. I do so love being 'Rockstar Nana Liz!'

In the end, I take full responsibility for any errors found in this book. The faults are all mine.

Liz van Santen

The naked woman's body is a portion of eternity too great

for the eye of man.

William Blake.

PROLOGUE

She lay still and opened her eyes. She often woke up in the middle of the night, this was normal. But something was different. Slowly, she raised her arm from beneath the warm blankets to turn on her bedside lamp and peer at her alarm clock. She sighed: it was only ten past three in the morning. She put out the light, tucked her arm back under the covers, curled her body into a tight ball and listened. Something was not right.

Please stop... not again; please God, not again...

As she became more alert, she realised that she was listening to complete and utter silence. Silence was a rare feature in her life and it hurt her ears. A strange grey light cast eerie shadows which danced across her bedroom wall. Her body stiffened. What was different?

The silence is overpowering, it is deafening...

Overwhelmed, she began to think. She hated thinking; thoughts went round and round in her head, always spiralling into a dark and dangerous place. It was going to be another long and lonely night.

It is my fault. I cannot tell anyone; I must not tell anyone...

She heard a muffled creak in the roof space just above her bedroom. She wondered what it was so she pulled

1

herself slowly out of bed, draped her long thin floral dressing gown around her shoulders and drew back the curtains. She could not believe the scene that met her eyes. The garden was covered in a thick blanket of snow which glittered in the moonlight. The boughs of the silver birch tree just outside her window were heavy with the burden of newly fallen snow. She took a sharp intake of breath and as she exhaled, the window pane became misty. She tried to wipe the mist away but she realised that the glass on the inside was covered in a thin layer of frost. She dragged her fingernails through the ice and inscribed her name, "Annie" diagonally across the pane.

Annie was seventeen years old and she thought her life was over.

CHAPTER 1

December 1973

Annie stirred, woken by the sound of her father going about his daily routine. Every morning Stan went into the toilet and retched loudly until he was able to dislodge his nightly buildup of phlegm and then spit the large globules into the bowl with a heavy splash. Seconds later, the shrill sound of the alarm cut through the air; it was time to get up and face another day. Drawing back the curtains, her eyes widened; deep snow drifts, moulded by the raging wind, partially obscured the back door and the steely-grey light of the morning sky promised another winter storm. Rummaging through her disorganised chest of drawers, she selected a crumpled pair of faded jeans, a purple T-shirt, and a baggy green jumper. Annie paused to look at her reflection in the mirror; greasy hair fell limply framing her pale gaunt face, and dark shadows surrounded her lifeless eyes; she looked grey.

I can't go on living like this. "Living?" I'm breathing, I'm alive, but I am not, "living."

She called her father Stan, because everyone did. Annie's mother had German ancestry - her great-grandmother came from Berlin - so Annie called her mother, "Mutti" and her late grandmother, "Oma." They lived together in a small end of terrace house in Clanford, an insignificant industrial town in the Midlands.

Some would say Stan was good-looking; tall with a muscular physique, a thick jet-black head of hair, striking green eyes and a deeply lined and weathered face. But he had a fiery temper, often erupting in unexpected and brutal ways, especially after he had been drinking; it didn't take much for him to lose control and when he did, she had learned to hide. But when he was in a good mood, he was a different person altogether, he was considerate and kind. How could he be so angry one minute and yet so loving the next? It was like living with a volcano, and yet, curiously, she loved him. And Annie knew that Stan loved her; deep down she believed that he loved her.

This particular morning she decided it would be wise to stay in her bedroom until he had left for work; she could hear him crashing about in the kitchen making breakfast, and muttering audibly to himself. He was a brilliant mathematician and taught maths at the local secondary modern school but he was disgruntled with his job. He felt that he was far too clever to teach a load of unmotivated, unruly kids, most of whom hated school, hated maths, and hated Stan.

He had a tough upbringing. He was brought up by his mother; his father left home when Stan was very young and he had no memory of him. His mother worked at the local grocery shop by day and struggled to bring in enough money to survive. She used to creep out after Stan went to bed to supplement her earnings by working at the local pub. When times were really hard she supplemented her income further by working into the night providing sexual services for the local men who frequented the pub. Stan knew he was far too young to be left on his own but he didn't tell anyone because he knew they needed the money to eat and have a roof over their head. He truly loved his mother but he didn't see her very much and when he did, she was too exhausted to give Stan much time and attention. He craved her love.

Stan never talked much about his childhood but when he did he was angry and bitter. He believed that his dad left home because he had a sordid affair, although he didn't know this for sure. Stan always told her, 'He just bloody-well buggered off, the old sod.' He was sad for his mother who worked all her life to keep food on the table and then died of cancer when Stan was twenty. Stan believed she was mentally and physically broken and simply lost the will to live. He was brought up in an impoverished home but his teachers at college soon discovered his unusual and exceptional mathematical brilliance. He was socially awkward and had no friends but he had an extraordinary mathematical ability, the likes of which no teacher in his college had ever seen before. His teachers found it challenging to harness and develop his mathematics when he was achieving at a far higher standard than they were. He was a nightmare to teach, but Stan was determined to further his education and, because his options were limited, he studied to become a teacher. The only problem was that he loathed children; in fact Stan hated people, except for his special Annie. But mathematics had become his obsession, his addiction.

Stan was fiercely determined to provide academic opportunities for Annie that he never had. He wanted Annie to become a fine mathematician and so he had paid for her to attend the local prestigious private girls' school but the family sacrificed a lot to afford the fees. There were no luxuries of any sort. Annie strived to make her father proud of her but she had only managed to pass five O levels. She achieved her highest grades in music and art, but Stan was quick to dismiss these as not "proper" subjects. But the most unforgivable thing was that she had failed her maths exam. She was hopeless at maths. The words that he uttered when he read her results would haunt her forever:

"You're a bloody disgrace. I have given you all the privileges I never had, and you Annie, are a dismal failure, nothing but a spoilt brat. You are not fit to be my daughter."

I will never be good enough...

He was well on his way to work by the time Annie came into the kitchen. She sighed with relief and welcomed the peace. Today the house felt cold and Annie shivered. Mutti was still in bed. She crept upstairs to check on her and found her mother curled under her eiderdown with her black curly hair half tucked under the covers. She emanated an earth-shattering snore and then appeared to stop breathing for an interminably long time before taking a huge and laboured intake of breath, and then, much to Annie's relief, she snored once again. Every time she heard this, she thought Mutti was dying. She quietly closed the bedroom door and returned to the kitchen. No wonder Stan slept in the box room. But Annie knew that her parents' problems were much more insidious and frightening than simply about snoring. She thought it best that she left her mother to rest.

Annie picked up a hunk of bread from the bread bin, inhaling the tempting aroma, and then carefully ate a few tiny crumbs from the soft centre, leaving a small irregular hole. Concerned that Stan may notice, she roughly sliced the nibbled end from the rest of the loaf and threw it into the garden for the birds.

She pulled on her old woollen coat, threw her duffle bag over her shoulder, and, as she stepped into the snow, she winced as the cold air seeped into her body and chilled her to the bone. The wind was bitterly cold and the snow was falling thick and fast hitting Annie's face and stinging her cheeks. Everything was silent now except for the odd car that slithered slowly and precariously down the road. Her canvas trainers gave no protection from the ice and snow and her feet were sodden.

Annie's life had changed dramatically since she had left the closeted environment of her private school at sixteen, to attend the local College of Further Education to do a vocational course in childcare. Her school had been a happy safe place, but it had not adequately prepared her for life in the real world. She had left school as a naive innocent young girl, and college was a rude awakening to the harsh reality of life. She felt different, a square peg in a round hole, a misfit…

The grey three-storey CFE building was a prominent feature in the town, an architect's dream, a modern eye-sore. There were usually literally hundreds of bikes stacked randomly in the bike shelter by the side of the main entrance, but today the shelter was half empty; perhaps because some students had wisely decided to take the bus or walk rather than risk their necks on the slippery roads. Or perhaps they had opted to stay at home. Young people congregated in small groups, chattering and laughing, as they waited for the doors to open. As Annie walked further, she noticed a group of students sheltering in the bike shed, pointing at her and sniggering.

'She thinks she's better than us, just cos she went to a posh school. Just listen to that la de da voice will you!'

Another girl that she recognised as Linda, mocked, 'I'm reel-eeeh reel-eeeh sooo much better than yooou…' They all collapsed with laughter as Linda, revelling in all the attention, minced towards Annie, wiggling her hips seductively. 'Golly gosh, I am simply perrrrfect, blah blah, blah…'

'Yeah, but look at her huge coat and baggy clothes, she looks like a walking jumble sale if you ask me!'

'Haha Linda, if you've got it, flaunt it huh?' Losing interest, Mandy turned to another student that Annie didn't recognise. 'You got a fag? Ah, thanks Bri.' She lit up, took a long drag, held her breath and hissed, 'She looks like the bloody bag lady who wanders round town with no-where to go… and, you know what, I reckon she's still a virgin!'

They think I'm posh, I'll change my accent. They think I'm like the "bag lady," I'll change my appearance. They think I'm a virgin, they could never imagine…

'For God's sake, grow up will you!' Annie turned sharply to see her friend, Franky, striding up the path towards them. 'Annie, take no notice, they're just jealous, that's all.'

Without another word, she brusquely propelled Annie by the arm, and together they strode towards the college without a backward glance.

Franky was the only student who had any time for Annie. She liked her, although they were very different. Franky had a well-rounded figure with a large friendly face. She was funny and always seemed full of energy; she never seemed to take anything in life very seriously. She was bright, beautiful - in Annie's eyes anyway - and always excelled at everything she set her mind to. Annie aspired to be as confident, clever and popular as Franky, but she knew it was not to be, it was not in her nature.

Franky put a reassuring arm around Annie's shoulder. 'Rise above them Annie, they're not worth the time of day.' Together they wearily climbed the two communal flights of stairs to room B109 where their course took place, and no more was said about the unfortunate incident.

Nearly three months had passed since early September, when Annie had enrolled on the childcare course. She soon discovered that the general standard of work was less demanding than O levels, and she was able to achieve high marks in her assignments. Recently, however, she felt distracted and unmotivated, and her grades had dipped. She was particularly interested in child development but, even in these lectures, her interest was waning.

My head is all over the place, my brain is scrambled... I must focus...

This morning's health education lecture was a session about conception and childbirth. Miss Lagon, a heavily breasted woman in her early fifties, introduced the lecture with a brief explanation of conception, skilfully and swiftly brushing over any embarrassing detail, before firing up the film projector to present a graphic film about childbirth. The students stared at the screen in hushed silence as a woman screamed out in agony, then a brief respite for heavy breathing, followed by more ear-piercing screams. The tension and the temperature in the room were mounting.

Annie's body stiffened and beads of perspiration started to appear above her top lip. She listened as the midwife tried to give words of comfort; 'Not long now until you meet your baby.' Then screaming and howling, heavy breathing, panting, agonising screams, ear-splitting screams, endless screams. The room was hot and stuffy, Annie's damp clothes clung to her, and she covered her ears to block out the high-pitched ringing in her head. 'Franky, I'm just going to the loo.' She pushed past the other students and staggered to the nearest toilets. Locking herself into the cubicle, she slid down the wall to the floor, forcing her head between her knees. The combination of the horror of childbirth, the sickeningly sweet smell of disinfectant and the rank odour of stale urine was overpowering; she retched into the stained toilet bowl until she had no bile, or strength, left in her body. She huddled into a tight ball for as long as she dared before returning to the lecture room. By then the baby was safely in the arms of her exhausted and dishevelled mother, the students had visibly relaxed, and thankfully no-one seemed to have noticed her absence.

The local Municipal cafe was frequented by many of the students at lunchtime. A selection of unrecognisable lumps of meat bathed in fat were on the menu today. Annie and Franky pulled their wooden trays slowly along the metal runners in front of the unappetising selection of food. Franky chose two slices of belly pork that were completely submerged in a thick layer of congealed fat, and helped herself to a large spoonful of soggy tired-looking chips. Annie always found it challenging to make decisions about what she ate, so she selected the belly pork as well, but with green beans that looked grey, as if they had been boiled to death. They sat together on one of the long benches and Annie watched as her friend tucked into her greasy, fried meal. Annie pushed her food aimlessly around her plate, cutting a pathway through the thick layer of solid white fat.

'Just imagine what this looks like in your stomach…'

'Stop it Annie, you're putting me off my food!' She held

a half-chewed lump of pork in her mouth, and wrinkled her nose. 'Do you know, lots of students here sleep around with anyone they happen to meet, they're not fussy.' She paused. 'It's a bit low if you ask me, they've got the morals of an alley cat. And besides, they might end up with a mighty big dose of the Clap… or, worse still, a baby!'

Annie shrugged her shoulders. 'If they want to sleep around, why shouldn't they? It's a free world, and anyway, it's none of our business.'

Franky, rather taken aback by Annie's dismissive attitude, added, 'But don't you think it's rather cheap and degrading?'

'Who am I to judge? I don't know what to think any more.'

Puzzled by Annie's words and sensing her sadness, Franky tried to lighten an increasingly tense atmosphere. 'And do you know, one of them told me that, if it's your first time, you can't get pregnant? I think some of them might be in for a shock! But actually they are way past their first time anyway, the old slappers.' She paused, suddenly becoming serious. 'But I don't think I'll ever have a baby.'

Annie shoved the pork slice aggressively to the side of her plate.

CHAPTER 2

She threw the window open, the icy blast chilled her body and numbed her mind. A shadowy figure towered in the doorway, silhouetted by the yellowy light from the landing. She cowered, gripping the corner of the sheet, her knuckles turned blue, then yellow, then white. She fought but she was unable to move, she screamed but she uttered no sound, she closed her eyes, but she could see. A weight bore down, flesh to clammy flesh, the stench of his breath hot on her neck. She couldn't breathe. She must surrender. The curtains billowed, the window swung on its hinges. The damage is done.

She ran her hand over the warm crumpled sheet where he had lain. She dug her nails deeply into the inside of her thigh until she drew blood. She felt nothing. Since that fateful day all those years ago, it consumed her with fear, every day, every waking moment. It rarely happened, but when it did, it was always after her parents fought. It was the "not knowing" that was the hardest to bear - always alert: waiting, watching, listening, waiting… She longed to tell someone, anyone, but she had promised to keep silent. He told her that this is what all loving fathers do. He told her not to tell anyone. She believed him, and she obeyed his word.

He loves me. He terrifies me and yet he loves me…

She screwed up her eyes and tried to imagine herself on a long sandy beach, listening to the sound of the waves gently rolling in, something she did to escape reality, but her thoughts quickly returned to the horror of what had just happened. Nothing made any sense.

He is my father, he must be right. This is what Daddy's do… How can I make it go away? Where can I hide? I could run away; I could disappear, I could destroy myself…

As night slowly turned to day, Annie gave up any idea of sleep and slowly dragged herself to the window. The snow was as deep as Annie had ever seen. Large snowflakes continued to fall. Yesterday's muddy footprints had disappeared, replaced by a chaotic trail of paw prints from the next door's cat. The trees were large ghostly shapes in the winter landscape. She dreaded her day ahead, lectures all morning, and trampolining in the afternoon. Gloom descended on her; all she wanted to do was to hide in her bedroom and be on her own to think.

What if Mutti knows? I feel deeply ashamed, if only I could make it all go away. I hate myself, and I would understand if she hated me too. If only I could recapture the special love she had for me when I was a young child. If only I could be someone else. If only…

Mutti became seriously ill and had to undergo brain surgery when Annie was six years old. Miraculously the surgeons managed to save her life; her body recovered, but her personality had changed beyond all recognition. She was no longer the warm loving mother that she once was; she had become cold and detached. Over the years, Annie had seen brief glimpses of how her mother used to be, a warm loving hug or an affectionate remark, and this gave her hope that one day Mutti would fully recover. But recently, Mutti had fallen into a deep depression, and it was becoming obvious to Annie that her behaviour was also fuelled by something else. She wondered whether it was because of the increasingly large cocktail of drugs that Mutti was taking; she often had a glazed expression on her face and a slight slur to her voice. What was making her mother so deeply unhappy? It seemed to Annie that, the more she reached out for love and affection, the more Mutti seemed to retreat into her own world. Annie's biggest fear was that her mother knew what happened in the bedroom in the hours of darkness.

***

The morning passed in a blur. Annie didn't listen to a word of either lecture.

'I'm going to test you on what you learnt this morning,' Franky said, 'you looked like you were a million miles away!'

'I'm just shattered… and the lectures were so boring!'

'Yeah, they were,' Franky conceded. 'But you looked sad and kind of haunted, are you okay?'

'Of course I am.' Quickly changing the subject she added, 'I think trampolining will wake us up!'

All students were offered weekly trampolining and gymnastics classes at the local gymnasium as part of the college drive to promote fitness. This particular afternoon John and Keith, two remarkably unfit-looking gym instructors, greeted the childcare students with the news that, instead of going to the gym, they were going ice-skating. The meadow had been flooded and was now a vast area of frozen fields and, quite by chance, John had discovered a collection of old skates in the storeroom.

When they arrived at the meadow Annie stared in wonder; heavy snow had abated and the ice stretched before her for miles. She laced up her uncomfortable white ice skates and watched as her fellow students took their first tentative steps onto the slippery surface. Some were fairly proficient, but most took a few gangly steps, sliding about like deer on a frozen lake. She wasn't at all surprised to see Franky confidently step onto the ice and gracefully glide away as if she had skated all her life.

Annie slowly and carefully stood up, placed one skate in front of the other, and gradually her skates started to glide. She needed her full concentration to stay upright on her skates and she forgot about everything except developing her new skill. The cold wind froze her jaw and the icy flakes hit her face but Annie felt happy for the first time in many months. In the distance she could just see the council estate where she lived but, at this moment, she felt far removed from her home. She felt free.

If only I could capture the feeling of exhilaration and joy in a bottle and then unleash the magical essence of happiness whenever I feel sad.

All too soon, John and Keith were calling the group together to return to college.

After an exhilarating afternoon, the students piled into the canteen to buy hot drinks and snacks. The room was airless, a cacophony of activity and noise, and condensation poured down the metal-framed windows obliterating the ever-whitening world outside.

How can I be in the midst of a crowd of people, and yet feel so alone?

She watched enviously as people around her ate scrumptious-looking chocolate bars and hugged steaming mugs of milky coffee. *If only I wasn't so fat…* Her body craved the warmth and comfort of food, but her mind was telling her something entirely different.

Annie wasn't fat, she had never been fat, but she believed herself to be.

When Annie arrived home from college that evening, something wasn't right. The kitchen was a mess and dirty dishes were piled high in the sink. Milk was spilt on the sideboard and Stan's half-eaten bowl of cornflakes was sitting just where he had left them that morning. The house was cold and Annie knew something was wrong. She dashed upstairs to find Mutti lying motionless on the bedroom floor, incongruously dressed in flouncy pink pyjamas. Her hands shook uncontrollably as she checked to see whether her mother was still breathing. Mutti's skin was cold with a yellowy pallor and her eyes were rolling in towards the back of her head, she was lifeless. And then Annie saw the empty bottles of pills and a half-drunk bottle of gin and realised with horror what her mother had done. At that moment Annie heard the front door open. 'Stan, call an ambulance, *now*! Mutti's swallowed all her pills.'

After what seemed like an eternity, Stan calmly replied, 'If she wants to die then let her.'

Annie ran downstairs and pleaded with him to dial 999, but he refused. She rushed into the kitchen, filled a large jug with salty water, and staggered back up the stairs, tripping painfully on the top step as she did so. By the time she returned, Mutti was semiconscious. She forced her mother to drink the salty liquid, and then dragged her floppy leaden body to the bathroom. Annie thrust her fingers down her throat and eventually water and a small number of undigested pills gushed out of her open mouth. Mutti gulped, struggling to breathe, and then she wailed. Annie shook her and slapped her to try and keep her awake. She knew it was vital to keep her awake; somewhere in the back of her mind she knew this was important. She then fled downstairs once more and begged her father again to call an ambulance. 'For Christ's sake, Stan, if you can't do it for her, do it for *me*...'

He slowly and deliberately held the phone to his ear and dialled the number of the local GP surgery. The doctor arrived within minutes and, as soon as he had examined Mutti, he called for an ambulance. As they waited for help to arrive, Annie told the doctor what she thought of her father at that moment: she hated him.

Mutti was rushed to the hospital for a stomach pump. Annie was told later that if she had been left for another two hours she would almost certainly have died.

After Mutti had been taken to the hospital, Annie fled to her room. She threw herself onto her bed, put her head in her hands and howled. What would have happened if she had decided to stay at college for longer that day? How could Stan have wanted Mutti to die? How she hated her father for this. Why did Mutti want to end her life? Annie heard Stan leave the house, slamming the door behind him.

She stood up, walked slowly down the stairs and returned to the kitchen. She filled the kettle and waited for it to boil. Longing to find some escape from the horror of what had just happened, she calmly poured the entire boiling contents onto her left hand. The exquisite and extreme physical pain replaced the acute mental agony that Annie felt. It worked.

CHAPTER 3

Mutti returned from hospital listless and vacant. These days she often sat in her armchair staring aimlessly into the distance. Annie yearned for Mutti to find happiness, but she doubted this would ever happen, unless something changed.

How can I protect Mutti and make her better? Think Annie, think…

Christmas was approaching and very early one morning Stan brought home a Christmas tree that he had dug up from neighbouring farmland. He had got up before dawn to procure the tree without the consent of the farmer. He had potted it in a large metal pail and dragged it into the lounge leaving a trail of mud and wet snow behind him. Annie came downstairs and looked at the little tree in disbelief. She had never seen such a beautiful Christmas tree; the branches were evenly spaced and still leaden with snow that had stubbornly stuck to the sharp pine needles. Annie smiled. Perhaps this would be a good Christmas.

'I thought a Christmas tree would make you smile, my beautiful A.'

Annie paused by the front door, before stepping out into the cold.

After college, Annie hurried home to decorate the tree. She rushed upstairs and positioned the rickety wooden ladder against the wall so that she could access the ceiling hatch leading to the attic. Using all her strength, she was able to pull the stiff door open and clamber up into the darkness. She felt around amongst many of the old and musty-smelling family possessions until she was able to locate the familiar basket that contained a small selection of Christmas decorations and the coloured lights. She climbed down the ladder carrying the basket, breathing out a deep sigh of satisfaction.

She crouched by the tree and emptied the contents of the basket onto the floor. Each decoration held a memory for Annie. The little wooden soldier had been given to her by an old school friend when she was six years old. The crumpled fading paper chains were something Annie had made many years before and now they were certainly worse for wear. Then she held the large angel in the palm of her hand, reflecting on the Christmas Story. The angels brought with them a message of hope and joy to the world telling the people of the oncoming birth of Jesus, but for Annie the angel resting in her hand brought back haunting childhood memories. She tried to push her dark thoughts to the back of her mind and focused on untangling the fairy lights, then she plugged them in. *Why do they never work?* Annie thought as she systematically checked each light in turn. She switched them on for a second time and, much to her delight, the multicoloured lights shone in the semi-darkness. The fairy lights symbolised hope and peace for Annie and she sat quietly for a few minutes feeling the gentle warmth of the lights resting between her fingers. She placed the lights carefully on the tree, making sure that they were evenly spaced with a golden bulb placed on the top branch to light up the angel. Annie carefully arranged all the decorations, tinsel and baubles on each branch and finally she reached up very precariously and placed the angel at the very top.

She stood back to admire her handiwork. The decorated tree surmounted by an illuminated golden angel looked truly magical. In some ways, Annie looked forward to Christmas.

When she was young her parents used to fill a stocking full of presents and leave it at the end of her bed early on Christmas morning. She recalled the excitement of rummaging through the contents of her stocking at dawn. Stan always lit the fire on Christmas Day. Annie loved to watch the flames dancing and listen to the crackling sound of the logs as they burned brightly in the fireplace. The open fire always lifted her spirits and warmed her body and she wished Stan lit the fire more than just once a year. The family used to enjoy a traditional turkey roast and plum pudding, but things were different now. Stan and Mutti didn't have money to spend on luxuries, and they no longer had the will to make Christmas into a special day. How Annie wished life could be as good now as it was then.

But perhaps her memory was playing tricks on her - were those earlier Christmases really happy?

A week had passed and the unrelenting winter storms continued. On Christmas morning Annie awoke to the strains of "White Christmas," coming from the radio in the kitchen. She smiled and rushed over to the window. The large icy flakes were still falling and the garden was blanketed in a thick layer of new snow. There was no doubt that this was to be a white Christmas. No stocking lay at the end of her bed but she marvelled at a group of cock pheasants in the garden eating grain that Stan had thrown out for them. The rich golden, red and green colours and the long, exquisite plumes of these majestic birds lifted Annie's spirits; she threw on her clothes and ran downstairs. As she sat at the table in the empty kitchen, she couldn't help but wonder why cock pheasants are so beautifully coloured and yet hen pheasants are plain and brown. Should it not be the other way round? It seemed to her that far too many women feel they *have* to dress up in ridiculously tight clothes, wear high heels and hideous makeup to look attractive, but men didn't seem to make much effort at all. She certainly had no desire to be trussed up in uncomfortable garish clothing, wear war paint, or have to stagger around in ill-fitting high heels. *What is it all about? Is it just to attract a mate?* At that moment, she felt an affinity with the plain brown hen pheasants. She did remind herself, however, that she had read in a recipe book that these birds were generally much plumper and tastier to eat than their spectacular male partners.

Her reverie was rudely interrupted by Stan who lunged awkwardly towards Annie putting his face very close to hers. 'Happy Christmas A!'

Stan rarely called Annie "A" but it was usually when he was in a good mood. Annie felt the small droplets of Stan's saliva as he spat out his festive good cheer and she surreptitiously wiped her face with the back of her hand.

'Merry Christmas Stan.'

Mutti was seated in her large armchair when Annie entered the sitting room. She looked tiny and vulnerable with a colourful crocheted shawl wrapped tightly around her shoulders. She looked up and gave a weak smile. 'Happy Christmas my love.' Mutti was clutching something tightly in her right fist. As Annie moved closer, she whispered, 'This is for you my dearest Annie.' Mutti put her finger conspiratorially over her lips, signalling that this was to be a secret between just the two of them. She slowly uncurled her fingers one at a time to reveal a small rectangular mourning brooch bordered by twelve red garnets contained within claws of gold. Annie looked closely at the brooch and noticed that in the centre there were strands of neatly woven grey and white hair contained behind a glass case. The glass was surrounded by a thin band of gold. Mutti carefully placed the precious item in the palm of Annie's hand, explaining, 'My father commissioned a highly reputable London jeweller to prepare this bespoke brooch when my dear mother passed away many years ago. It is your Oma's plaited hair that you can see behind the glass. My father left the brooch to me when he died and now dear Annie, I would like you to have it. Please would you love and cherish it forever? Will you do that for me Annie?'

Annie held the brooch carefully in two hands appreciating its exquisite beauty as it glittered and shone red and gold. She had no words to express her happiness but she marvelled at Mutti's generosity and hugged her gently. Eventually Annie found her voice and whispered, 'Mutti, I'd love to take care of this beautiful brooch. I will always keep it safe and I thank you with all my heart.'

At that moment Stan stumbled in carrying a large bucket of coal to light the fire. Annie hid the gift behind her back and hurried upstairs to find a safe place for her unexpected Christmas gift. She felt elated but she also felt fearful. Why did Mutti decide to give her this gift now rather than to leave it in her will, as her father had done before her? Why did she not want Stan to know? Perhaps Mutti feared that Stan would want to sell the precious family heirloom and spend the money. Maybe Mutti thought she might die soon. She had already tried to take her own life once and perhaps she was planning to try again. Many thoughts went through Annie's mind but she certainly loved this special piece of jewellery. She tucked the brooch carefully under her pillow and went downstairs to join her parents.

After breakfast, Annie excused herself, threw on her coat, and went for a walk.

Don't think of that fateful day all those years ago; lock those thoughts away...

The snow had eased and there were gaps in the clouds revealing deep blue sky. The low light of winter made long and beautiful shadows and Annie braced herself against the bitter northerly wind. As she passed the church, local people were gathering for the Christmas service. Annie listened to the chattering and laughter and longed to be part of a happy family. She crept into the back of the church and sat quietly on a hard wooden pew, hoping that no-one would notice her. As the congregation started to sing "Once in Royal David's City," Annie's eyes were drawn to the magnificent stained-glass window positioned high above the altar. Thousands of tiny pieces of glass had been crafted together to form a myriad of colours - reds, greens, blues and golds - to display a perfect image of Mary cradling baby Jesus. Annie wondered in which century this window had been created; how did people craft such masterpieces back in history when they must have only had the most basic of tools? The sun illuminated the window and coloured shafts of light shone down on the congregation. Annie could feel the warmth and love radiating between a mother and her child in the image. She reflected on her own relationship with her parents and she felt empty.

She admired the immaculate arrangements of holly wreaths with red berries that surrounded each of the flickering candles on every stone sill. A large, decorated Christmas tree stood at the front of the church and the lights twinkled. There was a deep chill in the church emanating from the cold, damp stone walls but the atmosphere was warm and cheerful. Annie listened with pleasure to her favourite carol, "In the Bleak Midwinter," and then quietly tiptoed out of the church, pausing briefly under the lychgate to appreciate the beautiful snowy scene before her and to enjoy the final strains of her much-loved Christmas hymn. She felt peaceful.

Everything had changed when she arrived home. The fire was still burning in the fireplace but Mutti had the familiar glazed look in her eyes. Her tiny frame almost disappeared into the worn fabric of her chair. Annie crouched beside her, gently shaking her body to try and rouse her. Her mother tilted her head to one side, her eyes were dim and sunken deep into their sockets, and then her tangled matted hair fell across her face as she collapsed forward once again. Stan was banging the pots and pans noisily in the kitchen, muttering to himself as he did so, 'Bloody Christmas, what's the point? I hate it!' He then turned slowly towards Annie with a sickly smile that chilled her to the bone. She felt fearful for Mutti but more fearful for herself. She offered to help Stan, staring at the pale unappetising chicken standing on the sideboard; the thought of eating anything made her feel queasy. As she peeled the potatoes, Annie wondered what was wrong with Mutti; had she taken an overdose again? Fear gripped her and she tried to focus on preparing the potatoes the way Mutti had taught her. She parboiled them, shook them up and then roughly added them to the hot fat sizzling in the roasting tin. As she did so, some fat splashed onto her hand and she felt searing pain. She rushed over to the sink and held her hand under the cold running water until the heat gradually subsided but the parts of her hand were left red and raw and a blister was forming on her thumb. The physical pain brought welcome distraction from the unfolding misery of Christmas Day.

The family sat in sombre silence as they ate their Christmas dinner. It was very rare for her parents to have wine on the table and Annie was surprised how much Chianti her mother drank during the meal. The round bottle was partially covered in a straw basket making it impossible for Annie to see exactly how much of the wine her mother had drunk. She reminded herself that today was Christmas Day, so perhaps it was acceptable for Mutti to have a few glasses of wine.

She looked down in horror at her huge plate of food. There were napkins on the table to mark Christmas as a special day. Stan and Mutti seemed to be preoccupied with their own thoughts so Annie was able to heap small piles of roast dinner onto her fork and then secrete the food, little by little, onto the napkin on her lap. Neither of them noticed, and she felt a quiet glow of satisfaction from her deception. She then folded the napkin under the table, stuffed it in her sleeve and excused herself. As she watched her Christmas dinner being flushed way down the toilet, she felt virtuous and strangely elated.

I don't need food, I just need self-control; I will be strong.

As Annie went to close the curtains early on Christmas evening, she gazed outside as the snow fell thick and fast. The wind was blowing and the snowflakes were forming huge snow drifts, now almost completely concealing the back door. This was indeed a hard winter. Her parents had remained quiet for the rest of the day, and Mutti had slept for hours. Annie had said goodnight and gone to bed, by the time the arguments began. She put her hands over her ears but she could still hear Stan's obscenities and Mutti's slurred words and wailing. She knew what was going to happen next. She felt underneath her pillow for her precious mourning brooch. She hugged it to her chest and then placed it carefully on the floor beneath her bed.

The silence hung in the air, sticky and damp. A foreboding figure loomed out of the darkness. Her body stiffened, her senses alert to every sound, every movement; she was ready. She drew her feet over the satiny edge of her eiderdown, deftly tucking the corner between her toes, meagre comfort. The weight was unbearable; suffocating, intense, airless and angry. A searing pain shot through her. She opened her mouth to scream, silent agony. He swiftly released her from his vice-like grip and paused. 'I'm sorry A.' Then he was gone, but the smell of sex and the stain lingered on her body. The damage is done.

She rubbed her sticky damp hands in her handkerchief and reached down and retrieved her beloved mourning brooch. She held it tightly against her body, and felt deep despair.

He loves me, just remember, he loves me. I must not speak…

CHAPTER 4

Life is simple with a list; it's like a rulebook for life. Rules take away decisions, just do it and then tick it off, simple as that! I am powerful. I am in control.

It was the first day of January 1974, a good day to write a list. She opened the first page of her journal:

1. I will lose two stone by April

2. I will get fit

3. I will look after Mutti and make her happy

4. I will get extra maths tuition.

Annie chewed the end of her pencil as she reflected on her list. She vowed to get fit by going to the local swimming pool three times a week after college. She had saved up enough money to do this, at least for a few weeks. Mutti seemed to be suffering from deep depression and Annie knew that her third point on her list would be more of a challenge. She couldn't control Mutti's emotions and she had no clear plan of how to achieve this. She would spend more time with her and help out more with household tasks. As for maths, Annie desperately wanted to make Stan proud of her, but she knew she was terrible at maths. Her shoulders tensed as she realised that the only aspects of the list that she could be sure of achieving was to lose weight and to get fit, because she could control these aspects of her life.

Annie held her beloved mourning brooch delicately in the palm of her hand and she examined the fine details of the exquisite piece of jewellery. She counted the shining ruby-coloured garnets that were held in place by elegant claws of gold. 'Twelve shining garnets, and there are twelve months in the year.' Suddenly everything became clear. Each red garnet would represent a month of the year, and if she fulfilled the promises she made to herself each month, she would earn herself the right to own this extraordinary piece of jewellery. If she did not, she would return the brooch to Mutti because she would consider herself unworthy. She held the brooch up towards the light and examined the plaited hair in the centre.

I will make Mutti proud of me. I can do this, and I will.

The word "calorie" was not familiar to Annie so she found a large dusty dictionary placed high up on one of the lounge shelves. She turned the thin crisp pages, squinting at the tiny print, until she found what she was looking for:

"Calorie: The energy needed to raise the temperature of 1 kilogram of water through 1 °C, equal to one thousand small calories and often used to measure the energy value of foods."

She read the definition several times before she realised that it made no sense to her whatsoever. She was convinced, however, that if she consumed less calories, she would achieve her goal. She remembered that she had seen a calorie chart in one of Mutti's cookery books in the kitchen. Annie searched until she found the large cookery book entitled, *Cooking for Today*. She leafed through the old and much-loved book, smiling as she noticed that most of the pages were covered with speckled ingredients of past cooking endeavours. She could identify Mutti's favourite recipes from the density of murky brown stains. Annie adored cookery books and she slowly turned the pages, pausing to savour at all the mouth-watering photos of food that she could no longer eat. Then she found the page that she was searching for, entitled "Calories and

Carbohydrates." She scanned the chart, noting all the highly calorific foods which she was determined to eliminate from her diet. She would start immediately.

The winter snows continued and frequent blizzards had become the norm. One morning as Annie arrived at the college gates, she was greeted by Linda, smirking, 'Annie, dare you to come to Paradise Disco with us on Friday night. Go on, dare you, you'll have a great time...' As she walked on, she could hear them mocking her. 'Bet she won't Mand, she's too bloody stuffy for us lot.'

Paradise Disco had a terrible reputation for being a place for young people to gather for casual sex, drink and drugs. The local police were called out on a regular basis to sort out fights and to call ambulances for numerous drunk disco-goers at the end of the night. "Paradise" seemed an ironic name for such a ghastly place. Annie trudged on with a heavy heart. She longed to be accepted by her fellow students, but she knew she was different.

Why do I feel like I come from another planet? They're so confident, so sure of themselves. When I'm slim, maybe I'll be confident too? And then maybe, just maybe, they'll leave me alone.

Annie resolved to go to Paradise Disco.

As Friday evening approached, Annie became fearful. She would have to creep out of the house without Stan or Mutti realising that she was gone. She knew she was underage and probably wouldn't be admitted into the disco anyway and that would be another humiliation. She wished she hadn't agreed to go.

That Friday, in the early evening before the disco was due to begin, Stan and Mutti seemed preoccupied. Stan was seated amidst a sea of marking showing reams of mathematical calculations, and every so often he would show his frustration by angrily screwing up his pupils' work and throwing it into the air, swearing and cursing as he did so. Mutti was curled up in her armchair looking very frail with her eyes closed. Annie thought, with some satisfaction, that they wouldn't notice her absence. She made her excuses to have an early night and neither parent looked up.

She dug deep into her wardrobe and found a purple cord mini skirt which she had purchased in a moment of madness a couple of months before. She teamed it up with a skinny rib brown polo neck, and a pair of tights which she had found in Mutti's chest of drawers - they were bright green but they would have to do. She struggled into Mutti's black high heels and looked at herself in the mirror. It was as if Annie was looking at the image of a different person; she thought she looked even more hideous than she normally did. She crept into Mutti's room and selected some makeup, which she then carefully applied: bright red lipstick, blue eye shadow and, for the finishing touch, she patted her face with horrible-smelling pink powder. She peered into the small mirror inside the powder compact and winced.

I look so cheap, how can I sink this low?

She glanced again at the tall mirror in her bedroom. Her hair was mousy brown, greasy, and hung lifelessly round her face. Her period was due and angry spots had appeared, congregating mainly on her nose, and even the face powder could not conceal them. She squeezed the large spot on her chin and the copious white contents oozed into her handkerchief. The bright green tights seemed to accentuate her heavy shapeless legs and her toes already ached in her agonisingly uncomfortable shoes.

As she crept out of the house, she paused to open the jar in the kitchen where Stan stored his loose change. She emptied it into her handbag, threw on her coat and closed the door quietly behind her.

Linda and Mand, and a couple of other students that Annie didn't recognise, acknowledged Annie, 'You, my darlin' are in for a treat tonight.' Annie wondered if they were already drunk. She was fearful of the girls and acutely aware that she didn't belong; she knew she was different. She limped forlornly behind them, wobbling precariously in her high-heeled shoes. When they arrived at Paradise Disco they were greeted by a huge intimidating man, smartly dressed in a suit and bow tie. He cast his eye lazily over the group, took their money and nodded his approval for them to enter. He didn't seem to notice that they were all underage.

Annie felt overwhelmed. The rhythmic and relentless bass of the deafening electronic music rang in her ears; the strobe lighting flashed continuously, revealing crowds of revellers gyrating on the dance floor. She stood still, realising with rising panic that she was no longer with Linda or Mandy. The bar was crowded with people pushing forward to buy drinks. Everything Annie touched was sticky, the air smells stale and she longed to go home.

'Can I get you a drink?' A rather good-looking dark-skinned man towered over Annie and smiled. Annie felt strangely comforted by his presence and nervously asked for a Snowball. She had no idea what this drink was except that she knew it contained alcohol and she had seen it advertised on the television in a rather exotic seaside location. While she waited for him to return, she smiled with satisfaction.

Well, I can't look too bad if he wants to talk with me.

He returned with two huge yellow frothy drinks. Handing one of the drinks to her, they locked eyes and clinked glasses. He shouted in her ear but the music was deafening. She tried hard to hear what he was saying by trying to read his lips but it was impossible. Instead she drank her Snowball at an alarming rate in order to give her something to do and to hide her embarrassment. The long, sweet drink made her want to gag but when he took her empty glass and offered her a second drink, she nodded her head and wondered again why she had agreed to come to this dive.

Towards the end of the second drink Annie started to feel dizzy and the bright lights started to spin and became a blur. The booming sound of the base resonated in her head and she began to feel very sick. Staggering towards the bathroom, she found it hard to negotiate through the throng of young people, and her legs kept buckling beneath her.

She just made it before heaving violently into the soiled toilet bowl. She obviously wasn't the first to vomit that evening. She found relief and a strange feeling of exhilaration as she emptied her stomach contents. After she retched for the final time, she looked in the mirror with horror at her pale face, dishevelled hair, smudged makeup and the splashes of vomit on her top. She quickly put a brush through her hair, splashed water on her face and rubbed her top to remove the vomit. She did look better than she did a few minutes before but the overwhelming smell of sick hung in the air around her.

After another Snowball the good-looking stranger pulled her across to the dance floor. She watched him with growing admiration as he moved his flexible perfect body in time to the music. Annie loved dancing and felt proud that she was with one of the best-looking men in the club. But suddenly everything became a blur, she felt as if she was falling off a cliff and her body was plummeting to the earth below. She had no control over her limbs and saliva was pouring out of her mouth. The odd thing was that her brain was alert and she was fully aware of what was happening to her. He caught Annie just as she was about to fall and manoeuvred her across the dance floor to a small fire door which opened onto a small outdoor space. She gulped the freezing air and fell into his arms. It was dark and there was no one around. Annie felt completely out of control but felt the warm comfort of the stranger's hand on her arm. She peered into the eyes of her rescuer and she felt his concern and tenderness.

'Are you okay beautiful girl?'

Beautiful girl, who is he talking about?

She felt his strong arms cradling her and warmth radiated through her body, releasing feelings that Annie had never experienced before. But then a vision of Stan flashed before her eyes and she shuddered. 'Get away from me, leave me alone…'

I fight but I can't move, I scream, but no sound comes out…

Then everything went black.

Sometime later Annie stirred, feeling cold, stiff and very sick. The dark-skinned stranger was still cradling her in his arms and she felt acutely embarrassed and deeply ashamed of her behaviour and lack of self-control, but she also felt a strange and inexplicable feeling of contentment.

He gently helped her out of the club and Annie quietly mumbled her address. He escorted her home, supporting her body gently and giving her words of encouragement to put one foot in front of the other in the deep snow. He stopped at the front door and then he strode away without looking back. As Annie crept upstairs unnoticed she realised with great sadness that she didn't even know his name.

CHAPTER 5

Linda and Mandy and their friends seemed to have changed their attitude towards Annie. They didn't know what actually happened at the disco on Friday evening but they noticed her leaving the venue in the arms of a very striking guy and they had just assumed what had happened next. As Annie arrived at college on Monday morning, she overheard them whispering, 'Can't believe it, Annie pulled! She's not too bad, and her bloke is a bit of all right… I wouldn't mind a piece of that!' They didn't ridicule her as they normally did, but instead, gave her admiring glances. Annie acknowledged them with a cheerful wave, and strode forward with renewed confidence and vigour. She smiled wryly as she reflected that she could put on a good show for the outside world.

If only they knew…

Over the next few days Annie thought a lot about her chance encounter at Paradise disco.

"A Chance Encounter in Paradise," now that would be a great name for a novel.

She had regrets about the evening, drinking too much and letting herself down so badly. She couldn't even recall part of the evening and wondered what on earth had happened during this time. She felt deeply ashamed. She didn't even like the taste of Snowball but it had slipped down her throat so easily. Annie's biggest regret was that she didn't ask his name. She would probably never see him again. The irony was that she went to the disco expecting to meet some bad boys and in fact she met someone who she thought might be special and far from bad. She reflected on his tenderness, concern and kindness; Annie had never known anyone to show this much respect for her. But then she began to question whether it had actually happened at all. Why did he choose her? How could anyone call her beautiful?

I told him to go away and leave me alone, when he was only trying to help me. I feel so ashamed. Why didn't I ask his name?

It was Friday morning in mid-January and today was no different from any other day. She lay in bed until she heard Stan throw his breakfast dishes into the sink, grab his bag and coat and run out of the house, shouting incoherent obscenities to nobody in particular before adding, 'See you later my precious Annie.' He banged the door so hard behind him that the whole house reverberated. Now was her chance. Annie quickly got dressed and dashed downstairs. The house was silent. Mutti was still in bed so Annie had time to do what she always did. She cut a thick slice of bread and put it in the toaster and then made herself a cup of black tea. When the kettle boiled she carefully poured the black unappetising liquid into a large mug and cradled it close to her body to warm her freezing extremities. She took a deep breath and savoured the tempting aroma of the toast. Annie allowed herself a moment to imagine that she was sinking her teeth into hot delicious toast dripping with melted butter. But she knew it was "forbidden fruit." She pushed the toast into the bottom of her duffle bag to dispose of later. She poured the crumbs from the bread board onto a plate and put a scraping of butter onto a knife to make it appear as if she had eaten her breakfast. She paused for a moment; she couldn't resist licking the remaining few crumbs left on the bread board until it was licked clean. She walked to college with mixed emotions. Annie hated deceiving Mutti and realised she probably wouldn't notice anyway, but she knew that she had to deny herself food in order to achieve her aim to become thinner and, she believed, more attractive. She didn't even seem to feel hungry.

After an uneventful day at college, followed by a rather cold and lonely swim at the local swimming pool, she arrived home to find the house empty. As she took off her coat, Annie heard a tentative knock at the front door. She wondered if it was yet another "hopeful" trying to sell his wares so she remained silent hoping he would go away. Then there was another knock, this time a little louder and more insistent. Annie sighed and realised that whoever it was would probably not go away until she had answered the door. She reluctantly opened it a little and peered out.

'Annie, I just wanted to check that you're okay. I hope you don't mind?'

She realised with disbelief that it was the stranger that she had met at Paradise Disco. She felt elated, tongue-tied and awkward.

How does he know my name?

Annie shyly invited him into the kitchen and offered him a cup of tea, which he gratefully accepted.

'Annie, I was so worried about you.'

Annie smiled, marvelling at the fact that here was somebody who was actually concerned about her. She was quick to find out as much information as she could about him.

Thanos was from the Greek Island of Rhodes and he was in England working as an apprentice engineer at the local airport. He rented a small flat in Clanford and was planning to stay for a further six months before returning to his homeland. 'I miss my parents and my brothers very much but I am learning a lot. It is so cold in this country.' Thanos suddenly gave an exaggerated shiver making Annie giggle; she loved the sound of his Greek accent and deep rich voice and she was amazed at how well he spoke

English. 'I don't have many friends here and it is rather lonely. My parents own a Taverna in Rhodes called Taverna Rhodos. We play music, dance and sing every night. Here I sit in my room and dream about my home.' Thanos looked pensive and Annie tried to imagine what life would be like in Rhodes; she had never been abroad but it sounded truly wonderful. 'I live for my music,' he said. 'I play a Greek instrument called a bouzouki and I sing with my brothers. My father plays the violin and we play together in a band every night in the Taverna for our guests. I often wonder how the band is getting on without the bouzouki.'

'I play the violin. Maybe one day we could play together. Do you have your instrument here?'

Thanos gave a broad smile which lit up his face and then he nodded. Annie felt a warm tingle of pleasure seep through her body.

At that moment the front door opened and Stan walked in. He looked shocked when he saw the stranger in his kitchen. Stan, his face etched with fury, bellowed, 'Get out of my bloody house!'

Thanos, terrified, glanced swiftly at Annie, and then fled. 'I'm sorry Annie...'

'How dare you let a greasy dago into my house? How dare you?' He lunged towards Annie with his arm outstretched but she dodged his blow and fled upstairs to the sanctuary of her bedroom. She threw herself onto the bed, buried her head deep into her pillow and sobbed.

Thanos really seemed to care about me. Why? He is so good-looking he could choose any girl, so why me? He probably won't come back now that he has met Stan. Who would?

Annie stayed in her room all evening. She consoled herself with the fact that she would be able to escape eating supper with Mutti and Stan. She calculated that college lunch must have been under five hundred calories, she had done a long swim, and she felt satisfied that today she would achieve her aims of losing weight and getting fitter.

As nighttime approached, Annie lay on her bed drawing

her knees into her chest as she listened to the arguments raging in the kitchen. 'Annie,' he spluttered, 'brought a bloody foreigner into my house - my house! Sitting at the kitchen table like he owned the place. Bloody greasy dago! After sex I bet. He wants to get it away with our Annie.'

'Maybe he…' Mutti stammered.

'Shut your mouth you crazy bitch. I will not allow anything to happen under my roof. He will not come here again, and that is the end of it. He can go to hell and so can Annie.'

Putting her hands over her ears, she didn't want to hear any more.

I will find a way to see Thanos again… I will.

Cowering under the covers, Annie could still hear the violent arguments and the crash of broken glass. She feared for Mutti's safety. Then silence.

She heard the familiar creak of the fourth stair. Her body was alert; listening, watching, waiting. He entered, her heart beat fast within her ribcage, every hair on her body upright, defending attack, ready. The dim light cast shadows on the wall, moving grey shapes. His body descended. She struggled for air, light turned to dark; she had no choice, she must dance with the devil. She emitted a silent throttled scream of anguish and despair; her whole body, and her whole world, ripped apart. But wait, there was someone else; a tiny, hunched figure stood still and silent, the glint of her steely eyes cut through the darkness… and then she was gone. The damage is done.

As the warm water of the shower trickled over her, she scrubbed herself over and over again with a large thick-bristled brush until she could see tiny pin pricks of blood appearing on her deeply bruised and battered body. She attacked herself further with the brush until a steady stream of blood and water poured down the plug hole. But she couldn't erase the filth of him. Patting herself dry and wincing with pain, she covered herself up with her long dressing gown and crept to the kitchen. In the gloom she boiled the kettle and poured the entire contents on her left hand. The extreme physical pain shot through her and, for a moment, she was in a world where she had control.

But why did she walk away? Why didn't Mutti help me?

CHAPTER 6

His brown eyes shone out from under a mass of curly black hair and he smiled raffishly at Annie. She looked forward to the secret meetings with her new-found friend. They met as frequently as possible in the late afternoon at a disused railway line not far from Annie's house. Annie adored everything about Thanos: his funny formal 'English' way of speaking, the lascivious looks he gave her, his ability to make her laugh but, most importantly, she felt safe when she was with him. It saddened Annie to realise that there was so much that she could not tell Thanos about her and her family. She knew that she must obey her father and keep a brave face for the outside world, but she hated the secrets. So many words must be left unsaid. She was thankful it was winter so that she could wear her coat and gloves to conceal the bodily scars of her life.

The chill of the wind and the silence of nature filled her with joy. Today they walked together through the dense ancient woodland, pausing in a sunny glade to marvel at the clusters of snowdrops pushing their way up into the light from beneath a thick blanket of snow. How are these fragile flowers able to overcome the ravages of winter? Huge frost-laden trees bore the brunt of the winter storms, their gnarled trunks partially covered in stubborn clumps of snow driven in by a northerly wind. Numerous animal tracks curved between the trees in random paths; perhaps foxes or rabbits, Annie wasn't sure.

'Annie, tell me about your papa. When he discovered us in your kitchen, I thought he was going to hit you... or me. Is he kind to you? Does he hurt you?'

The joy drained away in an instant and Annie stared at Thanos. She knew she had to remain silent but there was so much she wanted to say. She looked down at the ground, her eyes brimming with tears. Thanos gently drew his index finger over the angular line of her jaw. 'You can trust me, Annie, I really care about you,' he said, as his other arm snaked around her waist and pulled her towards him. 'I may be able to help you if you tell me what's going on.'

Annie stepped away, rejecting his warm touch and comforting words. 'Please understand, my life is complicated...' She shook her head sadly and gazed into his eyes, feeling his hurt and confusion; tension hung heavy in the air.

'Annie, all I want is to hold you close to me, feel the warmth of your body against mine, and tell you everything will be okay.' They faced each other in silence.

But is this what I really want? I can't bear him touching me...

Suddenly with one swift movement he scooped up a large solid ball of snow and hurled it towards her, hooting with laughter as he did so. She tried to duck but the cold snow landed square on her chin and then slid rather ungracefully under the collar of her coat, finding the cleavage of her breasts. Gasping for breath, she tried to retaliate but her snowball headed off in completely the wrong direction causing an avalanche of snow to fall off the branch of a tree that she had successfully hit. In an instant the tension drained away; they laughed and laughed until their sides ached.

The weak watery sun shone low in the sky casting deep shadows across the way ahead. Annie shivered. The melting snow inside her clothes brought with it a deep chill; it was time to return home.

'See you on Wednesday, Annie, same time, same place.' He brushed his lips lightly on her cheek before turning away.

When Annie arrived home she was nervous of what she might find. She gingerly opened the front door and found Mutti seated in her familiar armchair in her dressing gown, staring at an album of old photographs. Annie felt confused and angry that her mother had witnessed what had happened in her bedroom that night and had done nothing about it. She had considered confronting her but when Mutti looked up, something in her expression made her feel dismal; her eyes were hard and cold. Annie felt a sudden and inexplicable sense of loss. It was obvious to Annie that Mutti blamed her for the scene she had witnessed in her bedroom. Annie blamed herself too. She put her head in her hands and the tears flowed unchecked down her cheeks. The sight of her mother's face would haunt her for a long time to come.

The person I love, above all others, hates me now.

It was Monday and Stan was late home every Monday evening because of a staff meeting. Annie made Mutti a cup of tea and then escaped to her bedroom as quickly as she could. She leant on the back of the door and sighed heavily.

I cherish the memories I have of Mutti when I was very young. We were carefree and happy then; she was my world, my everything - I knew she loved me. But now my world has fallen apart.

Later that evening just before supper as the arguments began, Annie crept silently downstairs and hid behind the open door to the kitchen where she was able to peer through a narrow crack between the door and the wall and watch Stan and Mutti. She wondered why she hadn't just stayed in her bedroom, put her head under the pillow and pretended everything was okay.

'Where the hell is my money? The jar is bloody well empty. Oh I know, you stole it to buy booze didn't you, you old cow? Give it back now.' Stan slammed the empty jar on the table and waited for an answer. Annie froze, remembering that she had put the coins in her pocket to go to Paradise Disco. She had meant to return the money but she had completely forgotten and now it was too late. Mutti cowered away from him, shaking her head. Stan pulled away. 'Yeah and you expect me to believe you,' he said scathingly, 'you lying bitch.'

At that moment Annie knew that she had to leave the safety of her hiding place. She crept into a corner of the kitchen but remained silent, terrified of the consequences if she admitted her guilt. She didn't know what to do or say. She knew that it would be either her or Mutti who would be punished. Mutti stared silently at Annie as she was dealt a crushing blow across her face. Within seconds Stan had stormed out of the house. Annie watched in horror as Mutti slowly and painfully pulled herself up from the floor, her fragile body shaking as she dragged herself onto her feet before falling heavily across the kitchen table. After what seemed like an eternity, she stumbled towards the stairs and hauled herself up, one painful step at a time, to her bedroom. Annie, feeling powerless to help, was left shocked and alone. No one ate any supper that evening.

Annie lay in bed running her hands gently over her body. She felt her increasingly sharp and angular pelvic bones jutting out from beneath the covers and the deep hollow where her stomach used to be. She moved her hands upwards feeling her ribs as they moved rhythmically in time with her breathing. She sighed with satisfaction. At least she was in control of one aspect of her life.

That night Stan didn't come to her bedroom.

Over the next few days Annie watched Mutti retreat further into her own world. She was either dazed and vacant or fast asleep in her chair. One morning Annie delved into the depths of a high kitchen cupboard hoping to find a jar of marmalade but instead her hand landed on what felt like a square-based glass container. Puzzled, she reached behind all the jars of jams and pickles to reveal a large bottle of London Gin which was half empty. She hurriedly searched all the other kitchen cupboards and discovered six more bottles of gin hidden in unlikely places, even in the shoe cupboard. It slowly started to dawn on Annie that this was the reason for Mutti's vacant demeanour and slurred speech. Perhaps the gin helped Mutti escape from her miserable existence.

Annie knew that alcohol was not the answer to her mother's woes but, for the moment, she reconciled it in her mind as a way that Mutti had chosen to sustain herself and survive through hard times. Annie chose to ignore what she had uncovered. She replaced the bottles exactly as she had found them and then carried a tray of toast and a cup of tea upstairs, thinking that this small kindness might be a way of showing Mutti that, despite everything, she still felt some love for her mother. Finding Mutti asleep, she paused, wondering whether to wake her up but then decided this would not be wise. She placed the tray quietly on the bedside table and crept downstairs. She prepared toast for herself, stuffed it into her bag to throw away later, and stepped out into the snow. Annie reflected on Mutti's deceit but then she realised, with some sadness, that she was no better. She hated herself for being dishonest about so many things in her life; about food, about taking laxatives, about harming herself... and about Stan and her vow to keep silent.

The light and hope in Annie's life were her secret meetings with her wonderful friend Thanos. They walked, they talked and they laughed together. The woodland provided a magical place for them to appreciate the wonders of nature. Their senses were heightened; they saw and heard a tiny droplet of water as it fell from the snowy branch and wondered if spring was on its way. They breathed in the woody musty smell of the damp forest and noticed the mist circulating into the frozen air as they exhaled; they explored the deep crevices of the wide trunks of the veteran trees. They smiled in wonderment; if these trees could talk, what tales they would have to tell. As they stood side-by-side, he reached out for her hand, but she quickly pulled away, as she always did. She couldn't understand why the touch of his skin left her feeling cold.

Is there something wrong with me? Why does his touch make my skin crawl? Has Stan ruined everything? Or is it me? Do I have no feelings at all?

The last day of January dawned and Annie sat on the edge of her bed and clutched her mourning brooch close to her chest. She reflected on the start of her year and the promises she had made to herself. At least her diet was going well; she was satisfied that she had earned the first ruby-coloured garnet.

Twelve shining garnets and there are twelve months in the year. Each red garnet will represent a month of the year, and if I fulfil the promises I make, I will earn the right to own this extraordinary piece of jewellery.

She held the brooch up towards the light and examined the plaited hair in the centre. She uttered the words with grim determination, 'I can do this, and I will.'

CHAPTER 7

There was no let-up in the ferocious storms of winter, and the unrelenting blizzards and freezing temperatures continued. The tiny droplet of water that had fallen from a snowy branch in the forest had given false hope of the oncoming of spring.

Annie knew that she was losing weight, and this pleased her, but the worst thing of all was that she had no energy left. Her punishing diet and swimming regime was taking its toll; she found it increasingly hard to focus on her college work and feared that she was falling behind. Annie knew she had to find the wherewithal from somewhere to do well in her course. She knew that Stan expected her to achieve top grades.

Late that evening, Annie sat forlornly in the kitchen in semi-darkness.

'Annie, what the hell is the matter with you?' said Stan. 'You walk around here like a bloody ghost and I never see you doing your college work. You do nothing round the house, you disappear on a whim; you are a lazy good-for-nothing. What have you got to say for yourself?' He strode towards Annie, savouring each cruel step. He repeated the words slowly and with venom, 'I said, what have you got to say for yourself?'

Annie looked down at the floor and started to mumble.

'Speak up girl, I can't hear a word you say!'

'I'm sorry Stan, I will do better but I haven't been feeling very well.'

Stan turned his back on Annie, slammed the front door and walked out into the night.

Annie's whole body shook as she put the kettle on. She proceeded to pour the boiling contents over her left hand. At that moment she felt free.

***

During lunch break at college the following week, the health tutor asked to see her at the end of the day. Miss Lagon was a kind and caring person who always prioritised the welfare of her pupils, but Annie was concerned about what she might want to discuss with her and she felt unsettled all afternoon. Finally the last lecture of the afternoon came to an end and she was left alone in the lecture theatre with her tutor.

'Annie, I am worried about you. I would like you to reassure me that you are okay. You look pale and exhausted and the standard of your work has been deteriorating. When you first arrived at college you were one of our star students. Has something happened to upset you?'

Be silent, nothing is wrong; pretend nothing is wrong...

'I am fine thank you Miss Lagon. I've had a horrible winter bug and it has left me feeling very tired. But I promise I am okay, and I will get back on track with my work soon... I promise.'

'I'm pleased to hear this, but if the situation doesn't improve, I think we should have a meeting with your parents.'

'No Miss Lagon, there is no need to worry I promise.'

'Well, I am expecting great things from you, and Annie, please remember that if you ever have any problems, either at college or at home, I will always be here for you.' She smiled benevolently at her student but her concern for Annie's welfare was clearly evident.

As Annie walked home that day she felt desperately

worried that she hadn't fooled either Stan or her tutor. She held Miss Lagon in high regard and appreciated the concern she had shown, and she did not want to let her down. She didn't want to let Stan down either and she was well aware that her marks in her recent assignments were poor. The responsibility of not being a disappointment to others weighed heavily on Annie's mind.

I must do better. I will work harder...

The threat of Miss Lagon contacting her parents was terrifying and Annie resolved to try and avoid this at all costs.

She decided to take a detour to go to the chemist. She browsed the selection of laxatives and rejected one product because the laxative was contained in a chocolate bar and this was surely far too calorific. Annie finally decided to buy two large boxes of tablets, usually taken to ease the symptoms of constipation. As she bought the items, she noticed the chemist's puzzled look but thankfully she accepted the payment and asked no questions.

Annie was surprised to find that Mutti was out when she arrived back home. The house was empty so she was able to hide her shopping without fear of being seen. Opening the bread bin, she pulled out a loaf of bread and smelt its delicious aroma. She couldn't resist cutting the crust off and nibbling the soft crumbs from the centre of the loaf, savouring every tiny morsel. She paused for a moment before having a little more of the bread, knowing that she would regret her actions. Then her hands started to tear the bread into large chunks and she stuffed them into her mouth. Annie ate like a wild animal, attacking the food with her hands and cramming it all into her mouth. She gulped the food down so quickly and aggressively that she could hardly breathe. She searched the kitchen cupboards and ate anything and everything that she could lay her hands on: another loaf of bread, three packets of biscuits, a large chunk of cheese, chocolate bars and packets of crisps, all in one go. She continued to binge until all the food had gone.

There was no pleasure, no comfort, just anger, regret, pain and self-hatred. Above all, she loathed herself for being so wildly out of control. This would have to be another horrendous secret in her life.

I taste nothing but misery and shame...

She stared out of the window, shocked by what she had just done. She imagined slashing her stomach open with a large carving knife and digging deep inside to gouge out all the undigested food from her body; the image in her head was vivid, in colour and agonisingly tempting. Her uncontrollable bingeing had taken her to the dark depths of despair.

I want to go to sleep and not wake up...

Annie swallowed two handfuls of the laxative tablets and waited for the inevitable. After some time her whole stomach contracted and Annie doubled up in pain. She rushed to the toilet, getting there just in time. The entire contents of her bowels poured out of her in a violent, explosive and uncontrollable jet of brown undigested food. Beads of sweat formed above her top lip and she cried out in agony.

She felt exhilaration and despair in equal measure. Running a hand over her stomach she realised with satisfaction that, where there had been a large mound before, she now felt a deep hollow. She had successfully exorcised her body of food. But she knew what she was doing to herself was harmful and wrong. Her whole body was racked with pain and exhaustion.

Her legs gave way under her and she slowly sunk to the floor.

CHAPTER 8

It was Saturday morning and Annie lay on her bed. The sun streamed in through the window as she listened to the comforting and uplifting words of one of her favourite songs playing on her tiny radio. She felt more content than she had done for many weeks. Today she was determined to savour and appreciate every moment in time, and everything else could wait until tomorrow.

There will be an answer…

She thought about the day ahead. This afternoon she had plans to meet Thanos and she always looked forward to seeing his happy smiling face and hearing his deep accented voice. Stan would be watching the football with his drinking mates and Mutti would probably be asleep in her chair. Neither of them would notice her absence.

As Annie put her jeans on she was surprised to find how loose they were. She buttoned them up around the waist and then realised she could pull them down over her hips without unfastening them. The legs were enormously baggy and far too big. She dug deep into her chest of drawers and found an old weathered brown belt. When she threaded the belt through the loops at the top of her trousers she found that there weren't enough holes to secure the belt tightly round her waist. Luckily the leather on the belt was old and worn so she was able to force another hole with the prong of the buckle. She looked at her reflection in the full-length mirror. The belt was tight and uncomfortable and pulled the jeans into a most peculiar shape.

How can I feel so fat and yet my jeans are falling off me?

She looked more closely at herself in the mirror. She traced her fingers slowly over the prominent lines of her collar bone and into the deep recesses behind, finally resting on the sharp bones on top of each shoulder. Her breasts had almost disappeared except for her dark nipples which looked like cotton reels. Her hair was dull and seemed to be losing its colour. She had seen enough. She quickly pulled a large T-shirt and a huge jumper over her head. The clothes successfully concealed the shape of her rapidly diminishing body. Quickly slipping on her shoes, she went downstairs to find Stan towering over Mutti looking furious.

'The kitchen is bloody-well empty Mutti, where the hell has all the food gone?'

Mutti stared vacantly at Stan and shrugged her shoulders. All eyes rested on Annie. 'I'm sorry, I forgot to ask you. I took some food to college yesterday to share with my friends because we decided to have a winter picnic, a crazy idea really!' She was amazed at how quickly and easily she could lie to Stan and Mutti without even hesitating.

'Bit parky for a picnic if you ask me A.'

Annie realised with relief that Stan had called her "A" signifying that he was in a good mood today. She had got away with it this time. As she walked out of the gloom of the kitchen and into the outside world, she shielded her eyes against the welcome light of the new day and inhaled the bitterly cold air deep into her lungs.

She wandered into the local recreation ground and sat idly, pushing herself backwards and forwards on one of the empty swings. A group of adults were chatting and laughing together, as the children enjoyed climbing, swinging and balancing very precariously on the high narrow ladder between the two metal climbing frames. Annie resisted the urge to help one or two of the younger children who looked in serious danger of toppling off the high bars, but she reminded herself that the children were not her responsibility and that, by being allowed to take risks, they were enjoying freedom and adventure. She looked again at the adults who were still deeply immersed in conversation, everyone seemed happy; everyone except for one child who stood alone. The young boy was scantily dressed and looked freezing, desolate and friendless. Annie was reminded of the sadness, loneliness and desolation she felt in her own life; how she wished she could reach out and comfort this child. She glanced down at her watch and couldn't believe how much time had passed. She had promised to meet Thanos at two o'clock and so she decided to make her way straight to their agreed meeting place. She wrapped her coat tightly around her and shivered as she closed the gate to the playground and went on her way.

As she entered the forest, she was once again struck by the sheer beauty of winter. The deep mounds of snow were covered in a glittery layer which shone like diamonds in the dappled sunlight. Annie smiled as she listened to her own breath rising and falling like waves; she was really looking forward to seeing him again.

'Annie, it's good to see you!' Thanos stood some distance away, smiling from ear to ear. She smiled back shyly and felt a deep warm tingle of pleasure pass through her.

They walked side by side in comfortable silence until they reached a small brick-built bridge marking the entrance of a dimly lit tunnel. The old, damaged railway track ran underneath and disappeared into the darkness. Annie and Thanos paused before venturing a little way into the tunnel. Everything smelt dank and there were remnants of food wrappers and a lot of empty cans and broken bottles dumped on one side. She shivered and Thanos put his arm protectively around her shoulders. Annie flinched, almost imperceptibly. She slowly turned to face Thanos, her heart pounding, before stumbling back on the uneven ground towards the light. Thanos followed her out of the tunnel and noticed with dismay that there were tears streaming down her face. Annie looked into his sad confused eyes and fervently wished that she could share with him all the grief in her life. She knew that he cared deeply, but she couldn't bear him touching her.

'Annie, what's the matter? You look so thin and pale. What can I do to make you happy?'

'It doesn't matter, I'm okay. Let's just walk and enjoy the short time we have together.'

Annie quickly wiped away the tears with the back of her hand. Thanos shook his head sadly. 'Annie, please let me into your life.' He leaned forward, casting a dark shadow across her body, and drew her close, gazing into her deeply troubled eyes. She felt first warmth, and then terror. Their lips met and he started to kiss her, gently at first, and then with increasing strength and passion. Annie's whole body recoiled and she pushed him away as if she had been viciously attacked. 'No Thanos, no! Please stop. I can't do this...'

But why?' Thanos looked beseechingly at Annie, visibly shocked by her reaction. 'I thought you liked me.'

'I do...'

'Then why?'

Tears coursed down her cheeks; her face etched with pain. She wiped the back of her hand roughly over her mouth to rid herself of the stain of his kiss.

Stan, our secret is locked away forever; I will never tell...

Annie couldn't understand her own feelings. She yearned for his friendship and warmth, and yet she couldn't accept any physical affection. Stan had ruined everything, but was it just about him... or was it also something about her?

When Annie returned home later that afternoon she thought about what had happened. Thanos was a very special friend and her feelings for him were becoming stronger, as a dear friend, but she realised she couldn't give him what he wanted; not now, not ever.

He is good-looking, intelligent and talented; why does he choose me? He deserves so much better. I am soiled and filthy, I am used goods, I will never be good enough.

She looked sadly at her reflection in the bedroom mirror.

Perhaps I should stop seeing him. I should offer him the opportunity of freedom so that he can be happy again. I am not worthy of his concern or kindness.

Annie knew that she could not share much of her life with Thanos. She recalled Stan's mantra to maintain a brave face in the outside world and never to share any of her grief or hardship, and she knew this would probably mean that her relationship with Thanos would soon be at an end.

She reached for her precious journal as she recalled the image of the small child standing alone in the playground earlier that day, and she reflected on her own childhood. Her words flowed freely onto the page:

Child of our Time

I am a child of yesterday,
Free to roam like a bird in flight.
Chasing the wind through the cornfields of Summer,
Laughing and crying and feeling alive,
But the birds have deserted the sky.
The birds have deserted the sky.

I am a child of today,
I withdraw from the world and I dream.
I long to confide in a friend,
But instead, I stay silent and still.
For the birds have deserted the sky,
For the birds have deserted the sky.

What of the child of tomorrow?
Their hopes and dreams still to come.
How to recover the laugher and joy,
To be playful once again.
So the birds, they soar in the sky,
So the birds, they soar in the sky.[1]

She opened up her violin case and dusted her much-loved instrument; she hadn't played for a long time. She carefully applied rosin to her bow and tuned the strings. The tune meandered up and down the scale, reflecting the sentiment of her words she had just written, and finally rising and falling like birds that soar in the sky. She played with sensitivity and feeling as her whole body moved in time with the music.

Suddenly there was a loud knock. Stan put his head round the door. 'Annie my precious, are you all right? Are you ill?' He jeered at her, breathing out alcoholic fumes and then closed the door behind him.

She put her violin away.

The birds have deserted the sky...

As night fell, conflicting thoughts crowded Annie's mind.

Is it right that I should have to keep silent? I long to talk to someone. Anyone.

---

[1] van Santen L (2011) Child of our Time

CHAPTER 9

'What on earth are you doing to yourself Annie? You are so skinny, you're all skin and bones!' Franky stood and stared. She was shocked to see Annie's body as they changed for the trampolining class the following Wednesday afternoon. 'I can see every bone in your body!'

Annie realised with horror that everyone around her had witnessed the scene. Feeling completely mortified, she wrapped a towel tightly round her body and was quick to dismiss her friend's concern; 'Franky, I haven't been feeling very well recently. I haven't felt hungry and I couldn't eat. But I'm much better now so it won't take me long to get back to rights.'

Hide the scars, I am fine.

Franky was perceptive and Annie knew that she could fool a lot of people, but not her dear friend. As she walked home by herself after college she reenacted the scene in the changing room.

How could Franky do that to me? She is wrong, I am not skinny, I am fat. She humiliated me.

When she arrived home she immediately rushed up to her bedroom, took off her clothes and studied her body in detail in the full-length mirror. She had to concede that she did look quite skinny, but then she roughly pulled and pummelled a loose roll of flesh from around her torso and realised that she still had a long way to go before she would be truly happy with herself. She opened her trusted journal and started to write:

"When I think clearly I know that Franky highlighted my skinniness because she cares about me. I can feel my hip bones jutting out from under the covers when I lie flat in bed so maybe I am too thin? I don't get hungry or full, I don't feel anything. I hate food, I hate everything. The strange thing is that I feel so <u>fat</u>. My stomach feels so inflated and large and when I look down at myself my legs are like tree trunks. It must be an illusion because Franky said I was all skin and bone. It's a mystery; really odd. Everything is a nightmare. No, she is wrong, she has to be wrong. I know my own body and I am in control."

If I lose just a little bit more weight everything will get better, I know it will.

Annie looked at her image in the mirror again and she loathed what she saw. It was time to write another list:

1. No more overeating
2. Write down everything I eat (no more than 500 calories a day)
3. Wear baggy clothes
4. Put my sports gear under my clothes so don't need to strip off
5. Swim at least 50 lengths every day

The next day Annie started to write her eating journal in more detail than before:

14th February 1974
Breakfast: None (0)
Lunch: Shepherd's pie (400)
Supper: Cheese on toast (350)
2 drinks of black tea (0)
(750 - too many calories)

15th February 1974
Breakfast: 1 cup black tea (0)
Lunch: Mince and peas (200) (made myself sick afterwards)
Supper: 1 beef salad (200)
(400 calories-but probably only 200 calories because I was sick.)

16th February 1974
Breakfast: None
Lunch: One pork slice and green beans (300)
Supper: Chicken and a few peas (250)
(550 calories)

17th February 1974
Breakfast: None
Lunch: Ravioli (300) (made myself sick afterwards)
Supper: 1 boiled egg, toast (160)
(460 calories-but probably only 160 calories)

18th February 1974
Breakfast: None
Lunch: Pretended I was too sick to eat
Supper: one sausage and cabbage (100)
(100 calories - not enough!)

Annie studied her eating journal over the previous five days and satisfied herself that she was in control of her diet and that she had kept to her daily swimming regime which she knew would also burn calories. She went to the bathroom, stripped down to her underwear, and, leaning on to the edge of the bath, she cautiously stepped onto the scales, willing her weight to be less than it had been the previous week.

I am 7 stone 6 pounds... keep going! Just a little bit longer to be on the safe side; just a little bit longer...

Annie could not believe that it was nearly the end of February already; the weeks were passing by so quickly. She considered the list that she wrote at the beginning of the year, to lose weight and get fit, to support Mutti and make her life better, and to get some maths tuition.

She opened her journal and began to write:

"I am losing weight, and I swim every day. I just wish I didn't always feel so drained and exhausted. I have failed to help Mutti, in fact I think I have made her life worse. I can't help but feel betrayed by her; she witnessed everything that happened with Stan in the bedroom and did nothing. Aren't parents supposed to protect their children? She is my mother and I love her, but does she love me? As for maths, I have done absolutely nothing! I must sort out some tuition. I will work harder at college, I know I can do better. I will succeed."

I have so many things in my life that I need to sort out, but I do swim nearly a mile every day to get fit and, for this, I do deserve the second red garnet.

She clutched her beloved mourning brooch close to her chest and closed her eyes.

March will be a good month.

***

On Tuesday at the end of the last lecture of the morning, her tutor took her aside and told her that the Principal wanted to see her immediately. She liked and respected Mrs Granger but she was fearful about what he might want to talk about. She walked shyly through the open door into the light spacious office.

'Come and sit down,' Mrs Granger said kindly. She placed her hand gently on Annie's shoulder. 'I'm afraid I have some bad news about your mother.'

'Is she dead? Is Mutti dead?'

'No Annie, your mother was taken by ambulance to hospital earlier this morning because she wasn't well. The postman found her in the front garden. She had collapsed.'

'What on earth was she doing in the front garden? Where was Stan?'

'We don't know Annie, she might have been putting out

the milk bottles. Your father wasn't there, he had gone to work.' She paused. 'She is in the right place now, and she will be looked after well. Her condition is stable.'

Mrs Granger looked at the vulnerable young student in front of her with compassion. 'Would you like to tell me what is troubling you Annie? You look very frail. I'm concerned about you.'

Annie stared at the floor and remained silent.

'Why don't you make yourself comfortable and I'll get you some water?'

Annie sank into the deep armchair and pulled her knees into her chest.

Why are you destroying yourself Mutti? Is it because of me? Please don't die.

CHAPTER 10

The ward was large, dingy and impersonal. Mutti looked tiny and broken. She stared at Annie; there was no recognition, no words, no emotion: nothing.

'Mutti, I am so glad to see you. How are you feeling? I've brought you a magazine and some fruit. I'm sure the hospital food is disgusting.'

Nothing.

'It will be spring soon Mutti, I have seen the first daffodils. I'll pick a bunch for you. They lift my spirits, they are so cheery.'

Nothing.

'When you get out of here we can go for a walk together in the country. The snow is melting and grass is beginning to grow. The rooks are building their nests in the tall trees and early blossoms are appearing on the blackthorn. Please say you'll come with me Mutti.'

Mutti was lying in the bed, her body draped in a thin grey hospital sheet. She had been looking at Annie blankly, as if she hardly recognised her own daughter.

'Go away and leave me alone,' she whimpered, 'I don't want to see you or anybody.'

'But Mutti...'

'Go.' Mutti's voice was weak but insistent. 'And don't come back.'

The bleak words echoed in Annie's mind as she walked home alone. She felt complete and utter misery.

Stan didn't seem to care. He spent more and more time at work, and when he wasn't at work he spent a lot of time with his drinking mates. 'Annie, let the doctors sort her out, silly old bat.'

Annie did care a lot about Mutti and she resolved to see her mother every day. The visits always followed the same pattern: Annie always tried to be cheerful and chatty and Mutti remained listless and vacant. She had been in hospital for over a week when Annie was met by one of her doctors.

'Are you Helga's daughter?'

'Yes, I am.'

'We are very concerned about your mother. She has certainly damaged her internal organs by drinking too much and taking prescription drugs but, more worryingly at the moment, she is deeply depressed. She won't communicate with us at all. I would like to suggest that she attends one of our weekly group therapy meetings to start to address her addiction and her mental health issues. She needs someone to go with her to the first meeting. Is your father around? We haven't seen him here at all.'

Addiction... Mutti is an alcoholic, Mutti is a drug addict.

The truth hit home and Annie shuddered. She knew that there was no chance of Stan entertaining the idea of attending such a meeting. He hadn't even visited Mutti in hospital.

'My father is very busy at the moment, but I will come with Mutti if this would be helpful?'

'That would be very helpful, thank you. The next meeting is tomorrow at four-thirty and usually goes on for about an hour.'

She would just about be able to make the meeting after college and she accepted the invitation.

Annie rushed to the hospital after the final lecture of the afternoon and only just got to the meeting in time. Everyone was already sitting in a large circle and she felt very self-conscious as she clambered over the knees of one of the patients to occupy the one remaining chair. She looked at Mutti who was sitting directly opposite her and she was shocked by her appearance. She looked utterly helpless, and greasy strands of hair fell across her gaunt face. She let out an audible sigh, and then fixed Annie with a hard emotionless stare. It was clear that her mother did not want her to be there.

A young and empathetic therapist welcomed everyone to the session. They listened to individual stories of patients who were suicidal, had already attempted suicide, had manic depression, were drug and/or alcohol dependent or who were simply hopelessly lost in their lives. The therapist was skilful, encouraging the patients to talk and others in the group to respond. There were a few chinks of optimism but Annie found the session gruelling. The stories she heard introduced her to what she perceived as an underworld of darkness and despair. Mutti was encouraged on several occasions to contribute, but she was unable to vocalise her thoughts at that time and she certainly wasn't ready to admit to her reliance on drugs and alcohol. How could she take any steps towards recovery when she had not acknowledged or processed what she needed to recover from? After the group therapy Mutti walked away slowly and purposefully without acknowledging Annie at all.

At home Stan and Annie passed like ships in the night. Stan seemed strangely happier than Annie had seen him for ages but she felt vulnerable being left alone in the house with Stan. But then Annie received the unexpected and disturbing news that, after spending only two weeks in hospital, Mutti was to be discharged. Annie recalled how ill her mother had looked during her last visit, surely she wasn't well enough to return home?

It was during the lunch break the next day when Franky - determined to lift Annie's spirits - made an unexpected suggestion. 'We're going to the coast on Saturday for the day. Would you like to come with us? It looks like it's going to be a sunny day so we can eat whelks, make sand castles and walk along the beach.'

Annie thought that eating whelks sounded totally disgusting but she longed to escape Clanford and to be by the sea. 'I'll check with Stan but that sounds lovely. Thank you Franky.'

Stan agreed that Annie could go out for the day. Saturday was his football and drinking day and he didn't care two hoots about Annie or what she did. These days Mutti spent her time either in bed or slumped in her chair and, although she felt guilty, Annie thought she would probably be okay on her own for a few hours.

Saturday dawned bright and clear. Annie leapt out of bed, threw her clothes on and was excited about the day ahead. Before she had time to put the kettle on she heard the cheerful honking of an old Morris 1000 standing outside the front door. She squeezed herself into the back seat alongside Tom, Franky's older brother, and Franky. It was the first time that Annie had been invited to join Franky and her family for a day trip and it felt like an adventure.

Suddenly Tom burst into song, swaying as he did so; he wasn't the best singer in the world and everyone roared with laughter. Annie had met Tom a few times before and she always enjoyed his company. It took an hour and a half to reach Starmouth-on-Sea and Annie found herself thoroughly enjoying the atmosphere of this happy family.

'I was the first to see the sea,' Franky shouted.

The sight of the deep blue sea set against the even deeper blue of the sky took Annie's breath away. They passed through the scenic seaside town where shop owners were busily preparing for the summer season ahead. Shop fronts were being painted in pale blues and pinks and pots of colourful spring flowers were arranged artistically at the side of the narrow, cobbled streets. Annie's stomach lurched as the car weaved through narrow lanes of terraced cottages, and then rolled down a steep hill before finally stopping in a small, deserted car park. Stretching ahead of them was the most beautiful beach that Annie had ever seen. The small sandy cove was surrounded by huge grey cliffs and she listened to the cry of the gulls flying overhead. It was only the biting chill of the onshore breeze that reminded her that it was early March and not mid-summer.

Colourful beach towels were laid on the damp sand and the family settled themselves down to enjoy their day by the sea. The two friends took their towels and walked a little further down the beach. The spring sun provided some warmth and Annie felt deep contentment. They spent time exploring the rock pools at the edge of the beach, taking care not to slide on the green slippery rocks. Franky tried to pull a stubborn limpet from the semi-submerged rock and Annie examined the tiny shrimps as they darted between the small stones. There were shoals of tiny fish circling the small deep pools and a large crab sidestepped underneath an overhanging rock. Both girls were so engrossed in the miniature underworld that they didn't notice Tom as he ran up to them. 'Franky, Annie, what are you up to?' Tom knelt down beside them and grinned, looking into the pool. 'I think I could catch something here to eat for lunch!' He had an endearing roguish face and a tangled mop of straw-coloured hair. His lapis blue eyes shone and Annie found it easy to feel at ease with him.

'Oh no Tom, I couldn't eat any of these beautiful little creatures. They're happy where they are,' said Annie.

'Well, I suppose I'll have to make do with the best fish and chips this side of Grimsby then! Do you like fish and chips, A?'

Annie giggled. She loved the familiar way Tom called her "A" although it did remind her of Stan.

'Fish and chips, wow, what a treat!' Annie licked her lips in anticipation but then worried about how many hundreds of calories there must be in one portion of fish and chips. Almost as if he read her mind he smiled at Annie kindly and said, 'A, you are as skinny as a rake, there is more fat on a butcher's pencil! Fish and chips will build you up nicely.'

Annie knew that she did not want or need building up, but she loved Tom's openness and honesty. She was beginning to like him a lot.

'Come on you two, time for lunch I think.'

'Time passes so quickly when you're having fun,' Franky lamented. As they walked slowly back along the beach they saw Franky's mum returning from the shops carrying a large plastic bag. 'Fish and chips all round! I bet you're starving with all this sea air!' She handed out the hot parcels wrapped in yesterday's newspaper. Annie clutched her portion close to her, suddenly aware of the distinct chill in air. She slowly unwrapped her parcel revealing a huge piece of battered cod sitting on a bed of thick-cut chips. Annie's mouth watered as she watched everyone smear their feast with a thick dollop of tomato ketchup and then start to devour the greasy crumbs with gusto. Annie slowly broke off the end of her fish and nibbled. She hadn't tasted anything as good as this for a very long time. As she carefully removed all the batter, she forced herself to eat the soft white flesh and before long she had eaten the whole fish and a large amount of the chips.

How could I do this?

She licked her fingers, savouring the final morsels of salt and vinegar, but then she felt guilty and sick to the pit of her stomach.

After lunch the family cleared away the remnants of food and then lay down on their beach towels for an afternoon snooze. Annie stared up at the grey sheer cliffs and listened to the soporific sound of the waves gently lapping on the shore and the mournful cry of the gulls. She tried to relax her body but sleep evaded her so she threw off her shoes and socks and wandered towards the sea.

The soft sand was covered in a thin crunchy topping formed by recent rainfall and she enjoyed the sensation as her feet made footprints in the sand. She paused to gather a small collection of tiny, coloured shells which she placed carefully into her pocket to keep as a precious memento of a special day. She stared out towards the horizon and wondered if this masterful and powerful sea held any answers to the challenges she faced in her life.

'Are you trying to escape from this crazy family of mine?' Tom appeared beside her and laughed. 'I don't blame you A, they can be a bit much at times!'

Annie smiled, and thought how different her family was. 'No, I just didn't want to disturb you. You all looked so peaceful and content.'

'Ha-ha it won't last! I am very glad that you could come today A. Any friend of Franky is a friend of mine.' Tom threw an arm spontaneously around Annie's shoulders and she relished the warm contact of another human being. They stood together looking out towards the sea. All of a sudden Tom reached over and started to tickle Annie and they both collapsed into laughter.

'Come on Skinny Minnie, beat you back!' He sprinted back towards his family.

Annie lingered a while longer. Her whole body tingled with pleasure and she wondered why she could enjoy Tom's embrace when she couldn't bear Thanos to touch her. She was puzzled but her thoughts were interrupted by Franky bounding up behind her.

'Here you go!' Franky thrust a huge creamy ice cream into her hand. 'I'm sorry I slept for so long, I must have needed it! Ooooh isn't this delicious!'

Annie slowly drew her tongue over the creamy smooth ice cream and, at that moment, nothing else mattered.

'We'd better be going now before it gets dark,' said Franky.

'Okay, I'll just say goodbye to the sea.'

Annie walked over to the water's edge. The tide had come in and the waves were higher than they had been all day. She gazed as waves broke over a distant reef and smiled. It had been a wonderful day. She glanced at her watch. It was exactly four o'clock. Suddenly wave upon wave of pain and anguish pulsated through her body.

CHAPTER 11

At four o'clock on Saturday 4th March 1974 Mutti had a massive heart attack. She was very close to death but the medical team worked tirelessly and eventually her weakened heart started to beat once more.

Stan was waiting for Annie to arrive home. They sat at the kitchen table facing each other. His words were blunt and dispassionate, 'Her heart stopped but they got 'er back. Annie, she wanted to die and now she might get her way. She was bloody lucky I came home when I did...'

The agonising pain I felt on the beach yesterday happened at exactly four o'clock, and somehow I just knew...

The incident had interrupted Stan's Saturday afternoon football and drinking session; he checked the time and realised there was still an hour and a half before last orders. He ended the conversation abruptly, threw on his jacket, blew a kiss to Annie and rushed out of the house leaving her alone.

How could I have gone to the beach knowing that Mutti was so ill? I should have been there to hold her hand. I was laughing and joking while she was fighting for her life. I should have done more to help her.

She calmly boiled the kettle and poured the scalding water over her left hand. The physical pain brought immediate release from her mental torment. Her whole body heaved and she emptied the entire contents of her stomach down the kitchen sink until there was nothing left. She struggled upstairs feeling light-headed and giddy, everything was spinning in front of her eyes. She cautiously lowered herself onto her bed and buried her head in the pillow. She tried to imagine herself on a beautiful, deserted beach with the gentle waves lapping on the shoreline, but horrifying images of Mutti kept flashing into her head and she sobbed. Eventually she drifted into an unsettled sleep.

Stepping into the kitchen a couple of days after Mutti had gone to hospital, Annie was surprised to find a beautiful and striking black woman sitting at the kitchen table enjoying breakfast with Stan. 'Well, hello my darlin', you must be Annie. I am so happy to meet you!'

Annie stared open-mouthed. She had a huge mass of black curly hair tied back loosely in a messy bun with thick strands escaping everywhere. Her eyes shone mischievously and dimples appeared in her cheeks when she smiled. She wore a sky-blue dress with huge pink flowers which was tied back with a sash to reveal her extremely ample chest. Annie couldn't help but notice the way her feet bulged out of her startlingly pink stilettos.

'My name is Joycelyn but everyone calls me Joy... Joy by name, joyful by nature.'

Annie was completely lost for words.

'Well, Annie, you must wonder why I'm sitting at the breakfast table with Stanley.' Raising one eyebrow and pursing her lips, she continued, 'Darlin' I'm so sorry to hear about poor Mutti. You must be worried sick.' She shook her head and looked at Annie with concern. 'I used to see her occasionally out-and-about in town and we always passed the time of day pleasantly enough, but that was a long time ago and I wondered whether she had left town. Imagine my surprise when I saw her again a few weeks ago at the church bazaar. I was selling some of my Caribbean fabrics to raise money for an Easter party for our disadvantaged young people in Clanford. Oh my, did we have fun last year!' She shook her head and put her hand over her mouth to suppress a giggle. 'You should have seen us all jiggling about in time to the beat of the live reggae band!' She glanced at Stan and Annie, peering over her purple-rimmed spectacles. 'Your Mutti seemed to like rummaging through my collection of fabrics, but I recall she didn't buy any. I couldn't help but notice the sadness in her eyes. I was concerned for her, she looked like her spirit had left her. I didn't know her well, but she always seemed a very quiet and gentle soul… but oh my goodness, I can talk the hind legs off a donkey so she probably couldn't get a word in edgeways when I was around!'

Annie couldn't help but like this flamboyant joyful lady. She was like a ray of sunshine with her broad smile, velvety voice, empathic manner and warm presence. And she was definitely in stark contrast to the gloom, and the dust, that had descended on the house since Mutti had gone.

Joy by name, joyful by nature.

'Anyway, I've offered to come in twice a week to do some housework and keep this place ship-shape while Mutti is in hospital. Stanley has agreed to pay me a small sum for my efforts. Is this okay with you Annie?'

'The house is in a bit of a state,' Annie conceded. 'I think it's a good idea, Joy.'

'Pretty good huh Annie?' Stan had sat quietly while Joy was speaking, and Annie thought she could detect a hint of relief in his voice. She nodded, thinking that she had never heard anyone call him "Stanley" before.

'You never know, I might even do some cooking while I'm here… I do so love to bake!'

***

The bracing wind had swept through the town, and then quickly left, like Joy, the housekeeper. She made too much noise, sang to herself and moved every bit of furniture around, causing total chaos. But she always smiled, did the job in record time, and always left the house sparkling. She was like a breath of fresh air.

As Annie walked back home after another challenging visit to see Mutti, she was struck by how much had changed at home since her mother left two weeks before. Joy did the housekeeping at the weekends because she was employed in a nine-to-five-job during the week. In the short time since she had started, the house had been transformed, and Annie had begun to enjoy the cheerful presence of this hard-working, spirited lady. Even Stan seemed to be a little less grumpy, especially when Joy was around. But visiting her mother in the hospital was hard. Mutti was never pleased to see Annie, and often bellowed at her to clear off and to never come back; Stan had not visited the hospital, and he didn't even mention her name. He was unaware of Annie's visits; he had no interest in how Mutti was, or if she would ever recover.

Why should I bother when she is always so hostile and cold towards me? She has changed so much recently and I'm not sure I even like her any more. But, she is my mother...

She paused at the open front door and could hear Stan and Joy deep in conversation.

'Stanley, Annie is a real beauty but I think you should be mighty worried about her.'

'Why should I waste my time worrying about Annie, Joy? Let's just drop it shall we?'

'Stanley, listen to me, I'm being serious. Annie is real thin, she needs feeding up. I think you need to talk to her. She looks ill to me.'

'Okay, I suppose I'll have to talk to her, but she seems fine to me.'

'Thanks my darlin'' and in the meantime I will make her some of my finest ginger and molasses cake. I just know she won't be able to resist that!'

Annie didn't relish the idea of the talk Stan was planning to have with her, or of the ginger and molasses cake, so she crept upstairs to her bedroom. Her head was buzzing and she was exhausted. She needed time to think.

The day on the beach had been overshadowed by the news of Mutti's heart attack. Annie had enjoyed spending time with Franky, her lively family and particularly her funny roguish brother. She found it hard to stop thinking about Tom and the warmth and pleasure she had felt when he put his arms around her. She really liked him. But what about Thanos? Her relationship with Thanos was becoming increasingly intense and Annie knew that she was not going to be able to offer him the physical affection he so wanted; his touch left her cold; she no longer felt safe with him. Stan had ruined everything.

I must not get distracted. I must lose weight. I must help Mutti get better. I must work hard.

I wish I wasn't me.

CHAPTER 12

'Do you fancy a date, Annie? Tom and I want to take you to see a matinee performance of *Love Story* on Saturday afternoon. Say yes Annie, please say you will, it will be so much fun!'

The two friends slouched on the old and battered wooden bench in the airless cafeteria, surrounded by discarded cups of coffee, after an exhausting Thursday afternoon of back-to-back lectures. Annie smiled at Franky's enthusiasm and she paused to think about her response.

'Annie, *Love Story* is the most crazy, beautiful, funny, sad film I have ever seen and I want to see it again. And you will just love the music! Come with us.'

Annie nodded, realising that this might be a welcome distraction from her normal weekend drudgery of household chores and relentless hospital visits. Her daily visits to see Mutti had become a thankless task; Mutti was never pleased to see her.

Saturday morning dawned and Annie was looking forward to her outing to the cinema. Tom had made an impression on her. She was glad to be meeting him again, and she always enjoyed being with her lively, zany friend Franky. All too soon she heard a knock on the door and Tom's cheerful voice shouting, 'Come on Annie, for goodness sake, we're going to be late.'

The cinema was a short walk away on the main street in Clanford. After buying the tickets, Tom bought three cans of cola, a huge carton of popcorn and a packet of wine gums. 'We don't want to go hungry during the film do we?' He grinned as he propelled them into the back row of the cinema, making sure that he positioned himself in the middle. 'A huge bucket of popcorn, a good film and two beautiful girls sitting either side of me. What more could a boy want?' He chuckled loudly causing the people on the row in front to turn their heads.

Annie was wearing her treasured black PVC mac which she had found in a charity shop. It was extremely warm in the cinema and even before the film had begun she had started to sweat, but she knew she must keep the coat on to hide her body.

As soon as the theme tune began, Annie was transfixed. It was one of the most beautiful pieces of music she had ever heard and it transported her into a different world where everything was better. She smiled as she watched the young couple on the screen laughing and frolicking in the snow, just like she and Thanos had done. She reflected sadly that Thanos could never be her lover, and neither could Tom. They had both become very special people in her life; but all she wanted was their friendship, nothing more.

'This is such a great film isn't it Annie?' Tom said in a loud whisper, causing the people in front to turn their heads again. 'Isn't Ali McGraw a sexy beast?'

'Sssshhhhh!' The people in front were now annoyed by this disturbance. 'Be quiet will you!' hissed an older lady, who had turned in her seat to glare at them. Tom's shoulders started to shake with suppressed giggles until he could contain himself no longer and he roared with laughter. Franky gave him a deep and painful prod in his side. Tom scowled at her and then plunged his hand deep into the bucket of popcorn and devoured half the carton before offering any to Franky or Annie. Annie glanced sideways at him in the semi-darkness.

There is something about him that I adore; he is a gentle giant, a lovable rogue, and so funny.

The film was paused halfway through for a short interval. During the break, Franky, having devoured a large tub of ice cream, made a rather lame excuse that she had forgotten to run an urgent errand that their mother had asked her to do. 'I'm sure you two will enjoy the rest of the film and I'll see you later.' Not waiting for any replies, she waved goodbye and left Tom and Annie together.

A little way into the second half of the film, Annie stiffened as she felt an arm slowly and stealthily reach round the back of her neck and rest on her shoulder. She had feared he might do this, and, worse still, she was aware that she was now damp with perspiration, the PVC mac was a mistake and rivulets of sweat were running down the back of her neck. She rubbed her clammy hands together hoping that he wouldn't notice the damp patches that she could feel rapidly spreading under her armpits.

'Oh Annie, this story is so sad, I need a hug!'

Now it was Annie's turn to smile. Tom was rather like a wonderful big soppy bear of a brother and she relaxed into his arms. As the love story unfolded, Tom's grip got tighter and he was so close to her that she could smell the buttery popcorn on his breath. 'Annie, this is heartbreaking.' As the dying heroine asked her lover to embrace her before she died, Tom threw his arms around Annie and buried his head in her neck. 'It's no good, I can't watch anymore.'

The final poignant remark in the film brought Annie abruptly back to reality; love should mean that you never have to say you are sorry.

"I'm sorry A."

Haunting memories of Stan forcing himself upon her came flooding back into her head and her body contorted with deep silent sobs.

He loves me, he loves me not? He loves me, he loves me not...

After they left the cinema they slowly ambled back along

the road towards Annie's house.

'Wasn't that a wonderful film, Annie, but the ending was so tragic? I was willing them to live happily ever after but it wasn't to be.'

Annie realised with relief that Tom thought she was upset by the film. She nodded and then looked towards the ground, now shivering violently with the cold. Tom put his arm protectively round her shoulder to bring warmth to her freezing and damp body.

'Annie, I know that you're going through a really difficult time in your life. I don't know what's happening to you to make you so sad, but I *do* know that it is making you very ill. I am here for you Annie. You haven't known me for very long but I will do everything in my power to help you.' He gave Annie's arm a reassuring squeeze. 'Listen to me rabbiting on. I'm rather a baboon sometimes! All I mean to say is, let me be your friend, lean on me when you need to and life will get better; I promise, it will get better. Friends?'

'Friends...'

Annie closed her eyes and sighed with relief. He engulfed her tiny body in his warm, comfortable arms and they stood together in amiable silence.

CHAPTER 13

It was nearing the end of March. The warm gentle breeze brushed Annie's face as she followed the path by the edge of the forest to meet Thanos.

'Hi beautiful,' he said brightly, 'it's really good to see you.'

'Hello you.' She smiled, wrapping her thick winter coat tightly around her. 'It's March the twenty-first today - do you know why this date is so special?'

'Of course I do, it's because you're lucky enough to have a date with the man of your dreams.' His eyes twinkled with pleasure.

'Haha, very funny! Today is the Spring Equinox.'

'Spring Equinox? I've never heard of it.'

'It's the first day of spring. I think it is when the sun crosses from the equator moving from the southern to the northern hemisphere, or something like that anyway.'

Thanos raised his eye brows. 'How clever Annie, how on earth do you know all this?'

'We were taught about it at school. I don't understand the science of it all to be honest, but as long as the days are becoming warmer, I really don't care.'

'Oh, I can't wait, I love the hot sun and blue skies.'

They walked through the forest side by side. Swathes of wild garlic filled the air with an unmistakable scent, the small white flowers replacing the snowy blanket of winter. Clumps of daffodils brightened up the dark forest and buds were appearing on the wild honeysuckle.

Thanos turned towards her, his brow creased. 'I'm sorry if I upset you the other day Annie. The trouble is, I really fancy you, all I want to do is hold you in my arms and love you. Is that so very wrong?' A strong friendship had grown between them; they had many shared interests in music, poetry, nature and of being outside, but he was becoming frustrated as to why she always shunned his physical affection. He wanted more than just friendship; she had stirred his inner feelings. 'It hurts when you push me away all the time.'

'You don't understand where I am at the moment,' she hissed, exasperated by his relentless advances. 'The last thing I want, or need, is you pawing my body. I'm really worried about my mum - I can't think about anything else - Mutti is very sick.'

'What is wrong with her?' he asked abruptly, shocked by her harsh words and unexpected revelation. 'I'm really sorry to hear this Annie,' he added, his voice softer now.

She sank to the ground, and pulled her knees tightly into her chest. 'She might die Thanos. She's my mother and I might lose her.' Offering his handkerchief to wipe the tears away, he sat down beside her and waited; she had not shared anything about her life with him before; he knew this would be hard for her. 'Mutti had a heart attack. I should have been with her. Instead I was out enjoying myself while she was fighting for her life. I don't think I'll ever be able to forgive myself.'

'But you weren't to know Annie,' he said reassuringly, 'and anyway, it probably wouldn't have made any difference to her even if you had been there. Try not to beat yourself up about it.'

'But Thanos, I needed to be there for *me* as well as for her. I feel so guilty. If only I could turn back time, and help Mutti so much more than I have done. I'm a useless daughter and she hates me. What am I going to do?'

'You are warm, sensitive and loving. I'm sure your mother is very proud to have you as her daughter.'

'I wish that this were true. So much water has gone under the bridge and I would understand if she disowned me.'

'Tell me, please tell me, what has happened to you,' he pleaded. He was painfully aware that there was so much about Annie's life that he knew nothing about.

'Not now Thanos,' she said firmly. 'We should make the most of our precious time together...'

They walked further through the woodland. Words were left unsaid and deep sadness hung in the air. The sound of the drumming of a woodpecker tapping on a nearby tree distracted them briefly from their melancholy but all too soon it was time to return home.

'It is the first day of spring. It's a time to celebrate new life, and perhaps this day marks the beginning of something new and special for your mother and for you, Annie.'

She loved his optimism but she knew in her heart that she would not see Thanos for a long time to come.

As she walked home, she felt unutterably sad. Thanos was always there for her and she was not being honest with him. How could she tell him everything? Her life was spiralling out of control and she could do nothing to stop it. She knew she mustn't confide in him about her relationship with her father, she was sworn to secrecy. She had deeply conflicting and disturbing thoughts about her mother, but she couldn't share this with him either. She knew that her health was deteriorating and yet she seemed powerless to do anything about it. She liked Thanos as a friend, but not as a lover; she was fearful of sexual advances of any kind. She felt guilty about so much in her life and yet she felt she had to remain silent.

Later that evening Annie wrote some of her thoughts and feelings in her journal:

My Plea: Please God help me. Is there a God? I don't

know. I hope there is someone listening to me. My brain is being taken over by my obsessions. I am losing the battle.

Food
I love food, but I hate food.
I want to eat, but I can't eat.
I binge, but then I purge.
I dream about food, but to eat is a sin.
I long to eat, but I can't... so I starve, and then I will die.

Weight
Life will get better if I lose weight.
Just a little more, and a little bit more,
Even just a few more pounds,
And then life will get better.
But it never does.

Calories
What are they anyway?
I don't know, I don't care.
But I count them; every day I count them.
They take over my head.
But what are they anyway?

Me
I'm told I'm too thin, but I feel too fat.
I'm told I'm beautiful, but I feel ugly.
I'm told I'm clever, but I feel useless.
I'm told I'm worthy, but I feel worthless.
So what am I?

Relationships
Stan, Mutti, Franky, Thanos, Tom, and now Joy...

Annie put down her pen and sighed. She was too exhausted to think about all the people in her life tonight.
Tomorrow is another day... Please help me.

CHAPTER 14

'For God's sake Annie just eat, will you? What the bloody hell are you doing to yourself? Have you got a death wish or something? Just do what I say and get that food down you.' Stan sat at the head of the table and sputtered out his words, 'You don't know how lucky you are. There are some people in this world that don't have enough money to put food on the table. You're nothing but a selfish brat, I'm ashamed of you.'

'Stanley, that is enough! Go for a walk to cool off and I will stay with Annie.'

With that, Stan banged his fist down on the table and stormed out of the house. Annie and Joy sat in awkward silence for a few moments. Annie bowed her head, slowly fiddling with her congealed plate of sausages and mash.

'Annie, I know we don't know each other very well, but I would like to be your friend. There are things I'd like to share with you.' Joy spoke in a soft, kindly voice and Annie looked up and rather dubiously nodded her head.

'I'll begin by telling you a little about myself. I come from Jamaica and, my goodness, how I love my homeland.' Her voice was warm and passionate and she paused to have a chuckle to herself. 'In Jamaica I was brought up to believe I was somebody. I knew I was somebody. When I came to England some people thought I was a nobody but I knew otherwise. If we all believed that we are special and significant for who we are, as unique individuals, then we could all live together in harmony, whether we are black, white, blue or pink!' Joy took a sharp intake of breath. 'But something sad happened to me a few years ago. I was married, you see. My husband was the most wonderful man you would ever wish to meet. We were like peas in a pod. When Bill laughed I laughed, and when Bill cried I cried. One day he went on his bike to buy some groceries and he never came back. Bill was taken away from me by a reckless driver, Annie. I loved him so much and now he is gone.' Joy's face crumpled briefly but then she smiled again. 'Oh my darlin' from that day I have learned to be a strong woman. I am proud of who I am now. I came over here five years ago with my sister. We have found work and England is now my home. It hasn't been easy. Many people here hate black people. Some folk cross the road when they see me just because I'm black. I have had to stand up for my rights but, in doing so, I have made many good friends. It is what is inside that is important, not the colour of our skin.' Her eyes twinkled. 'Skin is only the stuff that holds us together. Black or white, it doesn't matter. We just need to be good people and be kind to one another. Do you agree?'

Annie nodded her head.

'Darlin' you are young and beautiful. You have your whole life to lead. You need to be strong and grab happiness where and when you can. And believe you me there is joy to be found in this world, you just have to grab it with both hands. My name, Joy, reminds me of this every day.'

Annie listened with interest, she welcomed Joy's warmth and wise words.

'Can I ask you something Annie?'

'Of course, but I may not have an answer for you.'

'Annie, please look at me… do you think I'm fat?'

'No, you are not fat, you are dazzling Joy.' Annie was surprised by her own words; Joy was undoubtedly overweight, but she was truly beautiful.

'Well, lots of people would say I am fat but I feel good. I'm glad to be me and I'm glad to be alive. It is the whole package that matters, not just the wrapping paper!'

Annie thought quietly about Joy's words.

'Oh but I do love to wrap myself up in colourful dresses. I am pleased that I'm in the sewing trade. I have freedom to choose my favourite fabrics and I stitch them up to fit. They make me think of Jamaica, dancing in the moonlight, joyful music and lying on those sun-soaked beaches. Shall I make a beautiful dress for you Annie?'

Annie smiled but before she could answer, Joy continued, 'I pray to the Lord God every day to give me the strength and courage I need...'

Annie was deep in thought. She looked at Joy and yearned to be like her. Joy had inner contentment that radiated from her, despite having suffered tragedy and discrimination in her life. She was indeed a strong and beautiful lady.

'What is it Annie? I know that something's hurting you inside and I wish I could help you.'

'Thanks, but I'm feeling very confused right now, I don't understand my own head. But what I do know is that I'm feeling sad, and I would like to feel happy.'

Joy put her arm around Annie's shoulder. 'Okay, you've probably heard more than enough of me for one day. I know I'm not your Mutti but if you ever want to talk about anything at all, I am a very good listener.' As she walked out of the kitchen she turned. 'And I have just the fabric for you Annie, you will look as pretty as a picture.'

Annie gave her a wry smile. 'Pretty as a picture?'

CHAPTER 15

Strange things were happening to Annie's body. She was growing soft downy hair on her face, casting a dark shadow around the edges of her jawline. Her eyes had sunk deep into the recesses of her skull. Her hair was falling out at an alarming rate. Her face had changed shape and her head seemed to be out of proportion to the rest of her body. Every day when she walked to college, she felt as if she was walking on razor blades because there was no padding on the bottom of her feet; her toes were swollen with chilblains and they throbbed with pain. Her monthly periods seemed to have stopped but this, at least, was a relief.

My body is my worst enemy…

'Stop fussing, Franky!'

'You look like death and I am desperately worried about you. And why is your hand always bandaged up?' Franky asked, looking searchingly at her friend.

Annie looked down, rather surprised that she hadn't asked this question before now. 'I keep getting a strange annoying rash so I've smothered it with antiseptic cream, and I think it's probably best if I keep it covered to stop it getting infected.'

'Okay, but you need help. I wish I could do something but I have no idea what to do.'

'Franky, I'm fine. I don't need you; I don't need anyone.

You don't need to worry about me.' She hated herself for uttering the words out loud, even to her best friend. She wished they were untrue but she knew better.

Franky and Tom are good friends and I know they want to help me. Why can I accept their friendship, but I can't accept their help? I suppose by accepting help, I would be admitting that I have a serious problem. I can't do that, I have to sort out my own life. But am I even worthy of their help?

Annie had little strength or fight left in her. Her whole body hurt and she was confused. She knew she was starving herself and yet she couldn't make herself eat; she had not eaten anything more than crumbs for the last few days and yet she didn't feel hungry. She knew she was painfully thin, and yet she felt unbearably fat. She forced herself to swim endless lengths every day, but this only made her feel weak and exhausted. She had been constantly punishing herself with scalding water and laxatives and she knew in her heart that this was wrong. She couldn't see any way out of the darkness.

***

She arrived at the swimming pool in the early evening, feeling exhausted and daunted by the prospect of the fifty lengths ahead of her. The shallow end was alive with young children and parents laughing and splashing, their squeals of delight reverberating around the high pitched roof. Without warning, a young child suddenly dive-bombed the group, creating a huge splash, and the decibels of sound reached an almost unbearable level. Annie eased herself slowly into the freezing water, her skin already transparent and blue. She had the fast lane to herself today. She gritted her teeth and began her daily mission, her mind focussed and intent on her goal; she stared ahead and pushed herself to the outer limits of her endurance.

I can do this and I will. Think about the calories I'm burning. Focus Annie... forty lengths to go... I can do this.

Her limbs began to feel heavy, her breath short and laboured and her heart beating fast within her ribcage. The families had now gone, and an eerie silence descended. Her eyes were smarting from the heavily chlorinated water, everything became misty, but she continued up and down, up and down, determined to reach her goal.

I have to do this, I must do this…

She concentrated her mind on counting each length, aware that the lifeguard was observing her intently. Her body was beyond exhausted, her throat dry from ingesting too much water, but she was driven to complete her goal. After the final length, as she hauled herself up on the side of the pool, her arms buckled under her and she collapsed back into the water, coughing and spluttering. The life guard stepped down from the high seat and rushed to her aid. 'I see you going up and down every day. Are you overdoing it my love? You look totally knackered.'

Annie, quick to find an answer, replied, 'I'm taking part in a swimming gala in the summer, so I'm building up my strength and endurance.' She fell back into the water once again, her breath rasping in her heaving chest.

He looked concerned. 'Good for you, I admire you,' and, as he leant over to help her out of the pool, he added, 'but look after yourself my darling, our health is the most precious thing we have in life.'

She nodded at the well-meaning life guard.

As she left the pool that evening she reflected on the wise words of the life guard. She knew that she was damaging her health, but everything was out of control. Her head had been taken over by demons, and her lonely long-distance swimming had become just one of her obsessions.

Two days later as Annie walked out of the education lecture with Franky, she was overcome by an agonising high pitched whistling sound in both ears which seemed to be coming from inside her head. She bent over to shield her ears and suddenly everything went black. Waves of nausea coursed through her body and she retched from deep in her gut. Her legs buckled under her and she felt sharp pain as her head ricocheted off the hard wooden floor. She briefly lost consciousness, and when she came round, Franky was kneeling beside her.

'Franky, go away... I want to go home. Please don't tell anyone, please...' Annie pleaded.

'But Annie, you have hurt yourself badly. I have to get help.' She gently supported Annie onto her side, and put her folded jacket under her head. 'Now try and keep still, I will be back in a minute.'

'No, no, please don't tell anyone. I'm so scared. I don't know what's happening.' Tears streamed down Annie's face and she realised that she couldn't go on. She was aware of a sea of faces looking down at her but she couldn't seem to move or speak. Everything was grey and out of focus. She heard the siren of an ambulance and a cacophony of voices and she could do nothing but let everything wash over her. This was her worst nightmare.

She was taken to the Accident and Emergency department of the local hospital. After a long wait she was transported by stretcher into a small room where she waited alone.

Why am I here? What happened? I have to get out of here.

The door opened and a slim Asian woman of about thirty years of age strode energetically into the room, her stethoscope swinging jauntily round her neck as she did so. She acknowledged Annie with a cheerful smile and then studied her notes. 'Annie, my name is Dr Sharm, I am very pleased to meet you.'

Dr Sharm had a friendly open face and hair was swept back in a stylish chignon. She wore a spotless white coat and flat well-polished brogues. 'Having read your notes, I am aware of some general details of your personal circumstances and family background. I now have a few questions for you, and then we will run some tests and send you for an X-ray. Does that sound okay?'

Annie reluctantly nodded.

I want to be anywhere but here...

'I believe you fainted and hit your head as you fell. Is that right?'

'I don't remember. It all happened so quickly.'

'Have you got your period at the moment?'

Annie shook her head, she hadn't had a period for a few months but she didn't mention this.

'Have you been feeling ill recently, Annie?'

I am falling down a black hole and I have no strength to save myself; I am falling deeper, deeper, and deeper into the darkness…

'I've been a bit tired but otherwise I've been all right.' Annie looked away, sensing that her answer had not convinced the doctor.

Dr Sharm paused. 'Okay, thanks Annie. I need to run a few routine tests.' She reached over to her well-equipped trolley and selected a large instrument which she thrust into both of Annie's ears. 'All looks fine to me.' She smiled and proceeded to examine Annie's throat. 'Good, no infection there either, so far so good!' She smiled again. 'Now I need to listen to your chest Annie. Lift up your top for me please.' As Annie reluctantly exposed her chest, Dr Sharm took a deep breath before placing the cold stethoscope over her heart. She then put one hand on top of the other and tapped on her chest and on her back. Annie saw her expression change and heard the hollow sound of her cupped hands against her ribs. 'It all sounds okay but we will need to run a few other tests.' She looked pensive. 'I'll ask the nurse to do these for me and I'll organise an X-ray and then we can have another chat.' Dr Sharm's voice was very calm and Annie started to relax. She led Annie out of the room and into the large, bustling waiting area.

After a long wait, Annie was called into another small room further down the corridor. She was greeted by a tiny and cheerful nurse. Her name "Betsy" was printed on a badge precariously placed on one side of her ample chest. 'Please can you roll up your sleeve for me my dear.' She wrapped the blood pressure cuff around her left arm and started to pump it until it felt unbearably tight; then, as the pressure was slowly released, Betsy's forehead creased with concern. 'In a minute we will check your urine and then I will send you off to "Bloods" for a blood test...' She took a deep breath and looked searchingly into Annie's eyes. 'But first I will measure your height and your weight.'

Annie looked at the ominous set of scales standing in the corner. She placed each foot slowly and tentatively onto the large black pad and looked straight ahead as Betsy adjusted the two weights carefully until everything balanced. Betsy peered over her glasses at the numbers. 'Annie, you are six stone and four pounds, and you are five foot three inches.' Betsy put a warm hand on Annie's arm and offered no comment. 'I just want to have a word with Dr Sharm. I'll be back in a jiffy.'

Annie was left alone and she started to shiver; she felt cold and tired and all she wanted to do was to go home. She started to feel uneasy.

What are they talking about?

After about five minutes, Betsy breezed back into the room. 'Sorry about the wait, Annie.' Thrusting an alarmingly small test tube into Annie's hand she continued, 'Please can you just pop to the toilet to give me a urine sample.' As if sensing Annie's thoughts, she added with a grin, 'Just do your best!' Having provided the urine sample, Betsy escorted Annie down the corridor to "Bloods." As the blood was slowly and painfully drawn out of her arm into test tubes, she did fleetingly wonder if having less blood in her body would make her weigh less.

After the tests were completed, Annie sat dejectedly in the large waiting area waiting to be called for her X-ray. She tried not to stare at the patients with more serious injuries. Two children were screaming and the sound echoed around the large impersonal waiting room.

I want to disappear...

When Annie's name was called she shyly entered a small room containing a huge X-ray machine and was greeted by the efficient radiographer who slipped a heavy lead apron over her head. 'This will protect your vital organs from harm. Just lie down here and relax for a moment while I organise the cameras. Now I believe you are having a head X-ray today. Don't worry, it's a simple process. All you need to do is lie very still when I tell you to.'

She stared at the large bright light as the cameras were placed either side of her head. Annie felt very alone, lonely and nervous. She had never had an X-ray before and she wasn't sure why she needed one now.

'Keep still my love and we will get some good snaps.' The radiographer disappeared behind the screen. 'Taking the photos now… there, all finished. Go and sit in the waiting room and the doctor will call you back in when she is ready.'

Before long, Dr Sharm welcomed her back into her consulting room. She moved her chair to face Annie in a reassuring manner, and began to explain everything in a calm and measured way: 'Annie, I hope it hasn't been too much of an ordeal for you. I have the results of all the tests except the bloods which I will receive in a few days. Most of the tests came back clear which is good news. I do, however, have one or two concerns which I would like to share with you. Is that okay?'

Annie felt herself start to sweat, her eyes fixed on the floor.

I have to get out of here.

'Although the X-rays showed no obvious injury, I am concerned that you may be suffering from concussion. For this reason I think we need to monitor you overnight, so I will arrange for you to be admitted.'

This was not the news Annie was expecting. 'But I need to go home…'

'Not tonight, but if all is well, we can discharge you tomorrow. I would like to talk with you about something else that is concerning me.'

"Hush little baby, don't say a word…"

'Annie, your weight is dangerously low. You are five foot three and you only weigh six stone and four pounds. I am very concerned about this.

But I feel so fat...

'Is anything going on in your life that you need to tell us about?'

Where do I begin?

Annie remained silent. How could she even begin to express in words everything that was "going on"?

'I'm sorry doctor, I don't feel well and I am exhausted.' She bent over and put her head in her hands. Her shoulders shook and she wept.

'That's okay Annie, I won't ask any more questions tonight. You will feel better after you've had a good night's sleep. I'll call for a porter to take you to the ward now and I'll come and visit you in the morning.'

The night staff asked Annie a series of questions every hour during the night to check that she wasn't suffering from concussion. 'What day is it?' 'What month is it?' 'What is the name of the Queen?' The ward was buzzing throughout the night with nurses tending to their patients and there was little chance of having any sleep. She thought about the events of the day before and silently cried into her pillow.

Dr Sharm told me my weight is "dangerously low." I don't believe her... but what will happen if I lose any more weight?

At six o'clock in the morning the day began with a burst of activity. The bright lights were turned up and the drug round was completed. Then a jovial member of staff came into the ward pushing a trolley full of food and steaming jugs of tea and coffee. He laughed and chatted vivaciously with all the patients as he dished up the breakfast. The patient in the bed next to Annie put her hand up to her mouth and whispered, 'We all call him George the dinner lady!'

'What can I offer you my duck? Cereal, toast, fruit, yogurt? What do you fancy?' The thought of eating anything was abhorrent and Annie declined everything except a cup of weak black tea. 'I tell you what, I'll leave a yogurt and a banana on your table in case you're hungry later. You need to eat, you know, to keep your strength up!'

She gave a weak smile, lay back in the bed and closed her eyes.

Am I losing my mind?

CHAPTER 16

'Annie, I think you are suffering from an illness called Anorexia Nervosa.'

Annie looked at Dr Sharm and wondered what she was talking about. 'Anorexia Nervosa? What is that?'

'Anorexia is an eating disorder where patients feel they need to keep their weight as low as possible, but I'm afraid I don't know enough about this illness. I would like to admit you to a hospital nearby called Ashmeade. This is a hospital that specialises in mental health and they will know how to help you.'

'So you think I'm losing my mind, do you? You think I'm crazy?'

'No, I don't, Annie, but I do think you need help.'

Annie thought for a moment. 'But I can't go to hospital, I don't have time. My mother is very ill and she needs me. I can't let her down. I need to go to college. Let me go home, I'll be okay. Please don't make me go there.'

'Annie, I would like you to trust me on this, you urgently need help and support and it is my job to make sure that you get it.'

'No, I can't and I won't.'

God, is it possible that I might die? What is happening to me? Should I listen to my head or should I listen to the doctor? I don't want or need help from anyone. I'm really scared. Perhaps I should agree to go to Ashmeade, but only for a few days… and on my own terms. I am in control.

***

An ornate wrought iron gate opened and the ambulance pulled up outside the main entrance to the building. Ashmeade was a huge red brick building set back from the road with rooms for fifty patients. The patients' rooms had large windows with views either onto the front garden or the grey courtyard at the back. Each window was encased by thick metal bars. Annie stared at the formidable, unwelcoming building and shuddered; it looked like a prison. The hospital was set in immaculate well-tended gardens and the whole estate was surrounded by a red brick wall surmounted by large rolls of barbed wire. The front door opened by a tall austere woman in her late forties.

'Hello. My name is Claudia, I'm the hospital manager here. You must be Annie Crawford, we are expecting you. Have you got any luggage?'

Annie shook her head.

'We will ask your parents to bring in some clothes and toiletries for you to use during your stay with us. Let me show you around.'

She briskly marched Annie down a long, dark corridor and into the residents' sitting room. 'This is where you can meet with other residents, read or watch television.' There were a few rather worn-looking chairs and a table with some old magazines and a pile of dusty board games. Faded floral curtains hung limply either side of the high Victorian window and the room smelt musty. A lone resident sat motionless in a chair.

I can't stay here, I have to escape.

Claudia led Annie upstairs into a large dormitory containing five beds. 'And this is where you will be sleeping. I will organise some night clothes for tonight and then tomorrow I hope you will have your own clothes and your own toothbrush.' Claudia was formal and unfriendly; Annie was beginning to feel that she disliked her.

How can she be this cold?

'The gong will sound at eight o'clock for breakfast, twelve noon for lunch and six o'clock for dinner. You must go down to the dining room for each meal. You will see a psychiatrist twice a week. You will also attend occupational therapy in an adjacent building. The communal toilets and bathroom are at the end of the corridor on the left hand side. You may walk in the grounds but you must get permission from one of the staff to do this. Do you have any questions?'

Annie realised that she hadn't listened to a single word this formidable lady had said and certainly had no questions. Claudia abruptly turned on her heels and marched towards the door, but just before she disappeared from sight she turned around. 'It will get easier once you get into a routine.'

So she is human after all. But why on earth did I agree to come here? In a bizarre way I feel like a huge weight has been lifted from my shoulders. I have escaped from my father. I am safe.

Annie lay down on the uncomfortable bed not knowing what to do. The place seemed deserted and she wondered where everyone was. All of a sudden the door opened and a teenage girl of about Annie's age ambled into the dormitory, and threw herself heavily onto the end of Annie's bed.

'Hello, you must be new here. I'm Jess. Who are you?'

'I'm Annie,' she whispered.

'Why are you here?'

'I have no idea. I just want to go home.'

Jess smiled. 'Don't we all!'

'Why are you here?' Annie asked, looking up at Jess.

'I get down and depressed... I tried to kill myself but I couldn't even do that properly. I've been stuck here for months.'

'Oh no, that must have been terrible.'

'Naah, it isn't too bad here. You get used to it.'

Annie thought about Mutti and her own circumstances. This girl seemed different; she seemed resigned to being in hospital, but there was a cheerful tone to her voice and Annie warmed to her immediately.

'That's my patch over there,' Jess said, pointing to a welcoming and cheery little corner of the dormitory. Her bed was covered by a luxurious brightly coloured eiderdown. An old tatty teddy bear lay on her pillow and well-worn baseball boots were kicked off randomly by her bedside cabinet. The walls behind her bed were festooned with intricate drawings and eye-catching paintings arranged rather haphazardly and held up with strips of yellowing sticky tape. A colourful mat made up of brightly coloured pieces of rag woven together, was placed beside her bed and it all looked very striking.

'It looks lovely. Did you do all those pictures?'

'Yes, we do art in OT and I must admit I'm quite pleased with some of my drawings.'

'OT?'

'Occupational Therapy… We draw, paint, use clay or make sculptures out of wood. I love being creative. It helps me escape from reality and I forget about everything for a few minutes… but they don't half moan about me using sticky tape on the walls!' Jess giggled. 'It's hard when you first arrive here Annie. It seems like a prison, and stone-faced Claudia doesn't help, does she?' This time it was Annie's turn to giggle. 'I have been in here for so long that I don't think I could do anything for myself any more. Everything is done for us here and I'm terrified of being let loose in the big wide world. I think I'd be lost.'

'Have you any family?'

'My parents were both killed in a plane crash years ago, so my aunt has reluctantly brought me up. She's my godmother and I think she promised my parents that she would take responsibility for me if anything should happen to them. But she hasn't been able to cope with me for years, I'm just too wild for her! When I came here she gave me an eiderdown, some slippers and a rug to try and make herself feel better about abandoning me here. I think she feels guilty about everything. She has never visited me, I haven't seen her for months. Good riddance to her!'

Annie listened sympathetically to Jess's story and closed her eyes.

Why is life so hard?

She felt comforted by meeting Jess; they were about the same age and Annie felt sure they would get on well.

Jess held her much-loved teddy bear close to her chest. 'Just do what they tell you and everything will be okay.' She turned to face Annie with an evil glint in her eye. 'But they don't know half of what I get up to!'

CHAPTER 17

The gong sounded six times for breakfast. After a long and restless night, Annie struggled to pull on her clothes and drag herself down to the dining room. She meekly followed her new-found friend. All the residents sat on long wooden benches, mostly in silence, eating their first meal of the day.

'Jess I can't eat this porridge. It's cold, lumpy and revolting.'

'When they're not looking just shovel it onto my plate Annie. I eat anything and everything.'

Annie scanned the room and then, when it was safe to do so, she discreetly piled her breakfast onto Jess's plate. She looked around the room again and was relieved that she had not been spotted by any member of staff.

This could be a very useful friend.

Annie looked around again and realised with horror that the four residents sitting across the table had all stopped eating, and were now staring at her with interest.

Oh no... please don't say anything...

A youngish man with alarmingly stern features leant towards Annie, pursed his lips tightly and eyed her up and down with disdain. She held her breath, dreading what he was going to do next. He shielded his mouth and whispered in her ear, 'If she doesn't eat it, I will!' He turned slowly to look at the others, cocked his head to one side and, much to Annie's surprise, he raised his eyebrows and winked.

No one commented, it felt like a conspiracy. Her secret was safe.

After breakfast, Annie made her way down the corridor to her first appointment with the psychiatrist. She felt apprehensive about the meeting and what she might have to talk about. She knocked on the door and stepped tentatively into the drab and sparsely furnished consultation room. The psychiatrist was seated behind a large wooden desk, deeply engrossed in one of the many coloured folders piled high in front of her. Quick to notice Annie's presence, she jumped up to greet her with a warm handshake and a wide smile.

'I am very pleased to meet you! My name is Patrice, and you must be Annie. Please make yourself comfortable and help yourself to water if you would like some.'

Annie smiled shyly at the psychiatrist. Patrice seemed friendly and approachable.

'I'm looking forward to getting to know you, Annie. How are you settling in?'

'I'm okay thank you.'

'That's good to hear. I'm sure Claudia and the team are looking after you well. I wonder if you are feeling a little nervous about our meeting today?'

Annie meekly agreed with an almost imperceptible nod of her head.

I'm terrified, I feel sick...

Patrice looked kindly at the vulnerable girl sitting in front of her. 'It is understandable that you feel a little nervous Annie. I'm going to keep this initial consultation quite brief, it will give us the chance to complete the initial evaluation and introduce ourselves. I have one or two questions I would like to ask you.' She smiled. 'And I'm sure you'll have questions for me too. How does that sound?'

'Okay,' said Annie quietly, as she shifted uncomfortably on her chair.

'But first I need to check a few things with you, your personal details, medical history, and family background. It shouldn't take long,' Patrice said, reshuffling her paperwork.

The initial evaluation was a lengthy process, but at last, Patrice put down her pen. 'Thank you for your patience Annie, I think I now have all the information I need. Let's move on to the practical arrangements. We will be meeting together twice a week for hourly consultations. During our sessions, I'll be asking you some challenging questions about your life, and this might involve discussing some sensitive or upsetting issues. Please let me know if, at any time, you don't feel comfortable, or ready to share your thoughts or feelings with me. All I ask of you is that you are open and honest. In this way we can make the best possible use of our time together. All our consultations are confidential, and I will be making notes as we go along. Have you any questions so far?'

How can I be open and honest? I must keep my promise to Stan.
Annie averted her eyes and shook her head.

'So Annie, what brings you here to see me today?'

'I'm not sure,' Annie muttered sadly.

'I see from your notes that you fell unconscious at college, and were taken by ambulance to A and E with suspected concussion. Is this correct?'

Annie stared gloomily out of the window, and nodded her head.

'Why do you think you collapsed?' asked Patrice.

'I really don't know - I can't remember anything about it. The hospital did loads of tests and they couldn't find anything wrong with me. I have been tired lately. Perhaps I was just exhausted…'

'The doctor at A and E has recorded in your notes that your weight is dangerously low. I wonder whether you lost consciousness because you have not been eating enough,' Patrice suggested quietly.

Annie shot a glance at her psychiatrist. 'No… but, when I think about it, I haven't been very hungry recently.'

'I wonder why this is…'

Where do I begin?

Annie's face contorted in pain. 'My friend, Franky, thinks I'm too thin. Maybe she's just jealous...'

'Do you think you're too thin?' Patrice probed.

'No I don't, 'she whispered, almost inaudibly.

Patrice bowed her head over her notes. 'Okay Annie, we'll return to this in our future sessions, but, for now, I'd like to ask you how you are feeling today.'

Annie's eyes welled up with tears. 'I feel beyond tired; sad, empty, lonely...'

How can you make my life better? There is no hope...

'I do understand this is hard for you,' she said, reaching over her desk to offer Annie a tissue. 'Thank you for sharing your feelings with me. In time, everything will start to make sense, things will get better. During our discussions, it is important that you feel that you can put your full trust in me. I think it will be helpful if I tell you a little about myself.'

But can I trust her?

'I am originally from Ghana - a country in West Africa - and all my family still live there. I came to this country to study to become a doctor. My mission is, and has always been, to help people in whatever capacity I can. I've specialised in mental health because I'm fascinated in the power of the human mind, and what happens when it becomes dysfunctional. I do believe that the invisible wounds are the hardest to heal. Do you agree Annie?'

The invisible wounds are the hardest to heal? Yes, maybe she is right. If I had broken my leg I could scream out in pain and people would help me; I could talk and people would listen.

Annie appeared deep in thought and so Patrice continued, 'Mental health does not get the focus, funding or status that it should have in this country, it is all swept under the carpet, as if these patients don't matter. Many people struggle during different stages of life, but are unable to talk about their problems, because there is a stigma attached to anything to do with mental health. I feel privileged to work in this area of medicine and to work with people like you Annie, and I hope that you will feel able to talk freely with me.'

Talk freely? There is so much I can't tell you. I can't even begin to understand what is going on in my head. If I can't make sense of any of it myself, how can I tell you?

'You will find that I have an unconventional and direct approach and I can be tough and challenging. I will at times be ruthless. I don't want to simply chip away at the surface, I want to dig down to the depths, to find out what is driving you towards starvation and ultimately towards self-destruction. Depriving yourself of food is the physical symptom of a serious and deep-rooted mental illness. It is *this* that we need to uncover and understand, Annie. Then, and only then, can we take small steps towards changing your life for the better.'

Self-destruction? Mental illness? Please tell me I'm not crazy…

'Just before we finish for today, I would like you to tell me some of your interests,' said Patrice with a smile.

'I play the violin, although I haven't felt much like playing recently.'

'That's great Annie, do you listen to a lot of music?'

'Yes, I find that when I listen to music - James Taylor, Carole King, Bob Dylan - I'm transported into a different place, a happier place,' she answered, her eyes shining through her tears.

'What else do you like doing?'

'I like drawing and painting, but I don't seem to have the energy or the will any more…'

'This all sounds wonderfully creative Annie. As part of our plan going forward, I would like to refer you for twice-weekly Occupational Therapy sessions, which are held here at Ashmeade. You will be invited to take part in a range of activities - painting, music, storytelling, dance, clay modelling, and much more. These sessions will help you to rebuild your skills, boost your confidence, improve your mood, and it is a great opportunity to meet other people too. Do you think this sounds like a good plan?'

'Yes, I think it sounds interesting,' said Annie, rather

hesitantly.

'Good, I will organise this today,' she said brightly.

***

Annie felt emotionally drained after her initial meeting with Patrice and so she retreated to the residents' sitting room, which was empty of staff and residents, and curled up in one of the faded arm chairs. Her head was spinning - full of questions she should have asked Patrice - and she needed time on her own to recover. But her peace was interrupted by an unexpected visitor. Joy swept into the room and engulfed Annie with a huge hug. She looked colourful and striking, in contrast with the greyness of Ashmeade. She was like a breath of fresh air, and Annie immediately began to feel brighter.

'Annie darlin', I'm sorry to find you here, but it is very good that they will be taking care of you.'

'Thank you for coming to see me. Is Stan with you?' she asked, looking over Joy's shoulder.

'No my dear, Stanley is just too busy to come, all that marking he has to do…'

Is he ashamed to visit me here at Ashmeade? Is he ashamed of me? Or does he just not care?

'I've brought a suitcase with some of your things for your stay here. I had to guess what you need and I hope I've brought everything.'

'Joy, please take me home. I don't know why I'm here and I need to go home to take care of Mutti. Is she out of hospital? Is she better now? When can she visit me?'

'Ah Annie, you need to use this time to relax and recover. And I need to tell you about Mutti. I visited her a few times in the hospital and I tried to brighten up her day.' She shook her head sadly. 'She seemed to be in another world and even the cheerful bouquet of flowers I took with me made no difference at all. Anyway, yesterday she was transferred to a drug and alcohol dependency unit in Birmingham. She will spend a few months in the unit drying out and learning how to live without her addiction. Nobody can visit her at the moment, so there is really nothing you can do for her right now. She is in good hands, and so are you.'

Annie thought about what Joy had just said and she realised the hopelessness of her situation. She couldn't help Mutti and she didn't feel ready to help herself either. She put her head in her hands.

'I hid a small mourning brooch amongst your clothing, Annie. I don't know why but I feel sure there must be a special story behind this beautiful piece of jewellery and I thought it may bring you some comfort.'

Annie smiled through her tears. How right she was.

'Now, there is something I want you to do for me. I want you to listen to these wise doctors because I think it may be a pathway to health, happiness and to finding the joy that is out there.' She knelt down in front of Annie and put a warm comforting hand on her knee. 'Find the joy, Annie! I know you will get there in the end.'

Annie listened to the wise words of her unexpected ally and friend. Since Joy had arrived, quite a few residents and staff had joined them in the lounge and Annie noticed that she was causing quite a stir. People were whispering – rudely, in Annie's view - but Joy seemed oblivious and she smiled broadly at everyone. 'I know what it's like to have to fight for your existence and that is what you need to do now. You are beautiful, brave and clever and you have your whole life ahead of you.' Drawing her face close to Annie's, she added in a whisper, 'I know it must feel strange being here, but you are strong and determined Annie. Keep your spirits up, and you will get through this.'

With that she strode out of the room, her head held high, wobbling on her pink high heels; her strong musky perfume lingering in the air long after she had left.

CHAPTER 18

Clutching her cherished piece of jewellery close to her chest, Annie wondered if she deserved the third of the shining red garnets. She reflected on the promises she had made to herself, to lose weight and keep fit, to support Mutti and to find some maths tuition. She had successfully lost weight and, even though she couldn't go swimming any more, she was satisfied that she had earned herself the first two garnets.

But I have lost control; I'm totally obsessed with food and calories. I know I have to eat to live, but my brain won't let me... No. I am in control. I decide what I eat and what I don't eat; I have self-discipline; I have self-control. I do deserve the third garnet.

Her heart sank as she thought about the promise she had made to herself to support Mutti.

I feel rage boiling up inside me every time I think about her. I am glad that she is getting the help she needs to overcome her addiction, but I am suffering too. I need her love and support - now, more than ever. Isn't that what a parent is supposed to do?

Annie put her head in her hands and sighed.

Am I being selfish? Mutti has her own struggles to face...

Annie felt guilty that she had failed to support Mutti to get better, but she knew that Joy was right; her mother was now in safe hands; she could do no more. This promise would have to be put on hold.

As for her third promise to herself, she still hadn't found time to find any maths tuition and she felt bad, knowing that she should have prioritised this. She desperately wanted Stan to be proud of her.

Joy had been very thoughtful with the packing of Annie's things. She had carefully chosen a selection of comfortable clothes, pyjamas and toiletries, including a bar of luxurious lavender soap. At the bottom of the case she found a pile of Vogue magazines. As Annie opened one of the glossy pages she noticed a small hand-written message which read, "Darlin Annie, 8 stone 4lbs is beautiful."

Annie knew that she was way under eight stone four pounds.

I think I would be too fat if I was that weight.

But she was touched by Joy's simple and clear message. Annie cast her eyes over page upon page of models wearing ridiculously outrageous outfits; they looked tall, willowy and beautiful, and she longed to be as skinny as they were.

As soon as Annie had unpacked her things, Claudia strode in and grabbed the empty suitcase.

Did she take my suitcase away in case I'm tempted to do a runner? Just as I thought; this is a prison and there is no escape.

Annie thought about Stan, and Joy's hasty excuse for his absence.

He would make time to visit me if he wanted to see me. It hurts… and yet I feel huge relief. He can't get anywhere near me in here. Hush little baby, don't say a word.

Annie reflected on Joy's kindness and wise words: "I know what it's like to have to fight for your existence and that is what you need to do now. You are beautiful, brave and clever and you have your whole life ahead of you."

I must keep fighting.

***

She lay still in bed staring into the darkness. It had been a week since she had arrived at Ashmeade and she longed to be able to sleep for more than an hour at a time. All of a sudden she felt a sharp nudge in her ribs.

104

'Annie, shhh, follow me.'

She blinked. Surely it wasn't morning yet. She felt another prod on her shoulder.

'Come on, quickly, come with me.'

'Leave me alone Jess, it's the middle of the night,' Annie grunted sleepily.

'Come on, you're in for a treat, trust me will you,' Jess said encouragingly as she pulled back Annie's covers.

'What on earth are we going to do at this time of night Jess? I haven't had a wink of sleep and I'm shattered!'

'Just shut up and follow me.'

Jess was very insistent and Annie realised that she was not going to give her any peace so she struggled out of bed and followed her out of the dormitory. They padded down the corridor in silence and crept in the shadows past the reception desk where the porter seemed to be fast asleep. Jess stealthily opened the front door and they escaped into the grounds. The air was cold and Annie shivered in her skimpy summer pyjamas. They ran across the wet grass and settled on the other side of a large bush. Jess dug deep into the pocket of her dressing gown and pulled out a rolled cigarette and some matches. She carefully lit the end. Her chest expanded as she drew in the musky smoke. She held her breath; her face radiating pleasure; before exhaling a line of immaculate smoke rings. Annie looked on in astonishment, aware of the earthy herbal smell of the smoke. 'Have a drag Annie, it feels really good!'

'I don't smoke.'

'But try this, you'll love it.'

Annie held the cigarette awkwardly between two fingers, inhaled and swallowed. Within seconds she felt as if she was falling into the abyss. But her friend kept plying her with more and before long they were both giggling uncontrollably.

'What the hell is happening to me Jess?'

'This is stuff that friends from the outside smuggle in for me. It makes us happy, right?'

'Right...'

As she had more drags Annie began to feel mellow and sleepy. 'Ah you're a good friend to me, Jess.' Then, as she tried to stand up, she stumbled and retched, bringing up an undigested pile of hospital food. Her whole body convulsed and heaved over and over again until there was nothing left.

Jess gently held Annie's hair away from her face. 'Annie, take another drag, it'll make you feel better.' Annie wiped her face roughly on her sleeve and inhaled more smoke. She felt mellow and sleepy again and strangely content to be sitting in the middle of Ashmeade gardens illegally smoking something - she had no idea what - with Jess. Nothing mattered any more. When the last piece of ash dropped to the ground Jess whispered, 'We had better go back now before Joe wakes up.'

Annie found it strange that she was aware of everything going on around her but she didn't seem to be in control of her limbs. She had to concentrate on putting one leg in front of the other, and every few steps she fell to the ground. Opening the door quietly, the two girls crept past Joe and he didn't move a muscle. Looking at him slumping in his chair with his mouth wide open Annie put her hand over her mouth to stifle a giggle, before lurching uncontrollably towards the floor. Jess managed to catch her just in time, avoiding a complete disaster, and together they staggered back to the dormitory. Annie threw herself extravagantly onto her bed and giggled again.

'That was fun wasn't it Annie?' Her body felt limp and heavy but her brain remained alert. She looked at Jess and felt an unfamiliar and powerful connection between them.

Nothing matters any more, I feel amazing. Is this what it feels like to be happy? But did it really happen?

The mud on her pyjamas was testament that it did.

During the days that followed, Annie began to understand the general routines of Ashmeade. Mealtimes were a huge hurdle but Jess proved to be a faithful ally and the staff were often too distracted to notice the subversion or the conspiracy going on between the residents. On the rare occasion when the staff were observing her, Annie would eat as little as she could and then rush upstairs to shove her finger down her throat and rid herself of the undigested food.

Friday was the day Annie feared the most because it was the day when she was weighed by Claudia. She soon found an effective way to deceive this cold, hard person. Early every Friday Annie would creep into the grounds past the porter and collect a pile of large stones. She wore multiple layers of heavy clothing and hid the stones in every available nook and cranny.

'Six stone four pounds, same as last week. You must eat more or we will need to revise your treatment plan.'

Annie nodded submissively.

Revise your treatment plan. What on earth does that mean?

It sounded like a threat to Annie but she had no intention of taking heed of the order given.

I have fooled her. She has absolutely no idea how much I eat, or how much I weigh. My plan is working.

CHAPTER 19

'I just can't do this, I'm sorry…'

'Annie, as you know, I will be asking you some challenging questions. I understand that, at times, this will be very uncomfortable for you, but it is important that you do your best to answer them.'

'But I just can't,' she wailed.

Today was the second consultation with her psychiatrist. The first session had gone reasonably well, perhaps because Patrice had not asked her too many difficult questions. Annie dreaded this meeting because she knew today would be different.

Patrice leant forward on her chair. 'I wonder what it is about today that makes you unable to answer my questions?'

Annie shrugged her shoulders.

I don't understand my own head, I don't have any words…

'Well, I'm quite happy to sit here quietly while you think about that, Annie.'

Shuffling uncomfortably on her chair, Annie stared out of the window and gazed at the open countryside beyond the confines of Ashmeade. How she longed to be walking in those hills with not a care in the world. Then her eyes alighted on the high perimeter wall and the barbed wire.

'I don't want to be here, I'd rather be anywhere than here.'

'This is a good place to start this session, Annie. Why do you think you are here with me today?'

'I'm not sure. I know my head is all over the place and I don't think you or anyone can help me,' she said sadly.

'Annie, I think you are suffering from depression. We need to find out what is causing your unhappiness and pain.'

'Depressed? Am I depressed? I *am* unhappy'.

'So, what makes you happy?'

Annie considered her answer carefully. It was not a question she had expected but, she realised with relief, it was something she could talk about. 'I love winter.'

'What is it about the winter that you like so much?'

'I love snow. It reminds me of when I was a little girl. I still feel excited when I see the first snowflakes fall.'

Patrice smiled. 'You must have loved this winter just gone.'

'I loved walking in the forest in a magical winter wonderland and skating across the vast expanse of ice on the meadow.' She shook her head sadly. 'But it's all different now.'

'What can you remember about winters when you were a little girl?'

'Mutti used to wrap me up in my thick winter coat, bobble hat, scarf and mittens and we would tramp hand-in-hand through the deep snow. We made a snowman or threw snowballs. We laughed together and hugged when we got cold.'

'Lovely memories Annie, what else can you recall?'

'On Christmas Day, Stan would light the fire. I can remember returning home after a long walk with Mutti and seeing the flames dancing in the fireplace. I couldn't believe how wonderful it was to get toasty and warm by the fireside. We used to put handfuls of chestnuts on a large bucket over the flames; I used to burn my fingers shelling the nuts, but oooh they were delicious.'

'I find the winters here so cold; we didn't get hard winters in Ghana. I can't believe you like the snow because

I don't like it one little bit,' said Patrice, hugging her body in an exaggerated shiver.

'Snow makes me feel happy.'

'Great Annie. What else makes you happy?'

It was warm in the room and the sun shone through the window. Annie was beginning to feel more at ease and engaged with Patrice and the words were beginning to flow more freely. 'I love to think about when I was very young. Everything was much better then. I was carefree and I had a lot of freedom to play out in the street with the local kids, just going home when I was hungry. I climbed trees and made dens with my friends. Yes, life was good then.'

'Climbing trees, making dens - it must have been so much fun. Tell me more, Annie.'

'I loved being outside, running and playing in the fresh air. We used to tell each other scary stories or play in deep muddy puddles. I was always filthy, caked in dirt after a day out with my friends. Stan would be grumpy but Mutti used to throw me in a steaming hot bath and sing to me.' Annie smiled wistfully. 'I loved listening to her singing. One of her songs - our favourite - was all about a baby swishing down the plughole; we used to howl with laughter.'

'Thanks for sharing your precious memories Annie. How did you feel in those early years?'

'I felt safe.'

'Good Annie, anything else?'

'I knew I was loved. And yes, I felt happy.'

'We have had a productive discussion today, and I think we should end the session now. I have a follow-up activity for you. I would like you to go out into the beautiful grounds of Ashmeade and walk all the way around the perimeter. Enjoy the colours and scents of the spring flowers and feel the breeze on your face, it really is a lovely garden. While you do this I would like you to breathe in the fresh air and try and capture those carefree happy feelings that you enjoyed as a young child.'

'I'll do that.' Annie smiled; she liked the idea of reliving some of her happy childhood memories in the garden. And then her thoughts turned to Jess and the mischief and fun they had had in the very same grounds.

In the afternoon, the clouds had cleared and the sun was shining. Annie thought she would take the opportunity of the blue sky and spring warmth to enjoy the garden, and do as Patrice had asked. But as she walked across the grass she felt pain, everything was hurting. Her clothes hung limply around her bloated tummy and every footstep was a struggle.

Why do I have to do this?

As she walked further she began to notice the abundance of spring flowers. The daffodils were just starting to lose their vibrant yellow colour and droop, and tall red tulips reached towards the sky. Bluebells had sprung up everywhere, turning the flowerbeds into a deep purple haze. Although these were very well-tended gardens, there was a certain chaos and wildness about it which Annie loved. It reminded her of happier times in the forest with Thanos.

Being happy when I was a young child was different to any feeling of happiness I have now. When I was young, I was innocent; I felt no pain, guilt, anguish or fear. My head was full of wonder and excitement about the life I had stretching before me. But then everything changed. My brain has been taken over by self-hatred and self-destruction; there is no room left for anything else.

She wandered slowly through the gardens, now following the perimeter wall as she had been instructed. Honeysuckle climbed the brick face reaching halfway up the wall, and as Annie breathed in the sweet, perfumed scent, she began to appreciate the calm beauty of the garden. Just beyond the trailing plant she discovered an old and weathered bench. On it was an unpolished aluminium plaque with a simple inscription:

"Cherished moments survive the ravages of time."

She wiped the plaque with the sleeve of her dress until it shone in the morning sunshine. Sitting down heavily, she thought about the inscription.

I wonder who wrote these words. Were they suffering? Magical moments in life are the most precious but they can pass all too quickly.

Annie recalled the magical moments of her youngest days, and how the most precious and poignant times were those that she had spent with her mother: the loving hug, the encouraging words. This special love was the most memorable for Annie.

CHAPTER 20

'Hello… is there anyone there?'

A solid beam of torchlight cut through the darkness. Annie and Jess froze and looked at each other in horror.

'Shh Annie, it's Joe,' hissed Jess. The elderly man, who worked on the reception desk as the night porter, swung his torch in their direction. 'Just keep still and he'll go away in a minute.'

Annie started to giggle. 'I can't help it, this is hilarious!' She took a deep drag and watched as the trail of smoke slowly drifted upwards.

I don't give a damn whether he finds us here or not. Actually I really don't care about anything at all.

She giggled again.

'I know you're there, come out and show yourselves.'

'I feel like I'm a prisoner of war trying to escape the enemy and if I show myself, I'll get shot!' Annie struggled to suppress her laughter.

Jess suddenly leapt on top of Annie and held her hand firmly over her mouth. 'Shut up or we'll both be in deep trouble.' Annie's words were muffled but her shoulders were shaking with uncontrollable laughter. 'Annie, you're a bloody liability, just for God's sake, shut up!' Jess's eyes glinted in the darkness.

Struggling to break free, Annie tried to answer back but

no sound came out. She was shocked by the harsh words of her friend and she felt Jess's fingers dig painfully into her cheeks. Suddenly they were trapped in the powerful light of his torch. 'Get your head down Annie, quickly…'

Joe walked within a foot of the girls and paused. Jess held Annie down in a vice-like grip with her hand still firmly clamped over her mouth. After what seemed like an eternity, Joe cursed, 'Humph, it must be one of those pesky deer again. God, I hate this job!' With that he walked slowly back towards the building, cursing and swearing as he went.

They remained still until they were sure the coast was clear and then Jess slowly released her hand from Annie's mouth. 'Oh Annie, you nearly landed us in deep shit!'

She stared at Jess, unnerved by her harsh words and painful grip. 'He's gone now so get off me, I won't make a noise.'

Jess gently stroked the side of Annie's face. 'I'm sorry if I was too rough. You have red scratches on your face and they look sore.'

'Don't worry, I'll live.'

'I didn't mean to hurt you, but if he'd caught us we'd have been dead meat, you know that don't you?'

'I'm such a liability Jess, I'm sorry.'

Annie felt the comfort of Jess's body gently intertwining with hers, and she started to relax into their warm and intense embrace. Jess slowly leant in and her warm lips touched Annie's, softly at first, and then with increasing fire and passion. Confused thoughts crowded Annie's head but her body tingled with pleasure;

How can I feel like this? My whole body is aching for more… Everything feels right.

Stan has ruined so much in my life. But this is different. I feel like the clouds have parted and the smallest chink of light has appeared in the darkness, I will never forget this special moment.

The spell was broken abruptly by Jess tugging Annie to her feet. 'Quick, we must go back. Old Joe is usually asleep at his desk but, for some reason, tonight he seems alert and on the hunt.'

'Perhaps someone knows more than we think about our nighttime escapades,' Annie whispered.

'Haha, perhaps…'

They crept in through the front door and spotted Joe deep in conversation with a man Jess didn't recognise: 'I could have sworn I heard people laughing and messing about out there tonight Mike. Perhaps it was just a deer; but I suspect that the rumours are right, something is going on.'

'Okay Joe, I'm depending on you to keep a watchful eye on the situation and call me if you discover anything; anything at all.'

'Of course Mike. Got time for a cuppa before you go?'

'Yeah, why not?'

The two men disappeared into the small office space behind the desk and Jess grabbed the opportunity to drag Annie to the floor and together they crawled stealthily past the desk, hardly daring to breathe, before fleeing down the long dimly lit corridor to the safety of their dormitory.

Jess breathed a sigh of relief. 'Shit, that was a close shave. I have no idea who old Joe was talking to tonight, but somebody here knows about us Annie; it makes it even more exciting doesn't it!'

Annie lay in the darkness and thought about her wild and reckless friend. She realised that they had taken such a risk, but her mind quickly returned to what had just happened. She wasn't sure if it was the dope, or the fear, or just something that had happened in the heat of the moment but, whatever it was, it felt magical.

Jess was a skinny girl with long legs, and she was about the same height as Annie. She had short spiky blond hair and piercingly blue eyes. When she smiled, a deep dimple appeared on the right side of her face which gave her a lopsided cheeky appearance. She had a tattoo of a long multicoloured snake on the top of her left arm, with the words "Be strong" inscribed in black lettering just above its forked tongue. She usually wore skin-tight faded jeans, a black T-shirt and her much-loved baseball boots that were coming apart at the seams. Jess was funny and sensitive, a free thinker - a non-conformist - and everyone loved her.

But Jess had a dark side.

***

The following afternoon Annie made her way to Occupational Therapy, which was housed in a separate one-storey block adjacent to the main building. She felt anxious but also rather curious about what her first session would entail. She opened the door and was taken aback by what she saw. The area was creatively messy and strangely ordered at the same time. The floor was a glorious pebbledash of years of dried splashes of paint, and the tables were stained dark brown from clay. The materials and utensils by contrast were ordered, attractively displayed, and readily available for all to use. Annie wandered around the room, marvelling at all the creativity. A wizened old man pummelled a large chunk of red clay on a wooden board, seemingly enjoying the solitude and making nothing in particular. A group of participants were hunched over their smudged chalk and charcoal drawings, their mouths opening and closing in a rather childlike fashion, in time with the movements of their hands across the paper. She didn't recognise the majority of people and assumed that they were out-patients coming in for their treatment.

The gentle, soothing sound of James Taylor singing "Fire and Rain" in the background completed the tranquil creative atmosphere and Annie looked forward to the session ahead.

A friendly member of staff wearing a white tabard and blue trousers bounced up to her with a beaming smile. 'You must be Annie, I'm Elaine, welcome!'

Annie scanned the room and then acknowledged Elaine with a smile. 'This place looks incredible!'

'We all enjoy ourselves here! We provide a safe and exciting space where you have the freedom to express yourself in creative and innovative ways, using an exciting range of materials. Does that sound good?' Without waiting for a reply she added, 'Ouch, that looks sore Annie. How did you scratch your face?'

Annie, rather taken aback by the direct question, was quick to respond, 'Oh, I just scratched myself on a branch in the garden, but it's okay.'

The Occupational Therapist seemed to be satisfied with her answer. 'What would you like to do today? Perhaps some painting, or drawing?'

Annie scanned the room and her eyes were drawn to her friend standing in front of an easel, in the art area mixing acrylic paint into various shades of green and yellow. She felt confused by her own feelings towards Jess, but she knew that something remarkable had taken place in the garden the night before, and she was eager to discover more about her new-found friend. She purposefully selected an activity nearby so that she could surreptitiously observe Jess at work. She sat down on a small table, on which was a round wicker basket containing a generous heap of colourful wooden beads with a hole drilled through the centre of each one. Beside the basket was a selection of dark leather laces of various lengths and some darning needles. The most challenging part of the activity was threading the leather through the ample eye of the needle and she was shocked to realise how much her hand shook. She acknowledged that she had felt increasingly weak and shaky recently, and feared that it was because she wasn't eating enough, but she quickly pushed her disturbing thoughts to the back of her mind and glanced around furtively, hoping that no one had noticed. She carefully selected six deep blue beads of varying hues and threaded them successfully onto the brown leather band. Finally she cut the leather to size with some heavy-duty scissors, loosely tied the ends and sat back to admire her work. This would be a handmade gift for her wonderful, funny, beautiful, wild and creative friend.

Jess was totally absorbed and Annie, having started to make another bracelet for herself, was fascinated by Jess, and she couldn't take her eyes off her, but she took care not to disturb her. When the paints were mixed, Jess scrutinised the selection of brushes on the table beside her, selected a thick brush, immersed it in the viscous dark green paint and splashed bands of colour deftly across the canvas. Her whole body moved in rhythm as she worked the brush across the surface; it was as if Annie was watching an exquisite dance as the picture started to emerge. Annie was transfixed as a deep forest appeared on the canvas, with a weak wintery sun in the background casting light and texture under each individual leaf; the veins highlighted by flecks of yellow, light green and brown. Then she paused and stood back to appraise her work. She shook her head slowly and mixed a deep red in another pot. She added a dash of red to the yellow of the sun, turning some of its surface into a rich orange and then dabbed orange flecks on the leaves in the foreground, giving the picture depth. She stood back and examined her art again. This time she seemed satisfied with her progress. She skilfully added texture using a spatula to sculpt the paint into raised areas to complete her forest scene. Finally, she returned to her selection of acrylics and selected three thinner brushes and mixed up some pink, grey, white and light brown shades. At the bottom of the page she carefully crafted the image of two bodies intertwined in the undergrowth. The figures were left largely undefined but Annie noticed a perfectly formed white breast and the merest suggestion of a snake tattoo. Having completed her creation, Jess stood back, took one last look at her work, turned towards Annie with a dimpled grin and whispered, 'For you.' As she ambled away, she turned and giggled, adding as an afterthought, 'And by the way, I knew all along that you were spying on me!'

Annie, completely lost for words, gazed at the finished painting in wonderment, and a rare feeling of happiness and hope bubbled up from deep within her.

CHAPTER 21

Annie wasn't looking forward to her meeting with Patrice. The art session the previous afternoon had lifted Annie's spirits but, after an unsettled night, she was feeling exhausted and just wanted to go back to bed.

'Follow me please, Annie,' Patrice said brusquely.

Annie followed her up a dark corridor and into a small dimly lit room. On the wall facing her was a long, full-length mirror.

'Stand in front of the mirror please, Annie.'

But the mirror lies...

Annie slowly walked towards the mirror, stopped, and then abruptly buried her face in her hands.

'Please look at yourself.'

Annie looked towards Patrice and shook her head. This was the fourth session with her psychiatrist and, although the sessions were tough, she had begun to trust Patrice, and had even started to like her.

'Claudia tells me that your weight has remained constant at six stone and four pounds, but you look thinner to me than you were when you first came here.' Her voice softened, 'I want you to look in the mirror and tell me what you see.'

Annie raised her head slowly and stared at her own reflection. 'I see me, Patrice. Nothing else. I see me.'

119

'Take off your cardigan, Annie. I promise I won't ask you to remove any other clothing.'

Slowly and painfully, she removed her cardigan and looked at herself again. Her whole body hurt, but the reflection that confronted her was far more agonising.

'Tell me what you really see.'

A single tear rolled down Annie's face as she gazed at her grey, haggard and ghost-like appearance. 'I look tired,' she conceded.

'And...'

'I look like I'm having a baby. Look at my belly, it's huge.'

'This often happens when the body becomes malnourished,' Patrice explained, 'the muscles stop working effectively and so the stomach becomes distended.'

Annie ran her out-stretched fingers slowly over the bulge of her belly and then she aggressively pinched the loose skin under her breasts.

'I look old...'

'And how do you feel, Annie?'

Annie spat out the words, 'I hate myself. I loathe myself with every fibre of my being.'

'Does being this thin make you feel better about yourself?'

When I can feel my skeleton through my skin, I have self-discipline; I have self-control.

'It isn't what I physically look like that matters, it's how I feel inside.'

'And how do you feel inside, Annie?'

All at once her spirit left her and she hung her head in shame. 'I feel like I am totally worthless. I don't matter anymore. My life has no purpose. I am nobody.'

Patrice looked at her patient benevolently, absorbing the significance of Annie's words. 'I do understand that this is painful for you, but you are making progress. It may not feel like it, but you are.'

Annie took a final look at her reflection. It was a mystery;

it felt like being in the "Hall of Mirrors" at the fair, where different mirrors distort the image of the body into strange shapes and sizes, making people laugh. To Annie, her reflection was grotesque, not something which gave any amusement at all. But her feelings about herself from deep within were far worse.

'During the next few sessions I would like us to explore why you have these negative feelings about yourself, Annie. I wonder what trauma has happened to you in your life that is causing these extreme feelings of worthlessness and self-hatred?' Patrice left the question hanging in the air. 'It's important to remember that we are all unique and special in our own way. But, for the moment, it has been a tough session and we will finish now.' She put a reassuring hand on Annie's shoulder. 'Until Thursday then.'

Feeling completely drained, Annie went up to the dormitory and lay on the bed. Her head was full of disturbing thoughts; her body felt heavy and every muscle hurt.

I remember watching horrifying scenes of starving children in Biafra on the news, with their skeletal bodies and swollen bellies. They needed food and water to live, but they were left to die. They had no choice. But I do have a choice; I could eat and I could live... but do I actually have a choice? I'm not choosing to be ill; no, I don't have any choice....

She was aware of the musky perfume long before she opened her eyes. A loud voice boomed, 'Oh my darlin' you're as thin as a toothpick! Are they looking after you properly?' Joy had arrived. 'What are we going to do with you?' Her lips formed a pink glossy pout and her forehead creased as she peered over her purple-rimmed spectacles. 'I think I need to speak to the doctor, Annie.'

'Oh no Joy please don't, I'm okay, really I am.'

'Well, my dear, I will just have to trust you I suppose... I have brought you a gift.' With that, she pulled out a flamboyant floral dress decorated in bright primary colours and finished off with an extravagant red bow. It was frilly, bright, flouncy and, in Annie's view, completely horrible, but Annie couldn't help but smile. Joy had made it especially for her but she wouldn't be seen dead in a dress like that. However, she was touched by Joy's kindness, and was able to thank her warmly for giving her this gift.

'Oh my, Annie, you will look a vision of beauty in this!'
Um, I would certainly look like a vision of something!

'I've also been to your college and your tutor has given me some Education and Health-care work to keep you busy while you're here. And Stanley gave me a couple of maths textbooks to bring as well.'

'Wonderful Joy, thank you. I need to work, and I was aiming to do some maths, so this is great.'

'They miss you so much Annie, particularly Franky and her brother Tom. He is mighty handsome and I have a feeling he wants to be your beau!'

'Ah, I wish I'd met Tom years ago. He's so kind and funny; just like the big brother I never had. And Franky is one in a million. I hope I'll see them again soon, I miss them too.' Glancing around the residents lounge, she noticed that Joy, as usual, was causing quite a stir amongst the staff and patients. 'Tell me Joy, where is Stan?'

'Oh Annie, Stanley is busy, busy, busy and I hardly ever see him myself!' Joy looked away and Annie knew that she was not being honest.

'He doesn't want to see me in here, does he?'

'You know what he's like…' She shook her head vigorously. 'Oh, and before I forget, I have made you another ginger and molasses cake. Shall we have a piece now?' Without waiting for an answer, Joy cut two large slices with the penknife she had in her handbag and handed Annie a huge piece wrapped in a lipstick-smeared paper hanky. Annie looked at it in horror and then took a small bite. The sponge was sticky and heavy and stuck in the back of her throat.

Almost whispering, Annie asked after Mutti.

'Well, I don't think she's too good, Annie. She'll be in the unit for a long while to fully recover and recuperate. No visitors are allowed and we just have to pray that she'll find the strength from somewhere to overcome her addiction. Poor love…'

Annie was almost overwhelmed by grief. It was as if her dear mother had died, since she never heard anything from her; no letters, not even a phone call. Crestfallen, she realised the hopelessness of the situation.

'All you need to do is eat, it really is as simple as that, just eat. Food is one of God's precious gifts and it will nourish you and give renewed life to your precious body and soul. Please, Annie…' With that, Joy took Annie up into her arms, giving her a warm and suffocating embrace.

'Find the joy, Annie, find the joy.'

If only life were that simple…

***

Annie and Jess sat cross-legged facing each other underneath the huge Victorian window which cast the shadows of late afternoon across the empty dormitory. A week had passed since the challenging meeting with Patrice, and even Joy had not managed to dispel Annie's feelings of despair. Annie knew that she was caught in the vice-like grip of her addiction. She knew that she had to eat to live, and yet the demons in her head were winning.

'I'm losing the battle, Jess. I can't do this anymore.' The tears were coursing down Annie's face and forming little puddles in the deep hollows on her inner thighs, visible through her flimsy pyjamas. Jess looked at her friend compassionately and placed her hands either side of Annie's arms. 'Annie, I think I might be able to help you.' Jess slowly rolled up the sleeve of her right arm to reveal hundreds of thin, white, irregular scars travelling across the inside of her arm. 'Look at these, Annie.' Jess appeared to be proud of the spidery patchwork of old wounds.

'What has happened to you?'

Jess pulled a small knife in a light-coloured leather sheath from the back pocket of her jeans. 'Watch me, Annie.' She drew the gleaming weapon out of the sheath and slowly and deliberately pulled the blade across the white flesh just above the elbow. As the blood started to ooze, Jess let out a deep-throated cry, closed her eyes, and finally all the tension seemed to vanish from her face and body; she looked strangely serene and beautiful.

I feel shocked and sad for her, but I understand. She has freed herself of all her pain and suffering... just for a fleeting moment in time... she has escaped.

After a period of silence and stillness, she mouthed her words over and over again, 'Thank you, thank you, thank you...' She slowly raised her head and their eyes met. 'Annie, it helps me. It would help you too.'

Annie held the knife tentatively in her shaking hand.

God help me...

She slowly drew the knife across her emaciated arm, cutting into the paper-thin flesh, and large droplets of blood appeared and spilled over her wrist forming globules of deep red on the brown floor. The pain was agonising but she felt her whole body relax, the tension flowing away like the ebbing waves of the ocean at low tide. Annie made a second cut just above the first and closed her eyes. She felt at peace.

The relief of a torrential downpour after a thunderstorm...

Jess moved closer to her friend and pressed her arm firmly against Annie's and their blood mingled together. 'Friends forever?'

'Friends forever...'

CHAPTER 22

'Hello my beautiful girl.'

Annie's eyes widened with surprise, this was not a visitor she was expecting. 'Hello Thanos, how did you know I was in here?'

His eyes darted round the room. He studied an elderly gentleman, his shoulders hunched in despair; his head bowed low as he emitted deep mournful cries, occasionally lifting his head, his face contorted by a lifetime of pain. Another elderly resident stood by the window clutching an empty cup of coffee between her gnarled hands. She stared intently into the distance, looking lost, broken and vacant. Thanos had never seen anything like this before and he was visibly shocked. His eyes finally rested on Annie.

'I went to your house and was met by Stan. Annie, he was so rude. He shouted a few choice words, which I didn't understand, of course,' he said, with a wry smile. 'And then he pushed past me and left, just like that!'

Annie shook her head sadly. 'Oh no, I'm sorry Thanos, you didn't deserve that.'

'But then I had the pleasure of meeting Joy! What a lovely lady! She offered me a cup of tea and a huge slice of her homemade cake. I think she felt embarrassed by Stan's behaviour. We had such a great conversation about her homeland and mine, and of the loneliness we both feel, living so far away from our family and friends. Anyway, she let me know where I could find you, so here I am.' He paused to watch the elderly man, struggling to lift his head, revealing his extraordinary weather-beaten face, as he let out another mournful cry. 'How can you bear to stay here, Annie?' He squeezed her hand. 'This isn't the right place for you, come home with me,' he pleaded. 'I'll take care of you.'

'You are wrong Thanos, this is exactly where I need to be. There are medical experts here, and they are doing their best to help me,' she answered curtly.

He withdrew his hand, surprised by her stern words. 'What has happened to you?'

Annie felt strangely disconnected from him. She held very dear memories close to her heart of their secret meetings in the snow-covered forest; the hilarious snowball fights and the warm amiable companionship; but everything was different now. She looked at this dashingly good-looking man with his beguiling eyes, and she felt absolutely nothing.

'There is nothing I can do to help you,' he acknowledged sadly.

'I'm ill, Thanos, I need professional help.' Annie thought about all the precious dreams they had of playing beautiful music, learning about the world together, perhaps even visiting Rhodes to meet his family and explore a different land. But she knew that this was not to be and would never be.

Thanos is kind and caring - I have treated him badly. I know that he wants more from me than I can give. He wants a physical relationship; he wants sex; but I can't bear to be anywhere near him. Am I unable to love? And, what about her? I can't stop thinking about Jess…

'I am so sorry, Annie, I'm sorry about everything.'

'I am too.'

They sat together in awkward silence for the rest of his visit.

As they parted, he placed a hand tenderly on the side of

her face and whispered, 'You are very special Annie, you deserve happiness in your life.'

She didn't know it at the time, but it would be the last time she would ever see her special friend.

She wearily climbed the stairs to the dormitory and threw herself onto her bed. She pulled the covers over her head and knew that, at that moment, she didn't want to face anyone, not even her crazy friend, Jess. She craved peace and solitude, but then the familiar dark thoughts started to invade her head and there seemed to be no tears left to fall.

We were never meant to be together, I have to let him go. But am I letting someone very special slip away from my life? Why do I feel so different when I'm with Jess? Is it simply because she is less of a threat because she is a woman? No, it is so much more; it feels right, we are perfect together; my whole body and soul aches for her...

Then she remembered the bulging rucksack that Joy had thoughtfully left beside her bed. She pulled out all her college work, and selected a brightly decorated text book entitled *Modern Mathematics* that Stan had asked Joy to bring. As she opened the book, she felt the familiar feeling of dread and total inadequacy. Annie wondered why she found maths so hard. She knew that Stan wanted her to excel in this impossible subject but how could she reach his high expectations of her? He had sacrificed a lot in his life to pay for expensive private schooling and she had failed her maths O level. Annie resolved to work hard in Ashmeade and try to improve her skills. There was so much in her life that was out of her control, but she could control how much she focused on her college work and maths.

She found a simple wooden table to work on in the lounge overlooking the immaculate green lawn of Ashmeade. Although it wasn't always peaceful, Annie found the frequent comings and goings of the residents quite comforting and reassuring, and she became strangely immune to the constant wailing of the gentleman sitting in his usual position in a corner of the large room. Since her arrival at Ashmeade, she hadn't spoken to many of the residents; she would always acknowledge them with a fleeting smile or wish them a good day, but she hadn't had any real conversations with any of them. She felt wary, never sure of how they would behave towards her. The only resident that Annie had regular contact with was Jess.

She resolved to make more of an effort, these were people struggling in their lives, just like her. She was determined not to be judgemental, they all had a lot in common.

She turned to the first page of problems and opened her exercise book. Her last attempts at maths had been a dismal failure, but here there was no one to answer to, and this realisation felt liberating. She knew all the answers were listed at the back of the text book and it was very tempting to cheat, but she knew this wouldn't help her at all, she needed to show how she worked out each answer. She chewed the end of her pencil as she considered the problem. She sighed and started to scribble down her first attempt at what she felt was an impossible mathematical challenge. After a few minutes she tore out the piece of paper from her exercise book and threw it on the floor in utter frustration. 'I just can't do this…' Much to Annie's surprise, someone reached down and retrieved the crumpled piece of paper, straightened it out, closely examined the haphazard figures on the page and then leaned over to look at the problem that Annie was attempting to address.

'Look, there…' The girl pointed to one of the calculations. 'That's where you've made a mistake. If you correct this sum, you'll arrive at the right answer.'

Annie looked at the short, rather overweight girl dressed in an A-line skirt down to her knees, white ankle socks and flat open-toed sandals. She wore a billowing white nylon blouse with a beaded necklace. Her mousy brown hair was tied back in a pigtail and she was the palest girl Annie had ever seen. She looked very frumpy and old-fashioned.

'How on earth do you know that?'

'Because I checked all your calculations and you've made

a mistake.'

'That's because I'm terrible at maths. I absolutely hate it!'

'But maths is fun. It's just a series of puzzles really, it's a great big, exciting game. Maths is so important in everything we do in our lives from the moment we get up in the morning until we go to bed at night. Think about putting on your clothes in the morning, it's all about awareness of position and space. How could you ever go shopping if you couldn't count your money and check whether you'd been given the right amount of change? Everything around us in the environment has shape, colour and form: this is all about maths.' She took a deep breath. 'Oh I could go on, and on. Yes, maths is integral to life itself.'

Maths is fun, she has to be joking! Integral to life, maybe this is where I've gone wrong?

Annie remained unconvinced. 'Do you really love maths?'

The girl smiled. 'Yes I really do love maths, and I think I could help you to love maths, too.'

'What's your name?' Annie asked, pleased that she was at last communicating with another resident.

'I'm Dee and I bet you're wondering how I ended up here, aren't you? I took my O levels two years ago and I passed all twelve exams with top grades. I'm lucky, I seem to have a brain that works well in all academic subjects and I like learning. It all seems to come very easily to me.' Her expression changed. 'But my brain is also my enemy. I have schizophrenia and I've had frequent psychotic episodes which I know nothing about. Thankfully it's controlled by medication at the moment so I'm able to concentrate on my studies again whilst I'm here.'

'I'm pleased to meet you, but I still can't believe you actually love maths!'

Dee sat down beside Annie. 'Let me help you, I have a suggestion. Why don't we do maths sessions together every day after breakfast for about an hour? I'd really enjoy that and we'd have some fun.'

Annie looked at Dee, not quite believing her words, but gratefully accepting her generous offer. At last she had found someone who was prepared to give her maths tuition. Then she noticed Jess at the end of the room, leaning nonchalantly against the wall, her legs crossed one in front of the other with one hand resting on her dropped hip. She was glaring steadfastly at the two girls, her face etched with anger; she looked menacing.

Could my dear friend be jealous?

CHAPTER 23

Holding the mourning brooch in the palm of her hand, Annie closely examined the twelve red garnets glinting in the early morning sunlight and thought about her mother.

I yearn for Mutti to wrap me in her arms and tell me that everything will be alright in the end, but I fear I have lost her now. We're so alike in many ways; the struggles we have faced in our lives have been very different, but now we are in the same place - we are vulnerable, damaged, and broken. We must find the strength to fight our own demons, not together, but on our own. We cannot help each other now.

She missed her terribly and her eyes misted over with tears as she recalled Mutti giving her this special brooch at Christmas. She must have known what was about to happen to her.

Annie thought about the promises she made to herself at the start of the year. Dee had given her hope that one day she might be able to retake her maths exams and she could eventually make Stan proud of her.

As she walked into Patrice's consultation room the next morning, Annie was feeling more optimistic than she had done for a while. 'Patrice, I have some good news.' Annie told her psychiatrist about the kind offer that Dee had made to her the previous day.

'This is wonderful news Annie. Dee is a remarkably

bright young lady and you will both benefit from the maths sessions.'

'But she actually enjoys maths!' she said, raising her eyebrows quizzically.

Patrice smiled, it was lovely to see Annie show pleasure in something; this was a rare occurrence in their meetings. 'Yes, that is rather hard to understand, it was never my favourite subject either. We'll come back to this Annie, but on Thursday we looked at your reflection in the mirror and discussed what you saw and felt about your appearance. Today I want to delve a little deeper and explore with you your *feelings* about yourself.'

'I've already told you, I hate myself, there's nothing left to say.' Annie suddenly felt deflated and the optimism that she came in with had vanished.

'Do you think you're a bad person, Annie?'

'I'm like a rotten apple, I'm rotten to the core.'

'Why do you think this?'

Annie paused and looked beyond Patrice to the hills in the distance.

'It's okay, Annie, we have plenty of time to explore your feelings, so take all the time you need to think about this.'

I can't and I will not tell her.

'I can't do this… please don't make me,' she pleaded.

They sat in silence.

'Has something happened to make you feel this way?' Patrice probed a little deeper.

'They said I was like the "bag lady" who walks the streets of Cranford.'

'Who said this to you Annie?'

'The students at college, I'm so different to them.'

'How did they make you feel?'

'Ugly, useless, worthless…' Annie answered angrily.

'Tell me about the bag lady,' Patrice asked quietly.

'She is an old homeless woman who walks the streets and she carries all her possessions in hundreds of carrier bags.'

'I wonder why they think you look like her...'

'I suppose it might be because I wear baggy clothing. They said I look like a walking jumble sale.'

'And why do you wear baggy clothing Annie?'

'I feel comfortable in these clothes.' As she said the words, she realised how deeply uncomfortable her body felt; her jeans were painfully cutting into the thin flesh covering her hip bones.

'I would like to suggest that you choose to wear baggy clothes to hide your body.'

'No, that's not right, I just like wearing loose clothes.' She scowled at Patrice defiantly. 'Anyway, the bag lady is strong - she doesn't care what people think - she's a survivor.'

'I'm sure she is Annie, to survive a hard life on the streets. But being different isn't necessarily a bad thing, in fact it is often a very good thing. Life would be very dull if we were all the same. Do you agree?'

'Yes,' Annie conceded, 'I suppose you're right.'

'We need to celebrate difference. We should all dare to be different, and not always conform to the expectations society places on us. You describe the bag lady as being a strong courageous woman, a survivor, surely being compared to her is a good thing. You could take their comments as a compliment and be proud to be compared to her.'

'The bag lady reminds me of something that happened to me a long time ago... Nessy...' Annie's voice trailed off.

'Would you like to tell me about Nessy?'

Annie looked stubbornly at her therapist. 'No, it was a long time ago and I can't remember anything.'

'But you remembered her name - Nessy. Was she homeless, like the bag lady?' Patrice asked, inviting Annie to tell her more, but Annie shook her head and resolutely remained silent.

Patrice found the therapy sessions fascinating, she always prepared an outline plan for her consultations, but so often the conversations would go in unexpected directions, often so much more valuable than she could ever pre-plan. She jotted down a few rough notes, and decided she would not pursue why Annie hides behind loose fitting clothes, or about her childhood memories of Nessy. They would explore these leads another day. She would probe further into Annie's childhood.

'I would like us to talk more about your family. During the last session, you described how your mother made you happy when you were a little girl. Tell me about your father, how did he make you feel?'

Think before you answer. I trust Patrice, but I must not be lured into saying more than I should...

'Everyone calls him Stan. When I was very little I remember he worked very hard. He has always been a brilliant mathematician, so he became a maths teacher. The problem is, I don't think he has ever liked children very much.'

'But you already described to me how he loved you when you were little.'

'Yes, I suppose he did. He used to hug me and Mutti, he used to laugh and look after us. He was grumpy sometimes but life was good.'

'So what changed?'

Annie hunched her shoulders and glared at the ground. No more words were spoken.

'I think we'll leave it there for now Annie. We will start the next session where we have left off today, but, in the meantime, I want you to give my last question some thought. What changed? What has happened in your life to make you want to systematically destroy yourself?'

***

25 December 1965

Everything was silent and still when Annie woke up early on Christmas morning. She was nine years old and, when she was younger, she used to adore everything about Christmas;

the decorated tree, the stocking at the end of the bed, the crackling of the open fire and the huge roast dinner, but things had changed since her mother had her brain surgery a few years before. She used to be warm, kind and loving, the best mother Annie could ever wish for, but since her operation she had changed, she had become quiet and often looked very sad; Annie missed the laughter and warm hugs that her mother used to give her. Stan had changed too and these days he was usually angry about something. Annie longed for her parents to be happy as they once were.

As she rolled over, she heard a strange rustling sound at the end of her bed. She reached forward and discovered a mysterious parcel wrapped in a brown paper bag. Puzzled, she felt the shape and form of the package, trying to guess what was inside. It was hard, but she had no idea what it was, so she slowly opened the bag.

The dull blue eyes stared upwards, unblinking, and unnervingly fixed on Annie's face. The colour and texture of the skin, pale pink, more intense across her cheeks, darker under the chin and the hairline, looked eerily realistic. Annie looked closely at the immaculately crafted features of the face; the slightly turned-up nose, the plump blushed cheeks, the tiny rose-bud lips and the thick brown painted eyebrows, all framed by a ring of coarse straw-coloured hair, drawn into two tightly woven plaits fastened together at the back of the head. Two curls fell stiffly in opposite directions, partially covering the forehead. She drew her fingers over the cold and unyielding features of the china doll in front of her; there was something about the gift that reminded her of Mutti, cold and hard, devoid of emotion, and yet, beautiful. Perfect.

She was just wondering who had put this gift at the end of her bed, when Mutti appeared in her doorway. 'Happy Christmas Annie,' she said, with a rare smile. 'Do you like her?' Annie leapt out of bed and gave her mother a spontaneous hug. 'Mutti, I love her! Did you buy this present for me?' Mutti reached over and gently placed the doll in her arms. 'When I was a little girl of about your age, Oma gave her to me for Christmas,' she said, looking down at the doll in her arms. 'She is a very special German china doll. I called her Greta and I loved her very much, and now that you are nine, I thought you might enjoy her, just as I did.'

Annie's eyes shone, although she wasn't quite sure that she loved the gift quite as much as she should. 'Oh Mutti, thank you, I will look after her, just as you did when you were a little girl.' The warmth of her mother's hug gave Annie hope that perhaps this Christmas Day would be a happy one after all.

She rushed over to the window and opened the curtains. The garden was cloaked in a thick layer of frost and the silver birch tree was a frozen silhouette. She scratched her nails over the ice on the inside of the window, but she felt warm inside in anticipation of the day ahead.

Stan was in the back yard whistling, whilst he filled the coal scuttle, and Annie could hear his heavy footsteps as he returned inside to light the fire. She felt relieved that he sounded in a good mood today. She threw some warm clothes on and ran downstairs for breakfast.

'Oh Annie, it's so cold the robin's skating on the bird bath!' Stan said cheerily, as she came into the kitchen. 'Happy Christmas!' He put crumpets and large mugs of tea on the Formica-topped table. 'I wish it wasn't so bloody cold!'

After breakfast they set out from home, and arrived at the church just as the service began. Annie cradled Greta close to her chest, and listened to the beautiful music. The fairy lights twinkled on the Christmas tree by the altar, everything was perfect.

After a simple Christmas lunch of chicken and potatoes, Mutti placed a small traditional Christmas pudding, decorated with a sprig of holly, proudly in the middle of the table. Annie was pleased to see Mutti looking happy, but she hated Christmas pudding and, as she reluctantly took her first mouthful, she bit on something hard; it was a shiny thrupenny bit. She wasn't sure if it was an old German tradition, but Mutti always hid a single coin in the pudding, believing it to bring good luck to the fortunate person who found it. She wiped the sticky pudding from the coin and slipped it into her pocket, and then she quietly pushed the rest of the pudding to the side of her plate.

In the afternoon, Stan and Mutti had retired to their armchairs by the fire for an afternoon nap. Annie looked out of the window, the ground was still covered with a thin layer of frost which sparkled in the low winter sunlight. She knew that her parents would be asleep for most of the afternoon, so she decided she would slip out for a walk, and return before they woke up. She pulled on her coat and stepped out into the cold, closing the door quietly behind her. She gasped when she breathed in the freezing cold air, everything was silent, except for the crunch of her own footsteps as she negotiated the icy uneven surface of the pavement leading towards the town. The hills in the far distance were sprinkled with a fine dusting of snow, partly shrouded by a layer of thick grey cloud. The trees lining the road stood like frosted statues and the first snow-flakes started to fall on her frozen cheeks, making her blink. It is a white Christmas, she thought, as she tucked her new gift deep inside her coat.

I promise I'll look after you and love you Greta.

Before Christmas, the streets of Clanford had been bustling with people rushing around doing their last minute Christmas shopping, and the Salvation Army played Christmas carols, inviting shoppers to stop and listen, and perhaps give a few coins for the homeless. But now the shops were closed and the streets were deserted. All the preparations for Christmas had finished and today, everyone was at home, enjoying the celebrations with their families. The only sound Annie could hear was the doleful chime of the church bell, as she wandered further up the High Street. Just as she was about to turn back towards home, she spotted a pile of cardboard, half hidden by the concrete pillars marking the entrance of one of the large department stores. She wondered whether someone had accidentally left a Christmas present outside the shop and she went to have a look. Beside the cardboard, there was a huge collection of grubby plastic bags, a few damp clothes strewn on the pavement, a half-drunk bottle of wine, and a curled-up sandwich. There was something about the scene which made Annie shudder, and she was just about to walk away when something moved and a pale wizened face appeared from underneath many layers of cardboard. 'Wait, my dear, please don't go. Stay and chat with me...please.'

Annie was feeling frightened and knew that she should go home.

'Please my love, don't be scared, I won't hurt you.' The old lady struggled to sit up. 'A merry Christmas to you!'

'Where do you live?' Annie asked curiously.

'This is my home, my duck, right here.' She pushed the layers of cardboard away and wrapped herself in an old, crocheted shawl, she looked tiny and vulnerable. 'I'm okay here, I can do what I want, when I want, *nobody* tells me what to do.' Her brown baggy dress rode up above her knees, revealing remarkably hairy white legs and long woolly socks. She wore old leather boots that were far too big, and full of holes.

'Don't you get cold?' asked Annie. She tried to ignore the stench of old bodies and stale food that was beginning to make her feel nauseous.

'I've lived on the streets most of my life, I'm used to it. I'm made of tough stuff, little girl.' She raised her eyes and jutted out her chin proudly. 'Yeah, you have to be tough to live on the streets, especially when it's parky like this!' She sat up and hugged her knees. 'I'm Agnes, but most folk around here call me Nessy. What's your name?'

'Annie.' She stared steadfastly at the old lady. 'But you must get hungry.'

Nessy pointed at her sandwich. 'People give me food

sometimes, and I can go to the soup kitchen in Castle Street if I'm really starving, but I don't go there often, because I can look after myself.' Her shoulders dropped. 'But it's hard when there's no-one around to beg for food… like today.'

'Oh Nessy, poor you…'

She folded her arms tightly across her chest. 'Don't you go feeling sorry for me, I'm fine, thank you very much. I told you, I can look after myself.' Her voice softened, 'Got any money love?'

Annie felt very sad for Nessy, and then she had an idea.

'I don't have much money, but you can have this!' She dug deep into her pocket and thrust the treasured thrupenny bit that she had discovered earlier in her Christmas pudding, into Nessy's upturned palm. 'Would you like to come back to my house? I could give you some left-over Christmas lunch. Would you like that?' Sensing that the old lady might be too proud to accept her offer, she added, 'If *you* don't eat it, Stan will probably throw it in the bin, or give it to the neighbours' cat. Say yes, Nessy, say you'll come!'

Nessy let out a deep sigh. 'I suppose it is Christmas, so I'll come with you, but only this once.' She slowly and painfully struggled to her feet, holding the concrete post beside her for support. Annie was surprised by how tiny she was, her back was doubled over, and Annie could only see the balding top of her head as she started to walk towards her. 'Follow me,' Annie said, sounding more confident than she felt. She was beginning to worry what Stan would think of her bringing this person back to the house. Surely he would be kind to her, especially on Christmas Day.

The walk back home was interrupted by Nessy's frequent coughing fits, and Annie wondered whether she needed to go to hospital. 'Don't you worry about me, my love, I'm starving, so let's keep going.' It was snowing hard now and the cold began to seep into Annie's bones. She pulled her coat tightly around her as she gently guided the elderly woman, one step at a time, through the newly fallen snow.

At last they arrived home, and Annie sat Nessy down on the doorstep. 'You wait here, I'll just go and get you a plate of food.' She was pleased that she could help someone and she quietly opened the front door. Stan and Mutti were still asleep and so she crept into the kitchen and opened the fridge. She tore a drumstick from the half-eaten chicken and put it into a bowl and piled it high with cold roast potatoes. She wondered whether she should reheat the food, but then she thought that Nessy really wouldn't mind either way. She grabbed a knife and fork from the drawer and crept quietly passed the lounge door and out into the cold.

'Oh my duck this looks wonderful.' Her eyes lit up as she started to eat hungrily. Annie stood back and smiled, it made her feel so happy to see this brave and proud woman sitting on her doorstep tucking into a plate of chicken and potatoes.

'What the hell is going on? Who is this? How dare you bring this sorry excuse for a person back to my house?' Stan towered over both of them, looking absolutely furious, and then he turned towards Nessy. 'Leave... Now!'

Stan raised his arm and Annie flinched, terrified that he was going to lash out at either her, or Nessy. 'Stan, Nessy was hungry and I thought...'

'For God's sake Annie, shut up. Once you bring someone like this here, you'll never get rid of her.' He strode towards Nessy. 'Scram, and *never* come back.'

Nessy slowly stood up to her full height and faced Stan, speaking her words slowly, 'You should be proud of your daughter, and you should be utterly ashamed of yourself.' Stan looked down at the tiny fearless woman in front of him, paused for a moment, and then spat out his words with venom, 'I said, get out of here now, and never come back.'

Stan turned towards Annie and grabbed her roughly by the arm. 'Get inside now.' He banged the front door behind him and then, without warning, he raised his hand and dealt Annie a crushing blow across her face. 'Go to bed, I don't want to see you again until morning.'

'But Stan, I only wanted to help her...' Annie said, rubbing the side of her face.

Mutti stood behind Stan - she had tried to restrain him, but to no avail. Annie rushed upstairs, slammed her door and hid in the relative safety of her bedroom. She was shaking and her cheek was smarting with pain. She had never seen Stan as angry as this. She hugged Greta close and thought about Nessy, the fearless lady, who lived on the street, and who had been brave enough to stand up to Stan. But what a sad end to Christmas Day. She hadn't even had a chance to eat. Annie shook as the arguments started downstairs.

'Annie is truly wicked and evil. How could she put us through this, especially on Christmas Day?'

'She was only trying to be kind, Stan,' Mutti stammered.

'How do you know, you stupid bitch? She is good-for-nothing and you are no better. What a bloody awful family I've got.'

Why did I do it? I could have stayed at home, but instead, I went for a walk. But what did I do that was so very wrong? I only wanted to help her. I'm stupid. It is all my fault...

She put her head under the covers as the arguments raged and objects were hurled across the room with the repeated and deafening sound of breaking glass. Then, silence.

Her body froze, petrified. But her mind was alert. She heard footsteps on the stairs, the creak on the fourth step, more footsteps, louder and faster this time, then silence. He waited. She stared into the darkness, and buried Greta deep in the folds under her chin. Keep me safe, please keep me safe. The door opened, the light from the landing cast deep ghostly shadows across the room. A huge figure loomed out of the darkness, his pale face, unrecognisable, misshapen, etched with anger. Don't, please, no, not again. He lifted his hand as if to strike, she cowered in the shadows and waited, her body braced for the inevitable. But then a heaviness descended upon her, she gasped for breath. Her mouth opened but she made no sound, there was no breath. She stared beyond him, the shadows danced like the devil, short to long, light to dark. Her blood ran cold, terrified, frozen in time. A weight bore down on her chilled frame, crushing, breathless, agonising; she gulped the rancid stench of his breath. The sudden pain was unbearable, her body was ripped apart. Make it stop, make it go away. A shrill deep-throated cry cut through the night, and then, silence. He turned towards her, paused, and then he was gone. Her waxen limbs lay motionless, her ribcage rose and fell, she fought for every breath. The shadows turned to darkness, she was paralysed with fear. She looked down to see the head of her doll, broken into three pieces, held together only by a single strand of woven hair; one eye staring up at her and the other eyeball rolling slowly from side to side on the cold hard floor. We are broken. The damage is done.

CHAPTER 24

'Anorexia Nervosa, isn't that an elegant name? Anorexia Nervosa...' Jess exclaimed. 'I think you have the "Anorexia" and I have the "Nervosa." It's a match, BINGO, what a pair!' She giggled, showing her irresistible dimple, as she continued to play with the words. 'My friend, Anorexic Annie. Anorexic Annie, I could call you "AA" but that stands for "Alcoholics Anonymous," so that wouldn't be quite right. If you think about it, your name is just perfect: "An" stands for Anorexic and Annie is your name, An-nie. Or I suppose I could call you An-née, which could loosely mean, born with Anorexia. What do you think?'

Annie grinned. 'Let's just stick with Annie, the name suits me just fine and certainly better than a lot of other names you could call me!'

The smoke gently curled up into the balmy air. It was early May; summer was approaching, and the evenings were noticeably lighter. Joe was asleep, as usual, when the two girls crept past reception and into the warm evening. They sat near the perimeter wall underneath a mass of climbing wisteria, and inhaled a heady mixture of its seductive perfume, and musky herbal smoke. As Jess gently removed a piece of tobacco from Annie's lip, she gazed at her friend and smiled. 'You're beautiful, Annie. You don't know it, but you are.'

Annie looked coyly at Jess. 'You do talk a load of rubbish sometimes.' As she took a drag from the diminishing stub of her joint, she began to feel the familiar sense of serenity and peace.

'Annie, I would like to ask you something.'

'This sounds rather ominous,' Annie said. 'You know I'd do anything for you,' she added generously.

'Can I paint a picture of you?'

'Of course you can. Did you really think I'd say no?'

'But there is something else… I'd like to paint a nude picture of you.'

'Naked, but why?' Annie roughly pulled away from her friends' embrace.

'Because I'd be able to capture every bone, every muscle, every vein and artery, every sinew; it would be an extraordinary study of the human form. I want to show you just how beautiful I find your body.'

'How can you expect me to do this?' Annie muttered. She dug her fingernails deeply into the bare flesh of her forearm, until she drew blood. 'You don't know me at all.'

'I understand you a lot more than you realise,' Jess replied softly.

'But how can I?' The idea of bearing her body to Jess, or anyone, was aberrant.

Jess gently squeezed her hand. 'Give it some thought Annie. I have faith in you, you *can* do this.'

Lying on her back, Annie considered her friends' daunting request. These days she was intent on hiding herself beneath layers of baggy clothing - being naked would be in stark contrast.

'Annie, I don't like her.' The mood changed in an instant.

'Who are you talking about?' Annie asked, still deep in thought.

'Dee. I don't like her. She's bad for you.'

'She's a good person and she's helping me with my maths.' Annie replied, bewildered by her friends' sudden outburst.

'I forbid you to see her,' Jess hissed. Her eyes glinted in the darkness.

Annie glared at Jess, shocked by her words. 'You can't control who I see.'

'For God's sake, listen to me Annie, I forbid you to see her.'

'I *can* see her and I *will*,' Annie said furiously.

'I'm warning you, she seems fine at the moment, but she'll demand more and more of your time, and then more and more of *you*. She'll eventually hurt you - hurt you very badly.'

Annie felt angry and confused by Jess's hash words, but she knew she must reassure her. 'Remember, *you* are my special friend.'

Jess's face softened. 'Promise me, Annie, swear on your life that I'm your best friend.'

'I promise.'

Jess seemed to be content, but the conversation had left Annie feeling ill at ease. Both girls lay on the soft lawn looking up at the big sky.

Hurt me? Dee seems well-meaning and just normal really. Jess can't control me. I must have freedom to make my own decisions about my own life.

Jess gently traced her fingers along the line of Annie's leg, sending intense tingles of pleasure through her body. As she moved towards her inner thigh, it was as if she was being sprinkled with magic fairy dust; she let out a sigh of extreme pleasure. Nothing else mattered.

***

The first two early morning maths sessions had gone well. Dee was an intuitive teacher and was quick to understand Annie's requirements. She had a clear and simple way of explaining how to solve complex mathematical problems and had a canny way of relating maths to everyday life. Everything was beginning to make sense.

'Read the question carefully Annie, and then make an

145

educated guess at the answer. This way your answer is unlikely to be wildly out. It's just like you do when you predict how much your supermarket shopping will cost. If you don't do this you may end up with a load of shopping you can't afford to pay for! How embarrassing would that be?'

There was always a lot of laughter and fun and Annie began to look forward to her time with Dee. She was, however, aware of a dark menacing presence in the corner of the room. Jess was always there, listening, watching and waiting.

Annie knew that with every day that passed, she was getting weaker and weaker. She could feel every bone in her body and see the tangled web of blue veins and arteries just beneath her skin. Part of her brain knew that, unless she ate, she would die. But the other part of her brain was much more powerful. It tired her to get out of bed and take part in the normal routines of the day. She knew she was losing her fight but she was too exhausted to care. But something was to happen that would change everything.

CHAPTER 25

The following evening, Claudia stopped Annie on her way to the dining room.' Annie, please come and see me in my office at ten-thirty tomorrow morning. I have something urgent that I need to discuss with you.' Claudia swept her hair back from her face, tossed her head back and marched back into her office, banging the door behind her. Annie was left wondering what could be so urgent? Had she found out about the secret nighttime dope-smoking rendezvous? Had Claudia suddenly realised that she was cheating during her weekly weigh-ins? What could it be? Whatever it was, Annie felt very nervous about meeting with the dreaded stone-faced Claudia.

Annie walked into the dimly lit office the next morning to find Claudia sitting behind her desk, steepling her fingers and peering over her half-moon glasses. 'Come in and sit down. How are you settling into Ashmeade?'

It felt as if she had entered an interrogation room and that her interrogator had absolutely no interest in her or her answer. 'I'm okay thank you, Claudia.'

'I'm going to come straight to the point. It has come to my attention that you are spending a lot of time with Jessica.'

It took a few seconds for Annie to realise that Claudia was referring to Jess. 'Jess is my friend and she's helping me to settle in here.'

Be careful Annie, be careful...

'Jessica has been an inpatient at Ashmeade for many months now and she is of grave concern to the staff here.'

'What do you mean?'

Claudia shook her head. 'She seems fine a lot of the time, but she has violent mood swings and we monitor her very closely to ensure she doesn't harm herself or others.'

You have absolutely no idea what she gets up to! I would hate to think what we could get up to if you didn't monitor her "very closely!"

'Perhaps my friendship will help Jess to get better,' Annie suggested optimistically.

'Jessica is cunning and manipulative and she will try and control your every action.'

Annie was already beginning to discover Jess's controlling behaviour, but she had no intention of being either passive or submissive. 'I won't let that happen.'

'You seem very sure of yourself.'

'I am,' said Annie firmly.

'Good.'

Feeling disturbed by Claudia's dismissive attitude towards Jess, she added, 'And she's one of the most artistic, creative and talented people I've ever met.'

'Hum. Very well, I won't limit the time you spend with Jessica, but I will continue to monitor the situation. Be on your guard Annie, be on your guard.'

As she walked out of the office, she felt annoyed by Claudia's attitude towards her friend but she also had lingering concerns about the stark warning that she had just been given.

Be on your guard.

Annie felt drained after her strange meeting with Claudia and her head hurt. Her feelings for Jess were developing into something special and unfamiliar. Could it be love? She lay on her bed, as she often did, to try and escape reality just for a moment.

'Annie, I'm so pleased to see you!'

Annie rubbed her eyes sleepily and was surprised to be warmly greeted by the broad, smiling face of her college friend, Franky. 'College just isn't the same without you. I miss you very much. What's it like here?' Franky scanned the dormitory and wrinkled up her nose. 'Poor you Annie, it looks a bit grim to me. What do you do all day?' Franky continued to talk without even drawing her breath. 'By the way, Tom has been asking after you. I think he fancies you. What about it Annie? It'd be fun if you went out with my big brother!'

Rather lost for words, Annie smiled weakly, overwhelmed by Franky's relentless monologue.

'Oh Annie, just listen to me going on and on... I haven't given you a chance to get a word in edgeways! Anyway, we're all getting worried about our exams and I haven't done nearly enough work yet. I'll probably pass them, but I do need to put my head down and stop watching Coronation Street, Top of the Pops, and all those other great programmes on the telly!'

Annie opened and closed her mouth like a goldfish in a goldfish bowl.

'Do you remember when we went to the seaside for the day? Wasn't that so much fun! I haven't had such delicious fish and chips since then...'

Annie had some good memories of the day, but also some very sad memories because that was the fateful day Mutti had had her heart attack and she hadn't been there to support her.

'I haven't been back to the seaside since then, but we will when we've finished our first-year exams. I just can't wait for the summer break.' Franky paused, realising how insensitive she was being. 'Oh Annie, why don't you just tell me to shut up. I'm only talking about *me* and I came here to find out how *you* are. How are you doing my dear friend?'

Annie waited, half expecting Franky to carry on with her continuous stream of conversation. 'I'm fine Franky, just a bit tired but otherwise I can't complain.'

Hide behind your mask Annie; don't show your wounds...

She had successfully circumnavigated her illness. She was convinced Franky didn't want to hear the truth, and being "just a bit tired" seemed to be an acceptable answer.

'Well, I wouldn't want to be here for any longer than necessary.'

'It isn't so bad, and they're trying to help me get better. I can't leave here until I do.'

'So how are you going to get better?' Franky asked.

Her direct question took Annie by surprise. 'I've no idea, but I hope that I'll find a way forward by talking to the therapist and allowing myself to accept help and support. But it's hard, I feel very confused and exhausted at the moment.'

'Oh my poor, poor love.' As Franky reached over to give her a hug, she realised with horror just how small and fragile Annie had become. 'Oh Annie, please get better, I need you to get better.'

As Franky left Ashmeade, she thrust a small black and white photo of herself, Tom and Annie all smiling, arms intertwined, barefoot on the white sandy beach with the wide expanse of ocean in the background. Annie stared at the photo for a long time and couldn't help but wonder if she would ever breathe in the salty air, run on the warm sand, or gaze out at the ocean ever again.

The following afternoon, just after lunch, she had another visitor. She was sitting alone in the sitting room, forlornly watching torrential rain batter the window pane, when the door flew open and a young and spritely man with messy blond hair and a large friendly grin strode towards her.

'Tom, how lovely to see you!'

'Cor, it's good weather for ducks out there!' He vigorously shook his head, spraying water everywhere. He then threw off his jacket and kicked off his sodden shoes, revealing bright red socks full of holes. 'Ah that's better! Now my Skinny Minnie, how are you doing?' He sat down in the chair beside her and gently took her hands in his.

'I'll be honest with you Tom, it isn't easy and I'm struggling... but I know it'll get easier.'

Tom looked at her with kind concern. 'Annie, I know I'm not very good at the emotions thing, but I'd lift heaven and earth if I thought that I could make things easier for you.'

'Tom, you are wonderful and I thank you from the bottom of my heart. They're looking after me well here but I'm beginning to realise that it has to come from me. I have to lift myself out of the darkness.'

'Yes, it is a bit dark and dingy in here isn't it.' They both smiled at Tom's literal interpretation of her sentiments, but Annie knew that Tom understood.

'I bet you didn't get a word in edgeways with Franky yesterday, but she cares deeply about you, Annie, and so do I.'

He dug deep into his pocket and carefully placed a large pink, white and fawn conch shell into the palm of Annie's hand. She examined it carefully, marvelling at the intricate patterns and curves of this beautiful piece of the natural world. She brushed her fingers over the rough outer shell and into the smooth and shiny interior; it was a priceless and precious gift. 'Tom, this means a lot to me, I will treasure it, thank you.'

'When you feel low or helpless, put the shell close to your ear, close your eyes, and, if you listen very carefully, you'll hear the distant call of the sea. Imagine yourself there on a beautiful beach, the sand between your toes, the sun bringing warmth to your skin and the wind blowing in your hair. One day you and I will visit the sea again, I promise.'

Although Annie hadn't known Tom for long, he had become a dear friend and today he had given her renewed hope that, one day, life would get better.

CHAPTER 26

'Come on Annie, you can do this.'

Annie hunched over her exercise book feeling beaten by the calculation. She had battled with the same problem for the whole session and couldn't fathom a way of working out an answer. She had tried everything.

'What have I told you about estimating your answer first?' she asked rather impatiently.

'I'm really trying, Dee but I just can't work it out.' It had seemed like a long and arduous session. 'Maybe we should stop for today. I'll work on my own and give you my answer tomorrow.'

'No, I want you to keep trying.'

'But I can't do it.'

'Yes, you really are as stupid as I thought!' Dee muttered, almost inaudibly. Her calm voice belied the words she spoke.

'What did you say?'

Dee turned and left the room, leaving Annie lost for words. She stared out at the immaculate lawns, feeling dismal.

I am stupid, Dee is right. Why did I ever think I could do this? But I must keep trying, it's important to Stan that I succeed. I will do better. I will…

***

It was developing into a beautiful late spring day after a chilly start and Annie wandered in the gardens, admiring the abundance of spring flowers and the deep pink flowers of the cherry blossom tree. There was a thin layer of dew remaining on the lawn and she breathed in the heady scent of the apple blossom and the clean fresh air. If she didn't think too hard, she could almost believe that everything was right in her world.

'Annie, oh *Annie*.' Jess ran up behind her and tickled her under both armpits. Both girls giggled. 'Have you thought any more about my request?'

'To paint me with no clothes on, you mean?'

'It'll be the most beautiful painting and I'd really like us to do it. Please, please say you will.' Jess's eyes glittered with excitement.

Annie paused. 'I was just wondering how we could organise it, even if I did say yes?'

Jess nodded her head sagely. 'Um, this shouldn't be a problem. I think if I asked the Occupational Therapist if I could do a life drawing of you, she may well agree to it. Life drawing, or painting in my case, is a popular and recognised form of expression in the art world. I should be encouraged to do this to extend my portfolio and improve my creative skills. My therapist would probably be in favour because it would be beneficial for my mental wellbeing. I'm sure they'll think it would be good for you too.'

'One thing's for sure, I am *not* going to strip off in front of everyone,' Annie said resolutely.

'I'll ask if just you and I could book a private early evening slot in the Art room every day, for as long as it takes, to complete the painting.'

Annie thought about this. She liked the fact that Jess wanted to paint her with full support of the staff, rather than trying to do the painting behind their backs. This seemed uncharacteristically sensible of her wild and reckless friend. 'Okay Jess, I've agonised about this but, if you get permission, I might do it - I'm not promising anything. And even if I decide to go ahead, I might bottle out at the last minute, in which case it just won't happen.'

Beaming from ear to ear, Jess threw her arms around Annie. 'I'll get permission, just you wait and see.' With that she bounded towards the Art room with gay abandon, stopping only to retrieve one of her untied baseball boots that had flown high into the air in her exuberance. Annie was left alone, her head full of mixed emotions; she dreaded bearing her body to anyone, let alone someone she cared about, but she was also strangely excited by the possibility of Jess creating an image of her. She knew that Jess was an extremely talented and extraordinary artist.

Annie decided to take advantage of her next meeting with Patrice to talk about the art project. She outlined their plans. 'What do you think, Patrice?'

'Tell me Annie, what are your thoughts about posing naked?'

Patrice had not beaten about the bush, she had cut straight to the chase, and Annie had not clarified her thoughts at all.

'I just don't know,' said Annie. She drew her fingers roughly through her hair. 'I have gone over and over it in my head.'

'What are you unsure about?'

'I hate my body...'

'And so...' Patrice paused, inviting Annie to expand on her answer.

'I would find it excruciating to take off my clothes and expose myself.' She bowed her head, clenching her hands until her knuckles turned white.

'Yes, I can understand that, there'll be nothing to hide behind. You will be totally exposed. How do you think this will make you feel?'

'Awkward, embarrassed, mortified, ashamed...'

'So it sounds like you're not quite ready for this. Have you any positive thoughts?'

'Jess is a brilliant artist and I feel honoured that she

wants to make a study of *me*.'

'And…'

'I'd be interested to see the final piece. She tells me she wants to show me how beautiful my body is… but Patrice, my body isn't beautiful, it's grotesque.'

'It might be valuable for you to see an image of your body portrayed by someone who cares about you.' Patrice stroked her chin, deep in thought.

'Yes, I think it would, but I just don't know if I'm brave enough,' whispered Annie.

'Well, there is undoubtedly risk in this for you and for Jess. It may affect your friendship, either in a positive or negative way. You may find that you simply can't do this at the present time, and that of course, would be absolutely fine, but you may be deeply disappointed with yourself. It's more than possible that you may not like what you see in the final painting, you may even hate what you see.'

'I don't know what to think.' Annie sighed. 'Half of me wants to say yes, but the other half wants to run a million miles away…'

'There is a lot to think about,' Patrice conceded. 'It might be a very positive experience for you both. Jess will have the opportunity to explore a different art form, and you may find that you have more confidence than you think. And you might learn a lot about yourself and your body by seeing an honest and true interpretation of *you*.' She studied Annie's face intently. 'It is a unique opportunity that you could grab with both hands, but I do have my concerns…'

'What would you do, Patrice?'

'That's not for me to say, I'm not you. But I would like you to consider the opportunity very carefully. I share Claudia's concerns about your friendship with Jess. She is undoubtedly a talented young woman, but she can be very manipulative and controlling. As your therapist, I would probably advise against doing this, for your own protection. I don't want you to be hurt in any way, or for the progress we are making towards your recovery to be hampered. But, on the other hand, if it is carefully monitored, this is a rare opportunity for you both. But I would like the final decision to come from you Annie. Whatever you decide, you must be content with your decision, and don't look back. Have no regrets.'

As Annie walked out of the meeting she had already made her decision. She would take the risk and rise to the challenge; there would be no turning back and no regrets. She would reject the warnings of the staff and grab the opportunity with both hands.

But the words kept going round and round in her head.

Be on your guard, Annie, be on your guard.

CHAPTER 27

It was early evening the following day when the two girls were led into a roomy studio adjacent to the main art room by Elaine, the occupational therapist. Annie had not been in the studio before, and she was surprised that the hospital had the funds to resource such a well-equipped, exciting, and creative space. The floor was made of polished pine, and a large rug made from reindeer skin lay at the far end of the studio. The room was illuminated by the fading natural light from the high window and there were a multitude of tiny lights like stars twinkling in the ceiling. The art resources were thoughtfully laid out to tempt any would-be artist and it seemed to be unbelievably well-stocked. In the centre of the room there was a solitary easel splattered with dried paint, and balanced on two pegs was a huge blank canvas. On a wooden table beside the easel was a selection of oil paints and little glass bottles containing yellow liquid. Rags of all shapes and sizes were available, and there was a kidney-shaped palette placed at the side of the easel for mixing the oils into an endless array of different colours. An upholstered sofa stood a few feet in front of the easel. Annie had remembered seeing something like this before in a book and knew it was called a chaise longue. The sofa was covered in deep red velvety fabric and it had a high curved back rest on one end. It looked quite elegant and luxurious.

The studio was very warm, heated by a small electric fire that cast a rosy glow across the room.

Annie glanced sideways at Jess who clapped her hands together in childish delight. Her faded ripped jeans and black T-shirt were protected by a blue overall, spotted with paint and tightly wrapped around her waist. Annie thought she looked every bit the artist that she was. Her eyes shone like sapphires and her whole body danced with pure joy. Annie had never seen Jess as happy as she looked at that moment.

'Ohhh what can I say? I can't thank you enough!' said Jess, giving Elaine a spontaneous hug. Annie smiled, she had liked Elaine from the moment she first met her in the art room during her occupational therapy sessions. She had a refreshingly creative "can do" approach, encouraging and inspiring the participants to play with new and innovative ideas, to develop confidence, and to have fun.

'Now, I'm going to leave you to your own devices and I'll return at eight o'clock. But girls, please don't abuse my trust in you.' They were both quick to affirm their good intentions to the therapist. 'Very well, I'll see you later. Good luck!'

Jess and Annie stood silently for a minute feeling rather awestruck by what lay ahead. 'This is simply perfect Annie, simply perfect.'

Feeling suddenly very nervous, Annie looked down at herself. She was wearing baggy trousers and an even baggier jersey with holes in it. As if she sensed the tension, Jess put a reassuring arm around her shoulder. 'Annie, it may be difficult for you today but it will get easier. Come on, come with me.' She pulled Annie towards the grey and white reindeer skin rug. 'Let's lie down and make plans.'

Lying on their backs, hand in hand, Jess explained that, before she could start her painting, she would like to make some quick pencil drawings of Annie's body in different positions to become familiar with the subject of her artwork.

'Before I commit to the first brush stroke, I will touch you, feel you and explore every inch of your body, as if I were unable to see. I want to discover everything about you Annie, your bone structure, your curves, every hollow, every crease, and every crevice. I want to explore the very depths of your body and soul.'

Discover everything about me? She can't; she mustn't...

Memories of him came flooding back into Annie's head. She recoiled as her recurring nightmare flashed across her mind; horrific images of his first brutal attack on her on Christmas Day when she was nine years old: the confusion, the pain, the terror.

'Annie, I'll be gentle and all I ask of you is that you relax; I'll stop at any time if it all becomes too much for you,' Jess said soothingly.

'I'm scared Jess, I'm truly terrified.'

Jess put a warm comforting hand on Annie's arm and waited; she wondered what had happened in Annie's life to induce such terror but she asked no questions. Annie knew she had to take the risk. After a long period of silence, Annie surrendered. 'Do with me what you will.'

Jess raised herself onto her elbow and, with the other hand, began to peel off Annie's clothing, layer by layer. As she did so, Annie curled up into the foetal position, drawing her knees tightly into her chest. She cupped her face with her hands and her long hair spread across her shoulders. Her thin and bony hands and feet looked pale and out of proportion with the rest of her body. Jess gave a deep sigh of pleasure.

"The naked woman's body is a portion of eternity too great for the eye of man."

She selected a sketch book and a thick pencil and, with a few lines, captured on paper the image of a tiny skeletal figure, detailing every individual vertebra, the dark shadow of downy hair at the base of her spine and the tangible hopelessness and fragility of her very being.

'To me you're like a rare butterfly fluttering through the

air, searching for something - anything - to make life better.'

Jess put her pencil down and stroked Annie's hair gently before drawing her finger down the bony prominences of her back, tracing the form of her bottom as she lay silently on the rug. Slowly her spine started to uncurl and Annie rolled onto her tummy, one leg straight and the other drawn up towards her chest, her arms loosely folded beneath her forehead. There she remained whilst Jess made a second rough drawing of her naked body, focusing on the sharp detail of her shoulder blades, and the deep ridges of her ribcage, barely disguised by the paper thin layer of skin that was like a fine yellow parchment, and the web of thin blue veins. She captured the dark shadows that formed at the base of her skeletal form. She followed the line of her toes, misshapen by chilblains, her enlarged knee joints, and traced the long bony flanks all the way up to the dark and secret area where her legs divided and merged into her torso.

'Roll over now Annie.'

Slowly and painfully, Annie turned onto her back, putting both hands over her face, and weeping gently.

'My darling Annie, you're doing so well. You're a natural model.'

'I'm ashamed of my body Jess, I'm sorry.'

Jess captured the mental anguish and shame as well as the physical image of Annie's emaciated body as she drew the pencil across the page. She was fascinated by the deep, dark hollows under her collarbone and her pale diminished breasts which formed tiny mounds above her concave tummy; her pubic bone rounded and covered by a small triangular pelt.

Annie pulled herself up to a seated position, hunched her shoulders forward and hugged her knees towards her chest. She bowed her head in shame and the tears flowed freely down her cheeks. 'I'm so sorry Jess.'

'But why? You're perfect.'

CHAPTER 28

She towered over Annie, flicked her wrist, brandishing the bullwhip high into the air and then forcefully down onto Annie's thigh with a deafening crack, each strike cutting deep into her flesh. Annie writhed in agony as the deadly cracks came down one after the other with no time to draw breath.

She spat the words out with the venom of an adder, 'I loathe you, you're worthless and stupid, you have no brain, you're nothing...'

Her face was covered by a beaded mask; her long white hair flowed behind her and she wore a black satin dress trimmed with intricate lace and gold braid. With the full force of her whole body, she cracked the whip again and again over Annie's limp and dying body.

'No, please no...'

Suddenly the mask was ripped from the face to reveal the twisted and grotesque form of a man: someone she knew; someone she feared; someone she hated. But as she watched in horror, the features became distorted, ugly, terrifying. The face slowly metamorphosed into a female form.

When she awoke her heart was pounding and she gasped for breath. Her whole body was bathed in sweat and everything around her was icy and wet; a deep chill swept through her exhausted body.

Is this what it's like to be dead? Am I in hell?

The terrifying image of her torturer coiling up ready to deliver another vicious blow cutting deep into her flesh would haunt Annie for a long time to come. It appeared to be Dee, but was her nightmare really about Stan; her nemesis?

You're worthless and stupid, you have no brain, you're nothing...

As she opened her eyes again, she shook her head, trying to rid herself of the terror of the nightmare.

It is an evil omen... There are dark clouds on the horizon.

After breakfast that day, Annie walked into her maths session with some fear and trepidation. She now viewed Dee with suspicion; she was on her guard.

Claudia warned me about Jess but nobody warned me about Dee.

To her surprise, Annie found Dee in a bright and cheerful mood today. They spent the session looking at algebra, and Annie was pleased to find that she could work out the equations fairly easily.

'Well done Annie. It looks like algebra comes more naturally to you and you've done really well.'

Annie did find algebra the least challenging branch of mathematics but she accepted the praise with relief and gratitude. She smiled to herself. Dee sounded so much more like a teacher rather than a seventeen-year-old girl in a mental hospital!

Suddenly Dee's face darkened. 'Back to trigonometry tomorrow.'

***

Annie was taken aback to see Miss Lagon, her college health education tutor, striding towards her later that afternoon. She had been lying in bed unable to doze off, feeling drained after her restless and distressing night.

'Annie, how lovely to see you.'

She blinked her eyes sleepily.

'All your friends at College send their love, we're all thinking about you.' She squeezed Annie's hand warmly. 'Are you okay?'

Annie hesitated.

Am I okay? Are you really asking me if I am okay? Actually no, I am not "okay." I am very not "okay." I am dying, falling into an abyss, and I can do nothing to stop it. My brain has been overtaken by demons and my body is broken. How can I tell her? Should I tell her?

'I'm all right thank you Miss Lagon, I'm just rather exhausted.'

Hide behind the mask…

Annie knew that she had again circumnavigated the truth of her illness, but she appreciated that her tutor's words were heart-felt and full of concern.

'Is there anything I can do to help?'

Can you work miracles? Can you save me from myself?

'I'm worried about my exams, and I would like to re-sit my maths exam, but I know I'm not ready to do this. I'm going to daily maths sessions with Dee, another inpatient, who seems to be brilliant at everything.'

'That's exactly why I'm here Annie, I wanted to discuss your exam options with you. In normal circumstances you would sit your first year exams in June.'

Annie nodded her head and listened with interest to what her tutor was going to suggest.

'But these aren't normal circumstances, far from it.' She paused. Annie waited with bated breath. 'So I think we should defer your exams until Christmas, or, better still, until next June. By then you will hopefully have made a full recovery and then you can confidently sit your exams and get the results you deserve.'

Annie felt the tension drain away from her body. 'I wish I was well enough to sit my exams. I've let myself and my family down, but when I feel stronger I'll make sure I work harder. I have to do well, I just have to.'

'Don't put yourself under so much pressure. You need to focus on getting yourself better now, put yourself first and the college work can go on the back burner for the moment.'

The relief was immense but then she remembered Stan. 'But what about…?'

'Don't worry Annie, I'll discuss the options with your father and it will all be fine.'

Stan… if only I could find the words…

'Thank you, thank you very much Miss Lagon.'

After her tutor had left, she slumped in an armchair in the lounge, and put her head in her hands. She felt a strange mixture of emotions; she was relieved that the pressure of exams had gone, but she also felt disappointed that she would lose a year of college; she felt that she had let her parents, tutors and friends down, but, most of all, she had let herself down; she had failed… again.

CHAPTER 29

Today was the second session in the art studio and Annie felt apprehensive. She reluctantly peeled off her clothing and lay down on the reindeer skin rug, fear coursing through her body.

Jess walked slowly towards her and lay down beside her. 'Why are you so fearful, Annie? You just need to let yourself go, relax, and allow me to explore the very essence of *you*. It'll be as if I'm blind. I may not be able to see you, but I'll explore every part of you using all the senses I have. I'll touch you, feel you, hear your breath, smell your scent, and taste your skin. All you need to do is put yourself in my hands.'

Why am I like this? Cold and unfeeling; frigid and incapable of love; destined to be alone. I am untouchable.

Jess was calm and her voice soothing and soporific.

Jess isn't "him:" she's a beautiful, gentle, and special woman; I am safe with her. I must take the risk and do this. Please God help me.

Annie surrendered her body for a second time.

'Focus on your breathing Annie: breathe in calm, breathe out tension. And again, breathe in kindness, breathe out fear. Everything in our world, at this moment, is beautiful. Breathe in peace, breathe out kindness, breathe in peace, breathe out kindness. Our breath is all we have, it is life itself.'

Slowly the tension began to ebb away as Annie drew her hands across her abdomen and felt it gently rise and fall.

'Our breath is our best friend.' Jess spoke in a soft creamy voice. 'It stays with us our whole lives. Breathe in love and kindness and it will nourish your body, from the tip of your fingers to the soles of your feet. Breathe in life and it will nourish your body and your soul.'

Then silence, just breathing, as Annie was held in a safe place of peace and tranquillity.

Jess ran her capable hands across the body laid before her. She raised each leg and, focusing on Annie's feet, applied firm pressure to the soft fleshy area of each foot then pulled and twisted each toe separately, and finally massaged each foot with warmth and close attention. Her hands moved up Annie's legs, pausing only to apply pressure to the middle of the calf muscle, taking care not to bruise the yellowing parchment of her skin. She worked towards her secret area exploring each leg in detail, gently working her fingers into every hollow and undulation. Placing a white sheet over her body, she ran her hands upwards and downwards over Annie's legs and warmth and kindness spilled into her body.

Peeling away the sheet, she moved up to Annie's abdomen, gently working her hands and caressing the soft hollow area and, in contrast, the sharp angular bones of her pelvis. Her index finger traced the curving bones of her rib cage and then the contours of her small white breasts as Annie breathed in calm and breathed out kindness. Intense sparks of pleasure shot through her whole body as Jess's fingers came to rest on her nipples. Jess lowered her head and drew her tongue around each dark area, tantalising and then withdrawing, spreading the thin trail of saliva round each breast with her finger. Annie drew a deep intake of breath and sighed deeply with pleasure. Then up towards the neck, working her fingers into each dark recess either side of her collarbone.

'These are the deep pools for your tears, Annie...'

Jess drew her fingernail lightly down the inside of each arm, nourishing Annie's body with delight and intense pleasure, and an extraordinary frisson of excitement emanated from deep within her.

Jess explored in detail the shape and form of her head, her fingers moving over her mouth and lips and bringing sensations that Annie had never experienced. She silently moved her body behind Annie's and cupped her head in her capable hands, taking all the weight, and Annie savoured the sense of being cherished rising from within. Her warm hands finally rested gently on Annie's closed eyelids, spreading kindness and light across her soul.

'Roll over now.'

This time Jess began her massage at the base of Annie's skull and her fingertips traced all the way along the line of sharp interlinked bones of her vertebrae. She felt the deep ridges of Annie's ribs and the bony prominence at the base of her spine.

'Oh Annie, I can feel everything.' There was an air of deep sadness in her voice.

Drawing her hands down the back of Annie's legs, she closed her eyes as she explored every fissure, every muscle, every tendon, and every bone. She licked the saltiness of her skin and breathed in her natural scent. 'Did you know that skin is the biggest and the most sensitive sexual organ we have?' Jess said gently. Finally she laid the sheet over Annie and her hands retraced their steps, moving gently but firmly up and down her body as she breathed in kindness and breathed out love.

Then the artist withdrew as Annie lay in complete stillness on the soft rug, her legs splayed and her palms turned uppermost towards the sky.

Finally she stirred, stretched her body, and gazed at her friend in amazement. 'Where did you learn to do this, Jess? I feel as if I've been transported to heaven and back.'

'Just something I've learned along the way,' Jess replied modestly.

I can't understand or believe what has just happened to me... I feel different somehow. I'm feeling sensations in my body that are unfamiliar and, yes, exciting. How can this be? At this moment in time I am happy.

Jess sat cross-legged beside Annie, and smiled. 'Tomorrow I'll delve deep inside your head to discover the unique and special qualities that make up your whole being. What empowers you? What are your passions? What drives you and gives you the determination to live through each day? I need to uncover the very depths of *you*. And then, and only then, will I be ready to commit my brush to the canvas. And I can tell you now with complete certainty, it *will* be a masterpiece.' Suddenly she threw her hands up in mock horror. 'Listen to me - I sound more like my bloody therapist than the wild crazy artist that I am!'

Annie pondered for a few moments and then it came to her.

I know just how I can express my inner passions, feelings and emotions and there'll be no need for any words to be spoken.

The session had finished a few minutes before Elaine was due to return at eight o'clock. She rose, dressed herself, and, feeling unusually rested and relaxed, she pulled Jess towards her and their lips brushed, soft and warm. 'I have an idea!' Her eyes shone with excitement. 'I have to go, see you later... and thanks Jess.' She hurried back towards the main hospital building, she had an important phone call to make.

CHAPTER 30

The following morning Annie sat in the drab consultation room, staring at nothing in particular.

'You're not focusing today, you seem miles away.' Patrice began to feel frustrated by Annie's lack of concentration. 'Come on Annie, I'm interested in what you have to say.'

'I'm all over the place, I'm sorry.'

'Why is this?'

'We've begun the art project and I can't stop thinking about it. My head is brimming over with conflicting thoughts.'

Patrice glanced at her notes. 'So, you decided to take the risk, a brave decision. How are the sessions going?'

'I'm glad that I agreed to do it, but it isn't easy.'

'Yes, I can understand this. When we discussed how you might feel posing naked, you said, "Awkward, embarrassed, mortified, ashamed..." How do you feel now?'

Annie stared at the grey linoleum, trying to make some sense of all the thoughts that were whirling about in her head.

There is so much I can't share with you...

'When I first took off my clothes I *was* mortified and ashamed of my body, but Jess gave me time and space. She seems to have a special gift...'

'She showed you empathy and understanding.' Patrice placed her pen down quietly on the desk next to her notes and leaned towards Annie.

'She said I was like a rare butterfly fluttering through the air, "searching for something - anything - to make life better." She's right isn't she Patrice? I am searching for something, but I really don't know what it is,' Annie acknowledged sadly.

'Everything will make sense in time, Annie, but, for the moment, let's return to the art session.'

'When we first went into the studio and I took off my clothes, I curled up in a ball like a baby in the womb, I just wanted to disappear. But as she spoke the words, my whole body began to respond.'

'In what way?'

Annie smiled. 'The tension slowly ebbed away and I felt like I was wrapped in a warm, comforting blanket.'

'And then what happened?'

'Jess drew some rough pencil drawings of me in different positions.'

'Did you feel relaxed and warm through each session? You mentioned having conflicting thoughts?'

'My body is grotesque, but she said that I was beautiful. How can I believe her? I cried.'

'Why did you cry Annie?'

'I cried because I am ashamed of my body. I wept because I am ashamed of me.'

'Did it help you to cry?' Patrice asked softly.

'I've always found it hard to cry, it's a very public expression of my feelings, which I don't usually share with other people.'

'This is deep analysis, Annie. We'll have you writing a psychology textbook next. But it certainly is interesting to describe crying as a public expression of your feelings which you don't usually share with other people...'

'I know it might sound weird, but I think some of my pain flowed away with my tears.'

'So, does this mean that crying is good for you, and for your health?'

'Yes, I think so, but it's very hard to do.'

Hush, little baby don't you cry…

'I wonder why, I cry at the drop of a hat. Just watching *Gone with the Wind* or listening to a sad song can make me weep,' Patrice said, raising her eyes to heaven.

Annie became pensive. 'I think it's how I was brought up.'

'In what way?'

'I've always been told not to share my true feelings with the outside world, always show a brave face and smile.'

Patrice scribbled down a few notes before asking, 'What are your thoughts on this, Annie?'

She shrugged. 'It's all I've ever known.'

'But what are your true feelings?' Patrice probed. She looked searchingly into Annie's eyes.

'I've become very good at not sharing my innermost thoughts with anyone. It's safer that way.'

Patrice wrote down some more notes. 'Who is it in your life that has persuaded you to keep silent about how you are really feeling?'

Annie paused, gazing forlornly out of the window.

Think Annie, don't go there…

'Annie, I'm losing you again, who is it that has influenced you in this way?'

'I suppose,' Annie said tentatively, 'it's my father, Stan.'

'Do you feel any anger or resentment towards your father?'

'I think he had his heart in the right place and was protecting the family.'

'Do you think he was right?'

'Stan and Mutti had many arguments. He felt the whole world didn't need to know about our private family upsets. He always told us not to air our dirty washing in public.'

'But you were a young child. Maybe you needed to share your thoughts and worries with someone? Talking with another human being can be very healing, it may have helped you to make some sense of everything?'

'Stan did his best and stood by his family,' Annie said stubbornly. She longed for the conversation to end.

He is my father, he must be right…

'I would like you to reflect on our conversation, Annie. Words are a powerful means of expressing who we are and, perhaps unwittingly, your father has limited your ability to express your individual and unique character.'

'I do find it challenging to find the right words to express how I'm feeling,' said Annie, 'but you have to be careful with words: words can hurt you, words can damage you, words can destroy you. It can be safer not to speak.'

'Yes, this can be true, so we all need to choose our words carefully. Can you tell me when words have hurt you?'

Annie considered her answer; there had been so many words that had hurt and damaged her in her young life. 'When I've been called "stupid" or "worthless." Words like that hurt me the most because I believe they are right.'

Patrice propped her head in her hands. 'We'll talk more about this in our next session, Annie. One careless word can change the course of our lives forever. And once a word is said, it can never be undone.' She paused for thought. 'This is significant and I think it would be helpful for us to explore this further. But for the moment, I'd like to suggest that it may be helpful for you, going forward, to start being more honest and open in expressing how you truly feel.'

'But I don't think I've been dishonest - I've been silent.'

The silence is overpowering, it is deafening…

'This is why I'm encouraging you to share your feelings with me in these sessions. I want to get to know you and understand who you are, what you are thinking and feeling, and what has happened in your life. But returning to the art project, I am proud of you. It was a tremendous leap of faith to take the risk and you have indeed grasped it with both hands; well done! Before we finish I'd like you to give me your final thoughts on today's session.'

Annie sighed. 'I think I can see a small chink of light at the end of the tunnel.'

'Now that's what I like to hear! We've talked about what makes you happy and a little about your relationship with Mutti. Next session I would like us to focus on the relationship you have with Stan.'

Annie's face darkened.

CHAPTER 31

Annie opened her violin case with great care, savouring the moment as she unwrapped the precious instrument from the turquoise silk scarf that was wrapped around it. She caressed the gentle curves of the violin and examined it lovingly, brushing off the remnants of rosin from each string and wincing from the familiar high-pitched squeaking sound that emanated from them as she did so. She sighed with pleasure as she examined the rich dark patterned maple on the back and the majestic scroll that held the four ebony pegs in place. She picked up the soft cloth inside the violin case and polished the instrument until it shone. Then she tuned the four strings; she had no tuner but she knew she had a good ear and that the tuning would be accurate. She placed the padded shoulder rest firmly in position and then, propping the violin in the open case, turned her attention to the wooden bow. Its white hairs had been blackened at either end from years of rosin but she knew it was a fine bow and she carefully tightened the horse hair and added sufficient rosin to enable her to play with a bright and clear tone. Her eyes rested on the Mother of Pearl decoration at the end of the bow; the deep purple, pink and blue of the iridescent shell fascinated and delighted Annie.

She was thankful that she had managed to contact Joy on the telephone following the art session the previous evening. Joy strode into the lounge just after breakfast, wearing pink high heels and causing quite a stir as usual, and swinging the precious instrument jauntily over her shoulder.

'Oh Annie my dear, I'm so happy that you'll play your violin. What a joyous sound you'll make!'

Music was central in Annie's life. She could express everything she was feeling through the strings of her violin; there was no need for words. Words were challenging but Annie knew she could communicate through her music and it came naturally to her.

'Thank you Joy, I'm looking forward to playing again.'

'Last time I was here I noticed the record player over there.' She pointed enthusiastically towards an insignificant and dusty blue box sitting on one of the side cupboards. 'It doesn't look like it's been used for years! I thought it might cheer everyone up if I play one of my favourite records. What do you think?' Without pausing for an answer, she took the record out of its colourful sleeve and placed it on the turntable. 'We used to dance to wild calypso and reggae bands under the blue Jamaican skies. Ooh those were good days, dancing on the beach with a glass of rum in one hand and an 'andsome man in the other. We didn't have a care in the world.'

Joy's voice reverberated around the hospital, much to Annie's dismay, but she certainly got a few chuckles from onlookers. She added in a smooth and creamy voice, 'Music be the food of love my darlin'. Oooh yes, music be the food of life itself.'

Joy stood up tall, threw her shoulders back, revealing her ample bosom trussed up in a tight pink and green floral bodice, and took a deep breath in. In that brief silence before the music began, Annie cringed as she watched the unfolding scene, worried that Joy's large floral bodice might split under the increasing strain of her expanding ribcage.

As the music began, Joy started to sing in a low, velvety, and tuneful voice, moving and gyrating in perfect time to the syncopated rhythm of the reggae beat. 'Oh, Toots and the Maytals, they sure were the best band in town!'

Annie marvelled at the colourful and extraordinary spectacle of a large Jamaican woman singing and dancing with gusto, her body twisting, turning, and pirouetting in perfect time with the irregular beat of the music, but totally at odds with the grey twilight zone of Ashmeade. She gazed around the room and couldn't help but giggle at the extraordinary sight of stone-faced Claudia beaming from ear to ear and swinging her hips under her rather prudish brown and green tweed skirt, in perfect time to the music.

As Joy started to sing the song all over again, and again, one or two residents tentatively joined in with "yeah," quietly at first, but then with increasing confidence and energy. As the music continued, more and more people, staff and patients, were drawn to the sitting room, to enjoy the rare scene and, one by one, they started to clap their hands and move their bodies in time to the music. "Yeah oh yeah!" The hospital was filled with the reggae music of Jamaica and Joy squealed with delight as she danced through the throng of people, pausing to acknowledge or offer a reassuring stroke of an arm to the few silent residents who had chosen to observe from afar.

The impressive brass interlude raised a ripple of laughter as Joy threw her head back and began to play her imaginary trombone with exaggerated arm movements and an accompanying sound that was incredibly realistic. Annie couldn't believe her eyes and her initial embarrassment was soon replaced by a real sense of pride in this amazing lady who had brought her magical qualities of happiness and joy. But the most joyful thing of all was seeing residents who were deep in their isolation and despair becoming joyful, if just for a moment in time.

And it was infectious.

After it was all over, there was a rare buzz of chatter and laughter in the room. A few residents crowded around Joy telling her just how much they had loved the music and dancing. Joy's face was radiant, she was brimming over with happiness. When the gong sounded for lunch, the residents made their way to the dining room, and Joy and Annie were left alone.

'Annie, I've had an idea and I can't tell you how excited I am!' With that, she smothered Annie with a suffocating, perfumed hug, and a wet kiss, and strode out of the room, her hips still swinging in time to the song she had just sung.

Annie smiled and the warmth and the sheer happiness of the moment stayed with her for most of the afternoon. The evening's art session would be another unique experience and Annie was looking forward to it. But she did wonder what Joy had in mind, and whether it would involve her.

CHAPTER 32

As Annie walked into the art studio her eyes widened in amazement. The room was bathed in a warm light created by a string of fairy lights arranged decoratively across the back wall, just above the reindeer skin rug. The warm yellow lights twinkled cheerfully, creating a magical glow, and she gazed at Jess, whose eyes were glittering and dancing in the semi-darkness. She thought once again how fortunate she was to have the creative attention of this talented and beautiful artist.

'Welcome to my magic grotto, Annie. I can't wait to find out everything about you: what empowers you, what drives you, what makes you into the special beautiful crazy person you are.'

Annie stood still to fully appreciate the beauty of the environment: the soft shadows around the room, the solitary easel standing proud, and the paints already for use to create a masterpiece. Yes, Annie was sure that Jess would indeed paint a masterpiece.

It was Jess's turn to be surprised as Annie opened her violin case to reveal her cherished instrument. 'Oh, I didn't know you played the violin, how amazing!'

Annie took out her bow and was about to play when Jess made a request. 'As I'll be painting your naked body, how would you feel about being naked when you play?'

Annie's body stiffened. She knew that she would feel far more exposed standing up naked than lying down on the rug. Jess would be able to see everything; her shapeless breasts, her bloated belly, the strange downy hair on her inner thighs...

Interrupting her thoughts, Jess added, 'I'll be making detailed notes and sketches of you and I need to be able to see you. All of you.'

Nodding her head slowly, Annie took off each article of clothing piece by piece until she was bare. She hunched her shoulders forward and lowered her head towards the ground, trying to shield her body behind the small violin that she clutched in front of her. She knew there was nothing left to hide behind.

'I know you'll feel more comfortable when you play your violin, trust me. I'm going to relax, close my eyes and listen before I draw or write anything. It'll be great to hear you play.'

Her comforting words helped Annie to focus on her playing rather than on her naked body. She lifted her violin under her chin, placed the bow on the strings ready to play and then she began. She played a slow and haunting melody that she made up as she went along. She started quietly, weaving in and out of the music, rising and falling. Her body started to flow and became a natural extension of the instrument she played. As the notes rose from low to high, the volume rose to a crescendo, pausing at the very top, before descending, meandering in the middle register for a few bars before falling to the lowest string as she played long, smooth, rich notes until the final note faded away. Annie had been carried away by the music as she played, and had forgotten that she was naked. The music transcended everything.

During the mesmerising and soulful piece, Jess had slowly lifted herself up from her reclining position on the rug and now sat cross-legged, her body erect and alert as she listened to the music, watching Annie's flowing body with keen interest. After the final note had finished, there was a silence: like the magical silence that happens in a concert hall after an audience has listened to a virtuoso performance - the final note ends, there's a millisecond of silence, before the rapturous applause begins.

'Annie, that was incredible, I had no idea you had this much talent. What were you dreaming about when you played this beautiful piece of music?'

Annie remained standing, holding her violin down to one side, immersed in her own thoughts. 'I often have vivid images in my head when I play: I was walking in a forest in winter. The trees reached for the sky, frozen in dignified silence, the branches heavy with frost. As I walked on, I came across a babbling brook, and I paused to listen to the water as it meandered over the rocks. It was eerily quiet except for the sound of my footsteps as they sank deep into the snow. Everything was silent and calm...' Her words trailed off.

Jess picked up her spiral-bound sketch book and thick pencil and started to draw, deep in concentration. She noted a few words and her face glowed with satisfaction. 'I'm really pleased with this Annie. When you described the scene, I could picture the forest so well. I feel like I've almost been there with you, walking hand-in-hand in the winter wonderland. I'm capturing the magic you describe through music and words, it's really exciting.' She hugged herself and sighed with pleasure. 'Now I'd love to hear a piece that makes you happy and joyful.'

Annie smiled as she recalled the joyful singing and dancing that had taken place that morning: the spectacle of the wondrous "larger-than-life" Joy, the extraordinary sight of Claudia's hips swinging in time to the music, and residents clapping and dancing.

She lifted up her fiddle - for this was what she called her instrument when she played folk - and the bow flew across the strings as she played a lilting and uplifting jig, sometimes playing two strings together, sliding up to each note, her fingers moving deftly up and down the finger board as clouds of rosin flew into the air. Her whole body danced with joy as she played, tapping her feet in time to the three-four rhythm and laughing as she did so. She was quite out of breath when she finished her tune.

'I can really feel the joy!' said Jess. She beamed from ear to ear. 'Where were you then? Did you have a picture in your mind again?'

Annie threw herself on the chaise longue, still clutching her violin, and breathing heavily. 'I was gazing out across the deep blue ocean, with the yellow sun making a band of dazzling light across the water. In the distance I saw a sailing boat bobbing up and down in the waves with its sails billowing in the breeze. I felt the gentle waves lapping against my feet as my toes sank deeper into the soft sand. I breathed in the fresh salty air and wondered at the beauty of the world; the sheer beauty and majesty of the ocean, far stronger and more significant than we can ever be. I celebrated the forces of nature. This is what makes me truly happy.'

She recalled Joy saying to her a while ago, "Find the joy, Annie, find the joy." She knew she had discovered the joy, only for a fleeting moment, but she had.

'My imagination is working overtime, I can almost taste the salty, fresh air. Ohh, I feel so happy.' She paused. 'Now I'd like you to play something sad. What makes you weep?'

The joy left Annie as rapidly as it had arrived and she stood stock still, her mind sharply in focus, wondering how she could move from joy to sadness in a trice. She reached into her violin case and found the small but significant piece of wood that would mute her violin. She placed it carefully over the bridge and lifted the instrument onto her shoulder. She placed the bow down beside her and started to pluck one note repeatedly and deliberately, her body framed by the gentle glow of the fairy lights. The relentless single note altered the atmosphere from light to darkness in an instant. She continued to pluck the single note with passion and intensity, representing the regular and life-giving motion of her heart beating in her chest. She slowly and deliberately picked up her bow, and drew it mournfully across the strings, the notes filling the room with the muted and heartbreaking sound of despair. The tears flowed freely down her cheeks and spilled over the curved edge of her cherished violin. She lowered her head and sank to her knees and, as she did so, she ended just as she had begun, with the relentless plucking of one note, getting slower and slower, and weaker and weaker, eventually fading away to nothing.

Jess moved gently towards her friend and hugged her tightly against her own body. 'My special Annie, what makes you so sad?'

Annie clung onto Jess, nestling her head in her shoulder. 'So many things make me sad, I don't know where to begin.'

Jess took Annie's hands gently in hers and she waited.

'My heart aches with sadness,' Annie whispered sadly. 'I understand the true meaning of a broken heart. I fear that, if I continue in the direction I'm going in my life, my heart will get weaker and weaker until it will eventually stop altogether and I'll no longer be part of this world. "Ashes to ashes, dust to dust." I'll fade away and turn into dust unless I overcome my illness. This makes me sad, Jess. I don't want to die, I want to live. But not as I am now.'

Wiping Annie's damp face with the back of her hand, Jess cupped her face in her hands and gently brushed her lips across Annie's wet cheeks. 'Annie, I won't let that happen to you. You're very special and I feel so much better for having you in my life. We'll come through this, I know we will.' Giving her a warm embrace, she continued, 'Now my last request: you have shown me what saddens you, but now I'd like you to show me what makes you angry. Give it to me. Let it all out!'

Annie pulled herself away from the warm comfort of Jess's arms and positioned herself squarely in front of her. She let her mind reel back to that familiar scene, the one that was etched in her memory, and her face contorted with anguish and fury. She gripped her bow in a vice-like hold and tore into the strings, carving out the short staccato notes with precision and aggression. Her angular, emaciated body attacked the instrument with a viciousness that made Jess stare at the frenzied vision of her anguished and deeply troubled friend. After the bow was finally flung into the air, Annie collapsed on the floor, exhausted and drained, and both girls were silent as they assimilated what had just happened. Jess was shocked by the show of anger from her gentle, kind friend; she had not seen this side of Annie before and she felt too choked to move.

'Oh Annie, what has happened to you? It must have been so terrible. I feel your pain, I share your anguish. What, or *who* has done this to you?'

The silence is killing me...

Annie slowly lifted her head, her damp hair falling across her face, and she let out a haunted cry of anguish.

CHAPTER 33

'Wake up Annie, come on. Joe's fast asleep at the desk and all's clear on the western front.' She prodded Annie in the ribs. 'Let's go.'

After the evening session in the studio, Annie felt unsettled. She had tossed and turned in bed, so she was relieved to be distracted for a while. They opened the front door and stepped out into the warm, balmy night and crept, one behind the other, to their favourite place in the garden next to the tall red brick wall. The honeysuckle had died down and had been replaced by an abundance of pink roses climbing towards the top of the old wall. The lawn was soft and sumptuous and the two girls lay on their backs and stared up at the inky-blue sky, full of stars.

'Look Jess, can you see the Milky Way?' Annie pointed to the hazy band of white light arching across the night sky. 'I wonder if we can see the Seven Sisters? Look, over there! It's like a huge mass of shining diamonds lying on a navy blue velvet bed. Have you ever seen anything more beautiful than this? It's like looking into eternity. Do you think heaven is up there? I wonder if there is a heaven...'

'Whoah Annie, you're tiring me out with all your questions. Now let me see. Yes, I can see the Milky Way now that you've pointed it out,' she said, 'although the name makes me think of a delicious chocolate bar. You know, the one with the blue and white wrapper!'

'But *do* you think there's a heaven somewhere up there?' Annie persisted. 'Is there such a thing as heaven?'

Jess nodded. 'I like to think so, Annie. I like to think that there's something to look forward to after we die, but I guess we won't find out until that time comes.'

'I hope there is a heaven, because otherwise everything seems very pointless. Why are we put on this earth if there's nothing before and nothing after? Are we just here to breed? Thinking about it though, maybe we should try to be wonderfully happy on earth first?'

Jess was not in the mood for deep and meaningful conversations. 'Eating a Milky Way is heaven on earth,' she said. Both girls giggled. 'Come on,' she urged, 'let's forget all about the philosophical "Meaning of Life" questions and have a smoke.'

Pulling out two rolled joints and a box of matches from her dressing gown, Jess lit them both simultaneously and handed one to Annie. Inhaling deeply, Annie felt the familiar feeling of euphoria and happiness, even Jess's joke about eating a Milky Way seemed funny now.

'Oh Annie, you are the most talented and amazing person I have ever met. Your violin playing gave me goose pimples, it was so expressive. How did you learn to play like that?'

Annie smiled, pleasantly surprised by the unexpected compliment. 'I started learning when I was six. Mutti used to love my playing.' She paused. 'But Stan hated it. I used to get up very early in the morning to practise before he was awake.' She shrugged her shoulders. 'I can understand why he didn't like it though, because when you first learn the violin, it can sound pretty horrible.'

'But, as your dad, shouldn't he have encouraged you to learn the instrument you love?'

'Yes,' Annie replied hesitantly, 'maybe.'

As the smoke coiled its way upwards, Jess reflected on her own childhood. 'I don't remember my mum and dad. I told you, they both died in a plane crash years ago, when I was a toddler. I wish I had had a chance to get to know them. I do wonder how my life would have turned out if they were here now. I really wish I'd had brothers and sisters, it might have been fun growing up in a normal family. And I probably wouldn't be here now.'

'What do you think they would have been like?'

'I often asked my Aunt about my mum and dad, but she didn't ever tell me very much. Instead, I like to imagine in my own head what they were like. My dad was probably quite a character, full of fun, crazy as the Mad Hatter, and an inspirational poet and artist. I imagine my mum being loving and caring, and she probably had a lot to put up with living with my dad... but I'll never know what they were really like,' she added wistfully. 'My aunt looked after me after my parents died and she did it because she had no choice. I was nothing but a burden to her and I knew she resented me. I made absolutely sure that I was as difficult as possible. I shouted at her, called her all the names under the sun, and often ran away from home not telling anyone where I'd gone. I don't care if I never see her again.'

Annie tilted her head on one side, listening intently. 'Did she show you any love or affection?'

'Are you joking? I'd have kicked her arse if she'd come anywhere near me. She didn't want to take care of me, and I hated her. Anyway, parents can mess you up so badly, it may have been just as bad living with my parents. I read a poem recently, written by a brilliant poet called Philip Larkin. His words really made me think about childhood: how parents can totally fuck you up - sometimes unintentionally - but they do. What do you think? Did your parents fuck you up?'

Annie took a sharp intake of breath, her hands shook as she spoke. 'Yes, Jess, *he* did.'

Jess was quick to surmise that Stan was at the heart of Annie's suffering but she sensed this was not the time to press Annie further. Instead she moved closer to her friend and stroked the side of her face with warmth and affection. 'It will get easier. I promise there will be better days ahead.'

She turned onto her side to face Jess and closed her eyes as her friend gently caressed her cheek, brushing her lips sensually over Annie's eyelids. Annie felt apprehensive, but also excited, as Jess gently peeled away her clothes to reveal her naked body. She felt less exposed than she had done in the studio, lying in the cover of darkness, but she was also acutely aware of the risk of being caught, which was dangerous and exciting. Jess paused to gaze at Annie; she looked carefree, young and happy, but at the same time, she could see her sadness and vulnerability. How she longed to find a way to ease Annie's burden. She quietly took off her own clothes and pressed herself firmly against Annie, both girls savouring the pleasure of the warm and close contact with another human being. Annie couldn't believe or understand how different she felt with Jess. She had always feared and recoiled from being physically close to anyone, but now she felt safe and warm. And, there was something else - something Annie had never experienced before - Jess's touch gave her an unfamiliar tingle of anticipation and longing, her whole body ached for more. Tentatively at first, she ran her hands through Jess's spiky blond hair and then lightly followed the line of her spine over her smooth flawless skin. Their bodies intertwined as they explored every part of each other slowly at first and then with increasing intensity. Annie breathed in the warm night air as she experienced sensations deep within her that she didn't understand or recognise. Jess expertly caressed Annie's body, tantalising and teasing her until her hands finally rested on her secret area, stroking, slowly at first, and then with increasing intensity, until finally, Annie's body arched towards the stars.

CHAPTER 34

The next morning, as she sat down in the consultation room, Annie felt a strange mix of euphoria and exhaustion after their exploits in the garden the previous evening. She didn't relish the thought of an intense meeting ahead.

'Tell me Annie, how is the art project going?'

The meetings with her psychiatrist often felt like a game of ping pong. Patrice would ask a question, Annie would give a brief response, and then it would be followed by another question. It felt like a long monotonous rally with no winning smash at the end.

Why do I have to answer her stupid questions? It's all so pointless. She won't give me any answers. It's so frustrating. A complete waste of time.

'The studio sessions are going quite well.'

'Tell me more...'

Annie stared out of the window, struggling to focus. 'Jess is trying to find out as much as she can about me before she starts her painting. During our last session, she wanted to explore my feelings - what makes me happy, sad, or angry.'

'How interesting, this must have been quite challenging for you?'

'Why do you say that?' Annie asked abruptly.

'It's okay Annie, it can be hard for us all to understand

our own feelings and emotions at times.' Patrice paused. 'Feeling sadness and anger can tell us a lot about ourselves. What makes you feel sad?'

'Today Patrice, do you know what, I really don't care.' Annie's eyes glinted with anger.

Patrice stood up and slowly walked towards the window. This was an uncharacteristically aggressive response, she must choose her words carefully. 'I think you do care. I think you care very much.'

Annie bit her lip. 'I just don't feel like talking today. I tell you what, why don't you tell me what makes *you* angry Patrice?'

'But Annie, we're not here to talk about me, we're here to talk about you.'

'It's always the same, you never give me any answers. How can I get better if you never tell me what I should do?'

'I'm here to encourage you to talk with me about what has happened. I promise we will find a way forward, once you're ready to face what has hurt and angered you.' Her voice softened. 'Until now you've been reluctant, but if we can talk openly together, we can then take the first important steps towards your recovery. I do understand this will be difficult for you Annie.'

'I need you to help me. Please help me,' she pleaded.

Patrice offered Annie a tissue and returned to her chair.

'Why do you always have to sit behind your desk, Patrice? It makes me feel like I'm being interviewed. I suppose I am in a way.'

Surprised by Annie's comment, she raised her eyebrows. 'That's an interesting point. Come with me.' She led Annie to one of two large arm-chairs in the corner of the room, separated by a light oak coffee table. 'Does this feel more comfortable for you?'

Annie suddenly felt rather exposed, but at the same time, she felt more able to talk in this less formal set up. 'Yes, the desk felt like a barrier between us, but everything feels more equal now.'

'Some psychiatrists use a couch for their sessions, so that the patient can lie down and close their eyes if they wish. However, I don't use this approach in my practice because I like to have eye contact with my patients, and be able to see their expressions. But thanks for sharing your feelings, we can sit here for the rest of our sessions if you like. Now, shall we start again?'

Patrice had left her large pile of records on her desk and, instead of constantly referring to her notes, she gave Annie her full and undivided attention. It was as if they were sitting in a comfortable living room. Annie's shoulders relaxed and she started to feel more focussed.

'So, tell me about the art project.'

'I sometimes struggle to find the right words to describe my feelings, so I decided to play my violin instead. I can communicate through music: I express my feelings and emotions through the notes that I play.'

'I think you use words very effectively when you have clarified your thoughts,' Patrice acknowledged, 'but what a great idea, I didn't know you played the violin. Tell me about the music.'

'I played melodies to express different emotions. I can see images in my head when I play, it's almost as if I'm there.'

'Do you need manuscript music?'

'No, I play by ear. I've never fully understood where the music comes from, I don't work it out, it just happens. I suppose it comes from my heart.'

'Wow, what a wonderful talent to have.'

Annie gazed into the distance. 'When I play or listen to music - any kind of music, classical, folk or pop - I'm transported to another place. I forget everything that's going on in my life.'

'Music can be such a wonderful way of connecting with your thoughts and emotions. It can enhance and enrich your life.' She studied Annie's face. 'I'm sure music can also help you to escape the harsh reality of life.'

Escape the harsh reality of life.

Annie played with the words. 'But when I am sad or angry, music certainly doesn't help me to escape; it makes me confront my own fears and anguish head on.'

'So you use the music effectively to connect with your true feelings. That's great Annie!' She smiled. 'What kind of music do you prefer to play?'

'I like to play mournful, haunting tunes, because they make me think.'

'So when you were playing your sad tune, what were you thinking?'

Annie's eyes filled with tears. She silently reflected on the piece that she had played to Jess in the art studio. 'That my heart aches with sadness; that I understand the true meaning of a broken heart. There is so much that has happened to me in my life that makes me sad. If only I could turn back the course of time and start again. If only I could be someone else. I know I can't change the past, but if I continue to follow the path I'm on, I will die. But the worst thing is that I am out of control. I can't seem to stop.'

'Why Annie, why?'

'I hate myself, I hate everything about me, but I seem unable to change. It doesn't matter what I look like on the outside, I need to feel good on the inside; but I feel worthless and rotten to the core,' Annie answered sadly.

'Why do you feel so worthless?'

'Because my mind has been taken over by ugly and destructive demons, I have the devil in my head and I can't rid myself of evil. I'm starving myself to death and I know that, unless I overcome this, I will die. My heart will eventually stop beating. "Dust to dust, ashes to ashes." '

'There is a saying by an old Chinese philosopher called Lao Tzu: "If you do not change direction, you may end up where you are heading." We *will* change direction in your journey through life, Annie, we *will* succeed.' She paused, sensing that she was getting closer to the heart of Annie's trauma. 'Now, returning to your music, I would be interested in finding out what you were thinking when you played your angry piece.'

Annie glared at Patrice and shut her mouth like a clam.

Patrice probed further. 'I wonder if you were thinking about your family, your parents? Do they make you feel angry?'

Annie said nothing.

'You described to me your earliest memories of Mutti taking you for snowy walks and Stan lighting the fire on Christmas Day. They sounded like wonderful memories. But what changed? Tell me about the later memories you have of your father.'

'Don't you understand me at all? I can't and I won't tell you.' Annie stared at the ground, folding her arms resolutely in front of her.

'Talk to me, Annie,' Patrice persisted.

Annie spat out the words with anger and venom: 'Parents fuck you up.'

With that, Annie stood up and stormed out of the room, slamming the door behind her.

CHAPTER 35

'What the hell has happened, Annie?'

Jess found Annie sobbing in the corner of the sitting room. Through her tears, Annie told her about the challenging and emotional session she had just had with Patrice.

'Come with me.' Jess took Annie's hand purposefully and led her upstairs to the empty dormitory. It was lunchtime and she knew that the other residents would be in the dining room, so they were unlikely to be disturbed. They sat together cross-legged and face-to-face. Jess reached into her back pocket, took out her knife, and carefully removed it from the sheath. As she spoke, Jess pulled the sharp blade across her arm and made several thin cuts just above the scars of the past. The droplets of blood dripped onto the wooden floor. 'Now it's your turn.'

Annie pulled the sleeve of her left arm up towards the elbow and, without hesitation, made several cuts into her emaciated arm. She breathed in the relief of the agony of her wounds. The tension left her body with the pools of blood that oozed out of her.

'Tell me what is haunting you Annie. What did he do? What did Stan do to cause you this much agony?'

'Stan, he…'

He told me not to. Hush little baby, don't say a word.

'They are just words Annie,' Jess urged, 'let them go.'

'It's all my fault.' As she spoke, Annie absentmindedly pushed the blade into her arm again and again. 'It was Christmas Day and I was nine years old. Mutti gave me a china doll called Greta. I wanted to love her, I really did, but she was creepy and cold.'

'Take your time. Breathe. Keep breathing,' Jess said soothingly.

'In the afternoon, Stan and Mutti were asleep, so I went for a walk. I don't know why. I was stupid Jess, really stupid.' Annie's face contorted with her painful memories, as she cut deeper into her arm. 'I walked into town, everything was silent, except for the toll of the church bell. I thought no-one was around, but then I saw her.'

'Who did you see?'

Annie was in a world of her own as she recounted her story. 'I saw a tiny woman wearing huge boots, lying in a shop doorway, half hidden by a pile of cardboard. She was old and wrinkly, with matted grey hair. She looked starving, but she was kind enough to wish me a happy Christmas. She told me her name was Nessy. There seemed to be no hope for her, but she was really spirited.'

'She sounds like quite a lady,' Jess acknowledged, 'but you were only a young girl, what was going through your mind?'

'She was starving. I wanted to help her.'

'I'm not surprised Annie, you're a kind and generous person.'

'Without thinking, I invited her to come home with me and have some chicken and potatoes. I should have known better. I was stupid. She had a hacking cough - I knew she needed help.' She paused, deep in thought. 'But I was scared about what Stan might say.'

Heavy silence hung in the air between them, as they faced each other in the large empty dormitory. Jess waited patiently while Annie collected her thoughts. 'When we got home, I was relieved that Stan and Mutti were still asleep, so I crept into the kitchen and got her a plate of food. You should have seen her, Jess, she attacked the food as if she hadn't eaten for months...' Annie's words faded away as she retreated further into her memories.

'And then what happened Annie?'

'Stan came out and he...' Annie stammered.

'Breathe Annie, breathe.'

'He was angrier than I had ever seen him before. I thought he was going to beat us both. But Nessy stood up to face him, she was tiny and he was huge. She told him that he should be proud of me, and ashamed of himself; but in the end she had to leave. She stuffed handfuls of potato into her pocket and scuttled away before Stan could hit her.' Annie dug the blade of the knife deep into her forearm. 'I didn't mean to cause harm, I was only trying to help,' she wailed.

Sensing that there was more to come, Jess gently urged her friend to continue. 'It's okay Annie, you're nearly there...'

'Do you understand? It was all my fault. If I hadn't gone for a walk, nothing would have happened. He slapped me across the face and sent me to bed. But then the arguments started. They were fighting because of me. Because of what I did.'

Jess listened to her friend, conscious that, as the story was unravelling, the cuts were becoming more erratic. She slowly and silently held Annie's arm and peeled each stubborn finger away from the bloody handle of the knife. She placed the weapon on the floor beside her.

'You're strong, keep going, tell me...'

Annie stared unblinkingly beyond her into her own private world. 'I put my head under the covers but I could still hear them Jess; the shouting wouldn't go away, it just wouldn't go away.' She rocked her body backwards and forwards as droplets of blood spilled across the floor.

Our little secret.

'Then there was silence. The silence was terrifying. I

didn't know what was happening. I pulled Greta close to me, to protect me, but she was cold and hard. I could hear my heart pounding in my chest.' She covered her face with her hands and sobbed. 'I heard him open the kitchen door and climb the stairs, slowly and deliberately, the creak on the fourth step...' She took a sharp intake of breath, 'I could see his yellowy silhouette in the doorway... and then he towered over me...' She pulled her knees tightly into her chest. 'I can't do this Jess, I can't...'

'Let it all out...' Jess urged. The true horror of Annie's story was just beginning to dawn on her.

'I thought he was going to beat me, but...'

'You're safe here Annie, keep going.'

'I felt a heavy suffocating weight on me, I couldn't breathe and he... he...'

The pain, the anguish, the sadness... there are no words...

'He forced himself deep into me. The pain was unbearable. I thought I was going to die. I tried to scream, but nothing came out, I couldn't move...'

'Oh no, Annie. No...'

Her breath had become shallow and fast. 'The sight of the broken doll on the floor in three pieces - one eye staring up at me and the other eyeball rolling away - will haunt me forever.'

We are broken...

Jess held Annie's hands in hers. 'How could anyone do that to a young innocent girl - to you Annie?'

'I was nine years old. He broke me and destroyed me.'

The damage is done.

Annie slumped back against the wall, exhausted and drained. Both her arms were riddled with small cuts and a pool of blood made a semicircle of red around her tiny broken body. 'If I hadn't gone for a walk on that Christmas Day...' She rocked her body backwards and forwards. Backwards and forwards. Backwards and forwards.

If I wasn't me...

'Was it only once?' She feared that she already knew the

answer.

'No. Please don't tell anyone, Jess, please I beg you. It can be our secret. You can't tell anyone, please.' Annie's mouth twisted with the emotion she struggled to contain.

Our little secret.

'None of this is your fault Annie.' She looked at her friend with true love and compassion. 'You will tell your story when the time is right, and it is then, and only then, that your healing will begin.'

Jess held Annie tight in her arms, both rocking backwards and forwards until their tears and blood mingled into one.

CHAPTER 36

'Annie, I have everything I need, I'm ready to paint the picture. We can start this evening. I can't wait.'

Annie and Jess sat together in the residents lounge the following afternoon, discussing the arrangements for the next studio session. Jess's excitement was infectious and, although Annie still felt apprehensive about posing naked, and uncomfortable about her body being studied so closely, she was looking forward to the evening session in the art room.

After supper, the two girls walked hand-in-hand to the Art room. The sun had just disappeared behind the distant hills leaving a deep crimson glow across the sky in its wake. They were met by Elaine who greeted them cheerily as she unlocked the door to the studio. 'Enjoy your session you two, I'll be back at eight.'

The studio was warm and cosy and all the art materials were laid out ready to use. The fairy lights created a warm and inviting atmosphere, casting a golden light across the studio. Everything was perfect.

'Annie, undress and then we can decide how you'll pose for the painting. We need to make sure you're comfortable because you'll need to stay still for a long time.'

Jess cast her eyes over all the pots and jars to check that she had everything she needed. She selected a variety of brushes and squeezed blobs of oil paint onto her palette. Her eyes shone with anticipation and she smiled, showing the mischievous dimple in one cheek. Annie was really looking forward to watching the artist at work. Jess pointed to the chaise longue which had been positioned diagonally in the middle of the room with the reindeer skin rug in the foreground and a standard lamp positioned to one side. 'All I want you to do now is find a comfortable position which you can stay in for a while.'

Annie draped herself rather self-consciously across the sofa. Reclining her back on the curved backrest, she straightened one leg on the padded cushion and crossed the other loosely over the first. She placed one hand on her hip and the other by her side. She tossed her hair back from her face and tilted her head sideways, glancing shyly towards the artist. 'Is this okay, Jess?'

'Simply divine. Wow, you're a natural! Now, I have a surprise for you.'

Jess wandered over to the corner of the studio, opened the lid of a large blue box, selected a record and removed it from its sleeve and placed it on the turntable. 'Stone-faced Claudia lent me her record player to play while I work. I was really bowled over because I didn't think she had an ounce of kindness in her!'

'Oh that is really generous of her.'

'I've got a few records here. Some are seventy-eights so they must be really old. I think I'll choose *The Unfinished Symphony* by Schubert because I adore this piece of music. It puzzles me that he wrote two movements and then left it unfinished, despite living for another six years.'

Annie was once again in awe of the depth of knowledge of her friend. How did she know about this classical piece of music? She was pleasantly surprised that Jess appreciated classical music as much as Bob Dylan, The Rolling Stones or Carole King.

'Schubert was supposed to be really absent-minded and disorganised, so he may have simply forgotten to finish it.

Isn't that hilarious, to forget to finish a masterpiece! If for some reason I'm not able to finish my painting of you - our masterpiece - we should call it *The Unfinished Symphony*. Actually no, I suppose we can't do that because there's already a symphony with that name.' She laughed. 'Um, I think we should call the painting *The Unfinished Symphony of Love*. What do you think?'

Annie smiled at her crazy creative friend. '*The Unfinished Symphony of Love*, what a beautiful title for a painting. I have no doubt you'll finish it, but not if you keep on talking like this!'

Jess ignored her obvious hint to shut up and get on with the job in hand. 'Can't you just picture Schubert, his brain full to overflowing with music, his wild curly hair flying everywhere, surrounded by bits of paper covered in random musical notes? Creatively brilliant and chaotically crazy.' Annie was surprised to realise how passionate Jess felt about this piece of music. Jess grasped the record's cardboard sleeve in both hands, looking at the faded illustration on its cover. 'There were fragments of two other movements but he just left them unfinished. How could he do that?' The music started to play. 'Listen Annie, it's ghostlike, such a haunting beginning, the sheer power and beauty of it, it reduces me to tears. How could he hear in his head how the instruments would sound all together when he was writing each individual part? He must have had an extraordinary brain.' She paused for breath. 'He died of syphilis. It's thought that when he wrote this symphony, he was in pain and suffering from depression because of his illness. Maybe that's why this incredible music can speak to other people who are suffering. Annie, we're suffering darkness and pain in our lives, and maybe something extraordinary will happen here in this room with this painting. I truly believe it will. Out of darkness comes light.'

Annie took up her position. Jess stood behind the easel and painted the first brush stroke onto the canvas. Annie listened to the enormity and sheer power as the orchestra played, the different instruments weaving in and out, rising and falling as the composer told his story through the music. It made her think of how she expressed herself when she played violin. The strength and power of being able to express emotion through music struck her again. There are only eight notes in a scale but the possibilities of those eight notes are extraordinary; endless; timeless.

Jess worked with concentration, only occasionally lifting her head to study the details of her subject. Her lips twitched in time with the movement of her brush; she seemed to be in a different world, completely focused.

Annie had time to reflect on her own emotions as she posed in stillness. She was beginning to feel different. She had initially felt very vulnerable and insecure about exposing her body for Jess to paint. She knew she still felt deeply ashamed of her body, but now something else was beginning to happen; she was beginning to feel more relaxed and in tune with herself, and some of her fears were leaving her. She felt calm and peaceful. Glancing at the artist at work, she felt true love and affection.

Jess stood back to review her artwork before acknowledging Annie. She breathed out a deep sigh. 'Oh Annie, I have some way to go, but soon I'll be able to show you just how beautiful you really are.'

'Can I see it now Jess?' Annie couldn't resist asking, feeling fearful, and yet longing to see the painting.

Jess laughed, shaking her head, 'Not yet, you'll just have to be patient...'

Later that evening Jess bounded up to Annie, carrying her notebook that she used as a diary. Her eyes glittered in the darkness. 'Annie, my dearest Annie, it's true, even after the agonising pain of darkness, light will follow. The sun will rise again.'

CHAPTER 37

Annie stared in astonishment and wonder: the gloomy room where she had her sessions with Patrice had been totally transformed. A large white fluffy rug lay in the centre of the room, replacing the old grey mat that must have been there for years. The walls were adorned with an impressive gallery of Ghanaian artwork showing life in the sixties: black and white photography of bustling street scenes, artwork of women dressed in traditional costume, incongruously set against a backdrop of a bright red saloon car of the era, and other eye-catching colourful works of art. The desk had been removed altogether and had been replaced by a low coffee table. In the corner of the room stood a huge green rubber plant in a large blue ceramic container. Bold print curtains hung either side of the Victorian window, enhancing the view of the spectacular gardens of Ashmeade. A striking ebony wood sculpture of a black nude woman, her legs drawn towards her body and her head bowed, was thoughtfully positioned towards the centre of the room.

'Patrice, I can hardly believe it. Your room looks truly stunning.'

Her psychiatrist's face radiated with pleasure, and even her clothes reflected this new, colourful approach: she wore a striking multicoloured patchwork fisherman's smock, with navy slacks and shiny blue flat-heeled loafers. Her hair was intricately styled into plaited braids incorporating tiny coloured beads.

'Annie, I have you to thank for this. Deep down I knew I needed to brighten up my work space and your words gave me the impetus I needed to actually *do* something about it. I hope this will help to put my patients at ease, but it also makes me feel more "at home" at work. I have reminders all around me of my homeland and culture, it will make a difference.'

Annie cast her eyes over the array of colourful and diverse art thoughtfully arranged on each wall. 'I love the pictures. Art can be so expressive. Did you already have these pictures or did you go to a print shop to buy them? They show a different country, a very different culture, I've never seen this style of artwork before. I love the colours and the textures, and the detail.'

'Yes, I had some of the pictures already,' she said, 'so the walls in my flat are rather bare now! The rest I begged and borrowed from my friends. Annie, I bought the sculpture especially with you in mind. Come with me.' Patrice led Annie over to the piece of art. 'Tell me what you can feel.'

Annie ran her hands over the rich, smooth ebony, feeling every line and contour of the curved and rounded body. She began by exploring the bowed head with the detailed carved lines of her hair falling over her body, then tracing the muscular shape of her arms which cradled her bent knees. She knelt down to feel her legs, the ample thighs, the calf muscles bulging with energy and the feet placed firmly and squarely on the ground. Finally she ran her fingers over the curved back, feeling each bony vertebra running all the way down to the base of her spine.

'I feel the body of a beautiful woman.'

'Anything else?'

'I smell the sweet scent of the wood under my fingers.'

'And…'

'I feel her pain, her anguish and her hopelessness.'

'What makes you believe that she is wretched and

hopeless?'

Annie hesitated. 'Because of the way she's sitting with her head bowed clutching her legs to her body. She's crying.'

'Annie, isn't it interesting how we can make assumptions about what we see. In my mind, she has just been for a swim in a cool lake and she now bows her head and closes her eyes to dream about the cool, delicious, silky feel of the water on her bare skin.'

Reflecting on this, Annie had to agree that she had made an assumption without any substance.

Patrice smiled. 'The artist called his creation "Beauty lies within." It is interesting how our mind can make assumptions, but there are other ways of looking at and assessing the same object, or the same situation, so it means that we can't always trust our own interpretations.' She brushed a trailing strand of hair away from her face, and waited for a response, but Annie seemed deep in thought. 'Annie, do you think the woman is overweight?'

'No, I think she is beautiful.'

Patrice smiled. 'I do too.' Now becoming more serious, she continued, 'I would like to suggest that the way you perceive your physical body, and how you feel about yourself, might not be an accurate way of seeing how your body actually is. You describe to me how worthless and ugly you feel on the inside, but for me, you speak with intelligence and insight, with love and compassion, and I see someone who has purpose and passion and beauty. The only outward sign I have that all is not as it should be in your life is that you are emaciated.'

Annie slowly looked into the eyes of her therapist and was lost for words: there was so much for her to think about, so much to absorb.

'It's tempting to assume that everyone around you is happy and content in their lives, but you can never know for sure,' Patrice mused.

'Perhaps you're right, I do make assumptions about people around me, that they are all leading happy and fulfilling lives.'

'But it isn't the case here in Ashmeade, is it?'

Annie shook her head. 'No, I see people struggle through each day.'

'I won't bore you with statistics but I think you may be surprised how many people suffer with some form of mental illness. You are not alone.'

Annie was already feeling rather drained from the intensity of the conversation and she wasn't quite sure where it was leading. As if sensing her thoughts, Patrice invited her to sit down.

'We need to find a way to help you to understand that you are beautiful, that you have value, and that you can accept yourself.' Patrice smiled compassionately. 'And how are the art sessions going?'

'Jess has started the painting at last.'

'How does it feel to be the subject of her art?'

She stared down at her feet. 'I'm so ashamed of my body,' she said, 'but I feel honoured that she wants to use me as her model, and I think I'm looking forward to seeing the finished painting.'

'This is good news, Annie. During the last session we began to think more about your parents, but I seem to remember the session was cut short rather abruptly...'

Annie bowed her head in shame. 'I'm sorry. Sometimes you ask me questions that I find difficult to answer.'

'I do understand, and I appreciate that there are some aspects of your life that will be challenging and painful to talk about. But, as I've said before, unless we dig deep into your life to find out what is at the root of your pain and misery, we won't be able to make any progress towards good health and inner contentment.'

Annie reluctantly nodded her head.

'I went to the library yesterday after work and looked up the poem that I think you were referring to during the last session, "This Be The Verse" by Philip Larkin. I searched for hours and finally found it buried deep in a magazine called *New Humanist*. It took some finding I can tell you!'

'Did you really?' Annie was touched by the time and effort that Patrice had given to this, particularly after her outburst at the end of the last session. 'Jess read the poem to me and it really resonated. It must be true for so many children. Parents can do untold damage…'

'And did your parents fuck you up Annie? Please excuse my language, but I'm simply quoting the *colourful* word used in the poem.' She put her hand over her mouth but her eyes were smiling.

Everything felt different today. The consultation room now felt like a safe and comfortable space and Annie felt more relaxed than she had done in previous sessions with Patrice. The words were beginning to flow more easily. 'Yes, I think they did fuck me up.'

'And did they mean to?'

'Mutti gave me unconditional love and affection from the moment I was born, but then she became seriously ill. She had brain surgery when I was a young child, and things were never the same again. She suffered from depression, she needed drugs and then alcohol as well to cope with her life. She can't help it, she is beautiful and talented, but she is suffering from an addiction.' Annie drew a deep breath. 'I do love her and I think she loves me too, but she did not do what any mother should…' Her words faded away.

'And what is that Annie?'

'She should have protected me,' Annie said angrily.

Patrice paused to write some notes in the file. Annie didn't feel that her mother protected her, but, from what? She would come back to this, but, for the moment, Annie was beginning to open up and she didn't feel she wanted to interrupt her thoughts. 'She did well to convey her love for you, despite her illness.'

'Sometimes I wonder if I inherited some of her addictive personality. She's addicted to drugs and alcohol, she has demons in her head. I'm addicted to starving myself, I have demons in my head. But I also inherited her love of music, and for that I'm really grateful.'

'Interesting, Annie, carry on...'

'But now we both share the same fight for survival. We're both in hospital and I believe that she's still struggling to recover.' She paused before adding sadly, 'I haven't heard a word from her, no letter, no phone call, nothing. I only know because Joy has told me that she is in hospital to overcome her addiction.'

'Do you feel she should be here to care for you now and help you to get better, Annie?'

'Really when I think about it, Mutti has rarely been there for me so, maybe she has fucked me up, but I know that it was never her intention to do so. She didn't mean to damage me.'

My words are beginning to make sense...

'Why was she so unhappy? Why did she need drugs and alcohol to deal with her life?'

'I don't think Stan and Mutti were ever very happy. They used to fight all the time. I hated it when they argued.'

'What kind of things did they disagree about?' asked Patrice, leaning forward a little.

'They used to argue about anything and everything. Stan would hurl anything he could get hold of towards my poor mother. They shouted and they screamed at each other.'

Annie, remember, don't air your dirty washing in public.

Annie took a deep breath and continued, 'But they both did their best, and Stan worked hard to earn money so that I could go to private school.'

'So, all this time you didn't share your unhappy home life with anyone? That must have been hard for you as a child.'

'Yes, it was but it's all I've ever known.'

'Annie, going back to the poem, you've told me about your mother. Did Stan fuck you up as well?'

'Yes, I think he did.'

'And did he mean to?'

'I'm not sure...'

Be careful Annie, be careful...

'You say he worked hard so that you could go to private school. Why do you think this was so important for Stan?'

'He's a brilliant mathematician and he wants me to be brilliant, too.'

'That's quite a pressure on you,' said Patrice. 'How do you feel about maths?'

'I'm utterly useless, I just don't understand a lot of it.'

'So it isn't your strongest subject...'

'No, it certainly isn't but I want to make him proud. Dee's giving me some coaching and I am determined to succeed.'

'That's truly admirable and I wish you luck with it. Do remember, though, that we all have different skills and talents, and that's what makes the human race so rich and diverse. I feel that your talents lie in music and the arts, and your considerable skills need to be recognised and celebrated for what they are.'

'But Stan doesn't think of music as a proper subject. All that matters to him is my academic success in English, maths and science - particularly in maths.'

'So you feel that you *have* to succeed in maths in order to earn his love?'

'I *must* succeed.'

'And how is Stan with you, Annie? Does he argue with you?'

Think before you answer. Beware, remember what Stan said, don't tell...

'When I was very young, Stan seemed to be much happier, but when the arguments with Mutti started, everything changed.'

'Tell me what changed?'

Why could I tell Jess and I can't tell Patrice?

'I was happy until I was nine years old.'

'So what changed?'

Annie shifted in her chair and started to fiddle with a piece of loose thread hanging from her jumper. She felt a rising sense of panic; her heart beat faster in her chest.

'Was Stan often angry with you?'

'Yes, he was sometimes very angry with me, but I made him angry.'

'Do you feel it was your fault?' Patrice offered Annie a tissue.

'Yes, because I was never good enough for him. I was too stupid.'

'Did he tell you that?'

'Yes, he did.'

'The problem is, Annie, if you are told something enough times, you begin to believe it.'

Annie raised her hands in despair. 'But don't you see, I am stupid and worthless. Stan is right.'

'Well, I would beg to differ.' Patrice said softly. 'We'll come back to this but, for the moment, let's carry on. How did he show his anger towards you?'

'He shouted at me.'

'And...'

'He made me feel small and insignificant.'

'And...'

'Sometimes he hit me.'

Patrice paused for a moment, and then asked quietly, 'How did you feel about him hitting you?'

'He had to teach me a lesson but I was scared.'

'Are you scared of Stan?'

The tears started to pour unchecked down Annie's face. Wiping them away, she meekly nodded her head. A little voice in her head was urging her to tell Patrice everything.

'You say that everything changed when you were nine years old. What changed, Annie? Did Stan hurt you?'

Yes, he took away my innocence, he destroyed my life.

Annie put her head in her hands in shame and humiliation. She recalled Jess's wise words: "You will tell your story when the time is right Annie, and it is then, and only then, that your healing will begin."

I want to but I can't, Jess...

She buried her head deep into the open palms of her hands in utter despair. 'I'm sorry. I'm so sorry Patrice.'

CHAPTER 38

Yesterday Jess had chosen *The Unfinished Symphony* composed by Schubert, to inspire both the artist and the model. Today she had selected something very different. She carefully placed the record on the turntable and stepped back. 'Listen to this, the best rock guitarist the world has ever seen. Can you believe that stone-faced Claudia actually had an album by Jimi Hendrix in her collection?' Jess laughed. 'Some say Hendrix never died, he still tours the Universe. Thanks for dropping in Jimi!' She turned away from the record player and walked over to Annie, who was sitting on the floor with her back resting against the chaise longue. 'Isn't that a beautiful way to think about it? He was ripped from this earth when he was far too young, but he sure left his mark on the world. His music will live on in the hearts and minds of people forever. Legends never die.' As Jess spoke, she moved rhythmically to the distinctive beat of the music. 'Just listen to the guitar - sheer brilliance; so young: so talented.'

Annie hadn't heard of Jimi Hendrix before. She listened intently to the first track, "Purple Haze" marvelling at the power of his words, and the metallic beauty - and yet harshness - of the strings. 'What happened to him?'

'I think he died of a drug overdose.' Her eyes widened. 'Perhaps it was the effect of the drugs that let him view life from a different perspective - a psychedelic and crazy angle. Perhaps it was the drugs that gave him brilliance? He was a truly untamed spirit.' Jess sang as she danced. 'Just listen to that guitar, it's almost as if it was invented just for him.'

Annie lay languorously across the sofa, enjoying the harmonious blend of Hendrix and Jess as they sang together.

'Listen to the words of the last line Annie: that girl is you - you've put a spell on me. You make me feel misery and joy in a heartbeat.'

Jess has certainly put a spell on me, she is the most extraordinary person I have ever met. Jess the artist. Jess the sensual woman. Jess, my friend and lover.

As she started to paint, Annie noticed that Jess had a different energy today. Her brush strokes were deliberate, fast and furious as she attacked the canvas, stopping only briefly to study her subject, select a different brush, or wipe her brow with a painting rag.

'He even set his guitar on fire on stage. Why the heck did he do that?' Not waiting for an answer, she worked the brush across the canvas. 'While he was performing "Fire" he struck a match and his priceless guitar went up in flames. Crazy, mad, and very cool!' The rock music inspired Jess to create and Annie found it a joy and inspiration to watch her.

After about half an hour of Jimi Hendrix and continuous painting, Jess set down her brush. 'Okay Annie, I think we should take a ten-minute break and then get back to work.'

Annie stood up and stretched her limbs: every part of her body ached - she wasn't used to being this still for so long. She realised with satisfaction that she felt less self-conscious posing naked than she had before: Jess had an extraordinary way of putting her at ease, and the music soothed her body and her mind. 'Can I look at your work?'

Jess giggled, shaking her head. 'No, you need to be patient. Tomorrow will be our final session in the studio. I have a few finishing touches to make and then I'll be able to show you the finished piece. I hope you'll like it.'

Annie felt a sudden sense of loss that their sessions were coming to an end. It had been an experience of a lifetime and Annie would never forget it.

Jess beckoned to Annie, and lay spread-eagled on the luxurious rug. 'Come and join me.' Annie smiled as she lay down beside her and together, they held hands and absorbed the magical atmosphere as the fairy lights twinkled and the music played. The minutes passed and before long Jess reached over and kissed her friend lightly on her cheek. 'I'm ready.' Annie slowly pulled herself up and took up her position once again on the sofa. The atmosphere changed as Jess turned up the volume and Hendrix played the eerie long note introduction of "Foxy Lady " and, as he started to sing, she started to paint, the rhythm of the brush and the rhythmic beat of the song working as one. Jess's voice rose tunefully above Hendrix, 'Oh, you little heartbreaker…' It was challenging not to giggle as Jess peered round the edge of the easel, and started to mouth each word in the most exaggerated, erotic and seductive manner, 'Ohhhh, you foxy lady…'

At last Jess put her paint brush down and stood back, as she always did, to review her work. Her face did not give anything away. Annie couldn't tell if she was happy with the progress of her portrait, or not. As she placed her brushes in the turpentine and wiped her hands on an oily cloth, Jess sighed. 'All good things come to an end, but we have some time left in the studio tonight. Come on.' She invited Annie to lie once again on the soft fluffy rug. 'I want to play a mellow, beautiful instrumental called "Little Wing." It brings tears to my eyes every time I listen to it.'

The two girls held each other in a gentle embrace, yearning for the moment to last forever. As the sweet music played, no words were needed. The tangible connection between the guitar, their interconnected bodies, and their deep love for each other transcended everything.

There was nothing left to say.

CHAPTER 39

Dee sat in her rocking chair moving back and forth. She stared vacantly into space; her mouth tightly set; her eyes expressionless. The only sound came from the creak of the rocking chair as it moved on the wooden floor. 'She's late, how dare she waste my precious time?' she hissed viciously under her breath. 'Who does she think I am? Does she really think I've got nothing better to do than pander to her every whim? She is a stupid, stupid child.'

The relentless rocking continued; her face remained blank. 'I'm such a fool, such a fool; she's not worth the time of day.' Her expression changed in an instant. 'Annie, how lovely to see you, I've been looking forward to our maths session today.' She smiled stiffly, showing her perfectly even white teeth.

'Dee, I'm so sorry I'm late, I didn't notice the time…'

'Let's make a start.' She held Annie's arm in a vice-like grip and propelled her firmly towards the wooden table by the window.

'I have some news. My tutor has suggested that I defer all my exams until next summer, so I have more time to improve my skills. Isn't that great?'

Dee's lips curled upwards into a tight smile. 'Have you no pride?'

Annie stared at her in disbelief. 'Of course I have pride,

Dee, but I think this is a good idea.'

'Have you no backbone, Annie? I fear not, but onwards and upwards,' Dee muttered. She rubbed her hands together, slowly, and deliberately.

Annie suddenly felt a deep chill run through her body. She began to question why Dee had offered to teach her in the first place. Did Dee even like her? But she was determined to continue with today's work; trigonometry, the area of maths she found the most difficult. 'Are you okay?' Annie asked cautiously. 'You seem a bit tense.'

'I'm fine thank you.' Dee's lips formed a broad smile, but it didn't reach her eyes. She pushed the text book into Annie's hands. 'Find page thirty-six and answer the question. I'll give you five minutes and then I'll ask you to explain how you arrived at the answer.'

Annie's hands shook as she turned the pages; her brain didn't seem to be working. She read the question and her mind went blank. She glanced sideways at Dee. Today some of her blond hair was tied in a large green bow on the side of her head; she wore a checked pinafore dress, short ankle socks folded at the top and flat brown Clarks shoes - the kind that Annie wore when she was five years old. Her style was more suited to the nineteen-fifties. There was something about Dee that was strange and rather foreboding today.

Concentrate Annie, you can do it.

Dee stared at the watch on her wrist and clicked her tongue against the roof of her mouth, indicating the passing of each second. Her left foot tapped in time with the clicking of her tongue. The sound echoed round and round in Annie's head. She knew she must focus.

'Three minutes to go.'

She broke into a cold sweat.

"The square on the hypotenuse is equal to the... sum of the squares... on the other two sides." I can't do this; I am empty and cold...

She looked at the diagram in front of her; her mind,

numb.

'One and a half minutes to go.'

Have mercy...

Annie still hadn't written a single calculation down in her exercise book. Dee had fallen silent some time ago but Annie could still hear the echo of the seconds passing, like the torturous drip, drip, drip of a leaky tap.

'Forty-seconds to go,' Dee said ominously.

The page was blank. The time was up.

'So where are your calculations?'

'I just couldn't do it today. I remembered Pythagoras but then I couldn't remember how to apply it to the problem. I think I need more practice,' Annie muttered.

'Well, I must say I'm not surprised.' Dee's foot started to tap again on the wooden floor, her face etched with anger. 'Go on Annie, tell me how to work it out. *Now.*'

'I can't.'

'You can. And you will.'

Annie bowed her head, desperately wanting to escape, but she felt afraid of what Dee might do if she started to walk away. They were alone in the sitting room; everyone else was still in the dining room at the far end of the long corridor. She didn't dare to cry for help, and no-one would hear her if she did. Dee continued to rock on her chair. She stared at her steadfastly with a face like thunder.

Tap, tap, tap, tap...

'Maybe if you stopped tapping your foot I could think more clearly.'

Dee drew her face up close to Annie's and she spat out the words, 'How dare you speak to me like that. How dare you! I give you my time and this is how you repay me.' Saliva dribbled down her chin. 'You have no clue, you'll never achieve anything in maths. You're stupid. Stupid, stupid, stupid...'

Dee rose to her feet. The nightmare which Annie had experienced that troubled night, with her tormentor, flashed back into her mind:

She towered over Annie, flicked her wrist, brandishing the whip high into the air and then forcefully down onto Annie's thigh with a deafening crack, each strike cutting deep into the flesh. Annie writhed in agony as the deadly cracks came down one after the other with no time to draw breath. Her tormentor spat the words out with the venom of an adder: "I loathe you, you're worthless and stupid, you have no brain, you are nothing…"

Annie's nightmare had become reality.

She watched in horror as the terrifying image of Dee, transformed into the grotesque image of her father. Her nemesis.

He towered over Annie, flicked his wrist, and struck one vicious blow across her face.

CHAPTER 40

'No, please stop, no…' Her blood ran cold. She flinched and screamed in the darkness. 'Please dear God help me.'

'It's over, Annie.'

Confused, she peered upwards. Everything was grey except for the dark outline of a figure standing beside her.

'Annie, you're safe now. I'll be looking after you.'

She listened intently, there was something familiar about the voice but Annie couldn't recall when or where she had heard it before.

'I'm Dr Sharm, you're in intensive care Annie. You had a serious blow to your head and you've been unconscious for some time. You may remember me, I saw you a few weeks ago in casualty.' Dr Sharm looked compassionately at Annie and smiled warmly. 'You're safe now. No one can hurt you.'

'But what happened to me?' Annie's body tensed as she looked around the semi-lit room: the air was heavy with the smell of disinfectant and sickness, and patients lay still and silent in their beds. 'Oh God no…' The image of her tormentor appeared before her. She cowered, covering her face with her hands. 'Please stop… I tried to shout…'

'Annie, I know it will be difficult, but I would like you to try and put it out of your mind for now,' Dr Sharm said soothingly. 'We will talk about this later, but now it is important that you give yourself a chance to rest and recover.'

'But I can't... she gave me five minutes... she kept clicking her tongue... tapping her foot... my brain wouldn't work.'

'Annie, take a deep breath...'

'I can see her face... smiling, but then... she spat.'

Dr Sharm leant forward and injected medication into the cannula in the back of her hand. 'Sleep now, Annie. Dee has gone; she's been taken to a place of safety to protect herself from harm and to protect others. No one can hurt you now.'

'But it was him. I saw his face...' Her words trailed off. She felt a wave of calm wash over her as she drifted into unconsciousness.

The next day, Annie - assessed to be out of immediate danger - was transferred into a small side room adjacent to the general ward. As she slept, she had a visitor. Claudia, the manager of Ashmeade, stood at the end of Annie's bed and stared open-mouthed at the horrifying sight that met her eyes. 'I'm so sorry,' she whispered, as if the walls could hear.

Just then Dr Sharm strode in behind her. 'Claudia, perhaps you can tell me what has happened to Annie?' she asked, in a hushed voice. 'I want you to look at her.' She carefully peeled back the sheet to reveal Annie's skeletal body, limp and pale, her face covered with deep purple bruising. 'I have never seen a body as emaciated and damaged as this.' It was as if they were looking at a skeleton of someone who had died many years before. Every bone was visible, there seemed to be almost no life left.

Claudia screwed up her eyes, trying to erase the image in front of her.

Dr Sharm gently cradled Annie's arm in her hands and turned it over. 'Look at these scars.' She traced her fingers lightly over the savage angry cuts. 'How could this happen, in this day and age, and in the confines of a hospital, where patients should be safe?' Dr Sharm spat out her words angrily, turning to face Claudia. The silence stretched for minutes as they stared at one another, neither daring to move or breathe.

Claudia hung her head in shame and stared at the ground. 'The sight of this poor girl will stay with me forever.' Claudia slowly raised her eyes to look at the vulnerable girl lying on the bed in front of her; it was the saddest and the most shocking sight she had ever seen. 'I will never forgive myself. I was sorting out a silly domestic dispute in the kitchen, something so insignificant, and I should have been there protecting my patients from harm. I should have been watching out for Annie.'

'But how has she become so emaciated under your watch?' Dr Sharm persisted. 'How has she damaged herself so badly under your watch? How has she suffered so much?'

'I don't know, I simply don't know,' Claudia murmured. She turned her back on Annie. 'I am deeply ashamed.' She put her head in her hands. 'It is my fault.'

Dr Sharm drew in a deep intake of breath. 'Claudia, I have serious concerns and I have no choice but to report this case to higher authorities.' She paused. 'There will be a formal review into Annie's individual case; the policies and procedures in place at Ashmeade for the treatment of illnesses such as Anorexia Nervosa will be scrutinised, and your own role within the case will be investigated.' She shook her head sadly. 'Measures will be put in place to ensure this never happens again.'

Claudia hung her head and nodded meekly.

They both turned to face Annie. 'She's very frail, she looks very near to death,' said Dr Sharm, 'I will monitor her very closely.'

Claudia stared at the horror that was Annie. 'Please don't let her die.'

***

'Help me, please... make him stop...' Annie said weakly. She had been in hospital for a week, slipping in and out of consciousness, and during this time, had been carefully monitored by the medical team.

'You're safe now.' Joy's creamy voice was comforting and soothing, 'You poor darlin'.'

'Something's wrong, I can't move.'

Joy put a warm reassuring hand on Annie's arm. 'Just lie back and try to relax, Annie, your poor body has suffered so much.'

'What's happening to me? What's this?' She tried to snatch the plastic tube from her nose. 'I can't breathe, take it out! My throat hurts.'

'Darlin' they're pumping goodness into your body, it will make you stronger.' She gently placed Annie's flailing arm back on the bed. 'I'll just ring the bell to call for one of those fine nurses.'

As the bell sounded, Annie stared at all the machines surrounding her bed.

Pumping goodness into my body? Oh God, are they force-feeding me? I have lost control. Please don't let me put on weight. I don't want food, I don't need anything... I have to escape...

She covered her face with her hands as she felt warm liquid trickle between her legs and spread out onto the sheet below. Soon the sheets became cold and damp; Annie shivered with the chill of her urine, and the deeper chill of her humiliation. 'I think I've wet myself.'

All of a sudden a cheerful bustling nurse appeared from nowhere.'Don't worry my duck, we'll soon have you cleaned up.' She rolled Annie over roughly and efficiently as she deftly changed the sheets, causing pain to shoot through Annie's body. She didn't utter a word. She sobbed silently.

Please dear Lord, help me.

As soon as Annie became stronger, she was moved to the general ward where she stayed for a further two weeks. This particular morning Dr Sharm came bustling into the ward, followed by a group of medical students. 'Good morning Annie, how are you feeling today?' Without waiting for a reply, she continued, 'I'm sure you will be pleased to hear that I believe you are now strong enough to return to Ashmeade.'

Annie smiled weakly at the doctor; she would be glad in many ways to return to the more familiar environment of Ashmeade, and she longed to see Jess again, but any change made her feel anxious.

'There have been a few changes, Annie. There is a new hospital manager who you will be meeting soon. Her name is Elizabeth Granger. She is well clued-up on your condition. I know she will look after you well.'

'But where's Claudia?' Annie asked. She feared that Elizabeth Granger sounded rather formidable.

'Don't worry yourself about Claudia, I'm sure Elizabeth will take good care of you.'

Later that day, Annie was transferred by ambulance to the familiar confines of Ashmeade. She was greeted with a firm handshake and a bright smile by Miss Elizabeth Granger. 'Annie, welcome back to Ashmeade! I am Miss Granger, but I'm happy for you to call me Elizabeth. I've been looking forward to meeting you.' She put her hand lightly on Annie's shoulder. 'Let's go and settle you in and we'll talk later.'

Elizabeth was more friendly than Annie had imagined, but there was something about her demeanour that gave Annie the feeling that she would not be able to pull the wool over her eyes, as she had with Claudia.

Looking across at Jess's empty bed, her collection of art stuck haphazardly on the wall and her colourful mat rucked up in a heap, she longed to see her friend. 'Where's Jess? Can I see her?'

'I'm afraid not. Jessica is receiving therapy and may not be back in the dormitory for a while.'

'Please can I see her?' Annie pleaded. She felt a gnawing sense of unease.

'We need to focus on you Annie, and you have arrived just in time for supper,' Elizabeth said firmly.

The thought of eating anything brought with it a feeling of nausea but Annie knew she had to try. Elizabeth had helped her into a semi-reclining position in the newly made bed, making it possible for Annie to eat. She reluctantly opened her mouth and the thick, smooth liquid trickled down her throat. She could feel the warmth and comfort of the soup permeating through her starving body. Elizabeth fed her slowly and with care; she was able to accept small amounts of the liquid but most of it was regurgitated into the bowl placed beside her.

'I need to see my friend, I must see Jess.'

'We cleared the dormitory to give you the time and space to begin to recover from your ordeal. Jessica is in good hands.'

Annie felt too weak to argue as she sunk into a troubled state of semi-consciousness. Night and day seemed to roll into one. The nights were the worst; with the darkness came her terrifying nightmare. She would wake with a jolt, bathed in sweat.

Her face was covered by a beaded mask; her long white hair flowed behind her. She wore a long black dress trimmed with intricate lace and gold braid. With the full force of her whole body, she cracked the whip again and again over Annie's limp and dying body.

The days passed in grey silence until one day she woke up and felt a little more alert. She lay still for a while, too frightened to move. She looked down at her body shrouded in a thin crocheted blanket and noticed that her right toe was twitching, making the bed clothes lift almost imperceptibly. Annie slowly peeled the covering away, and stared with horror at her emaciated body. She was deeply shocked by what she saw.

What have I done? I have nearly starved myself to death, I may die. How can I let Jess see me like this? I'm terrified about seeing the finished painting, and yet I long to see it. I long to see my wonderful, creative, crazy friend; to hold her close and never let her go, and yet I am ashamed of my body. I am ashamed of me.

A week had passed when Elizabeth gave Annie the welcome news that she was well enough to see her friend.

'Jess, my beautiful Jess, I've been longing to see you.'

Jess looked forlorn, her cheeks were streaked with tears.

She walked slowly towards Annie, her shoulders rounded; her eyes steadfastly fixed on the ground. She looked pale and sullen.

'Oh Jess, say something, hold my hand,' implored Annie. 'Tell me what's wrong.'

'Annie, I'm so sorry for everything,' said Jess. Her face was contorted with shame, twisted with guilt. 'I don't know where to begin.'

The atmosphere was tense. This was not what Annie had hoped or expected.

'I felt very jealous of the time you were spending with Dee,' Jess said sadly. 'I didn't know what she was capable of, or I would have been there to protect you. I'm so sorry, I wish I'd been there. I've let you down so badly.'

'But you're not to blame Jess, something went wrong with Dee's medication, nobody could predict what she would do, not even Claudia. Dee was unstable.'

'But there was always something that worried me about you spending so much time with her, I needed to protect you... and I wanted you all for myself.' Jess wrung her hands together. 'But, how are you? I can't begin to tell you how worried I've been.' She clenched her hand into a fist and nervously bit her thumb nail.

'Don't worry about me, I'm okay now. Dee hit me on the head and I can't remember much after that, except that they put a tube up my nostril and forced food into me. Jess I had no control, I had no choice; it was simply horrible.'

'Do you feel stronger now?' Jess asked.

Annie felt unnerved by her question. 'Yes, I guess...' she stammered.

'Then it was good that they took the decision out of your hands wasn't it? Annie, I can't confess to understanding your illness, or why you want to starve yourself,' she acknowledged, 'but I'm glad they gave your body some food, because you are too thin. The doctors and nurses probably saved your life.' She paused. 'I love you - all of you - but you need to eat to live.'

The poignancy of the words were hard for Annie to assimilate; she fell silent, lost in thought.

'Annie, I've not been good for you in so many ways. I'm different: I'm wild and impetuous, but *you*; you are strong and wise. I've led you into the darkness. I goaded you into cutting yourself. I now realise it's just a brief relief from the deep pain in our lives - just a short-term fix.' Jess looked over towards her own bed and folded her arms resolutely. 'I suppose it's a bit like using sticky tape to fix my paintings to the wall: it works for a short while, then it goes yellow and curls up at the edges, and then eventually it stops working altogether and the paintings fall to the floor. Look at the dirty marks the tape has left on the wall.' Jess rolled up one sleeve to reveal her damaged arm. 'These scars will never leave me. They're a tragic map of my life: a permanent reminder of my sadness and pain, they will stay with me forever. Harming ourselves is not an answer to anything. I was wrong, Annie. Please forgive me. And promise me that you'll never do it again, please…'

'But Jess…'

'Just promise me…'

Annie calmly nodded her head, knowing that she would try her best, but that she might not succeed.

'And I guess the dope-smoking wasn't a great plan either.' She looked at Annie with the familiar dark glint in her eye. 'But we did have a lot of fun, didn't we?'

'And we will again,' Annie said. She felt a growing sense of unease.

Jess hid her face in her hands. 'I'm no good for you. You deserve so much more.'

She felt a heavy ball of sickness welling up in the pit of her stomach. 'But Jess, I don't want anyone else. I want you.'

'We've had a wonderful time.' Gazing at Annie intently, she reached out and took her hand. 'I'll cherish our time together. I'll cherish the memories forever.'

'Stop talking like it's all over,' Annie implored. 'I love you as high as the sky, and to the moon and back. I'll love you until the last breath leaves my body.'

'I love you too, as deep as the ocean and high as the heavens above. In the darkness we saw the stars Annie. I'll be in your heart forever and you'll be in mine.'

A warm beam of sunlight shone in through the high window of the dormitory, but a cold shiver ran through Annie's body. 'When can I see the painting?'

'Ah yes, *The Unfinished Symphony of Love…*' Jess said distantly.

'But it'll be finished soon.' Annie clamped Jess's hands in her own.

'We were always meant to be, Annie.'

Jess gently brushed the hair away from Annie's face and gave her a long and heartfelt kiss, and then she walked slowly towards the door. Just as she was about to disappear, she paused to gaze once again at Annie, and, with a broad grin and a lopsided dimple, she purred, 'You sure put a spell on me, you foxy lady.'

CHAPTER 41

Annie tossed and turned all night following her meeting with Jess. She sensed that something was very wrong. Jess had made everything sound as if she was leaving, but why? And where?

Early the next morning she asked to see Elizabeth.

'Where is she? Where is Jess? Please tell me.'

'Annie, I want you to stop worrying about other people. Just focus on getting yourself stronger.'

Annie sensed that Elizabeth was not being honest with her. 'I need to see Jess now,' she said, through clenched teeth.

Elizabeth averted her eyes and said nothing.

'Please can I see her?' she implored. 'She'll help me to feel stronger. I need her.'

'I'll be back in a moment.' She turned away from Annie, her footsteps echoing in the empty dormitory.

A few minutes later Elizabeth returned with Patrice. 'Annie, we have some very sad news for you.'

Annie's heart pounded in her chest. She hardly dared to look at the two women in front of her.

'Jess died this morning. There was nothing anyone could do.' Patrice shook her head sorrowfully. 'I'm sorry, Annie. I know Jess was a good friend to you.'

Annie sat bolt upright. Her hand shot to her mouth in

horror. It was as if she had been dealt a blow to her stomach; she felt sick. The room seemed to tip sideways, like a boat lurching on a stormy sea. Jess wouldn't leave her. She couldn't leave her. 'No, this can't be right, I saw her yesterday. Tell me it's not true.'

'I wish I could. I so wish I could,' Patrice said.

'She wouldn't leave me. Jess loves me.' She felt as if her limbs had been ripped from her torso. Life was over.

Elizabeth gazed out of the window, unable to meet Annie's eyes. 'We found her in a beautiful part of the garden near the brick wall under the climbing rose. She was lying on the lawn.' Looking directly at her now, she added kindly, 'She looked at peace, Annie.'

Our special place...

Annie turned to Patrice. 'But how did she die?'

'She used a knife to cut her wrists. She lost a lot of blood, but we don't yet know the exact cause of her death.'

'So do you think she meant to die?'

Patrice sighed. 'Yes, I'm afraid it does appear that she took her own life, Annie.'

My Jess has gone forever. How could she leave me? How dare she do this to me? Killing herself is the easy way out, the coward's way out. She didn't care about me or anyone. I'm furious with her and even more furious with myself. How could I put my trust in her when she deserts me in this way, with no explanation? Nothing, nothing, nothing...

Annie shook her head. 'This can't be happening. How could she do this to me?'

Elizabeth reached across to the trolley beside her, poured a glass of water from the jug, and handed Annie two tablets. 'Take these, I think you should sleep now.'

Annie frantically drew her fingers through her hair. 'I should have seen this coming. I should have known.' She let out a desperate cry. 'I wasn't here when she needed me the most. Oh God, it's my fault.'

'We will talk about this Annie, but it is important that you realise that none of this your fault. Jess was concerned about how fragile you had become…' She gazed at Annie sadly. 'But this was just one of many things that had been building in Jess's life which led her into turmoil. It will always hurt: you have lost a dear friend, but I promise you that with every day that passes, it will get easier. You will find some peace and acceptance.' She gently stroked the side of Annie's arm. 'But, for now, I would like you to take the medication, and allow yourself to sleep.'

'I will never forgive myself.'

As Annie began to drift into a deep sleep, she breathed in a familiar musky aroma and felt a warm and comforting hand in hers. 'Oh my darlin' I'm here now and I promise I won't leave your side until you wake up.'

'Joy, please tell me that Jess is still alive. I love her and I need her to be here with me.' Her eyes started to flicker; her words faded away.

'I'm not sure if you can hear me, but my dearest mother used to read me the twenty-third psalm: "The Lord is my shepherd" when I felt sad or lonely. The words always comforted me.' She squeezed Annie's hand gently. 'I understand that you may not share my belief in the Lord my darlin' but, if you can hear me, I hope the sentiments might bring some comfort to you, too.' As she recited the words of the bible in a low soothing voice, Annie felt an overwhelming sense of tranquillity and peace wash over her.

Joy kept her vigil by Annie's bedside during the dark and timeless hours that followed. Annie seemed to be suspended in a twilight zone of semi-consciousness - at times peaceful, and then crying out in pain and anguish. Joy mopped her brow as Annie flailed her arms in the air around her. Nothing would or could erase Annie's pain.

I long for us to be together again. Oh Lord, please help me. But wait, there must be a way. I could go to the special place in the garden where Jess lay down, and I could make the same deep and fatal cut. It would be easy. Yes, I could do that. Wait for me, my darling… we can hold hands for eternity. Jess, wait for me…

Annie felt a gentle warmth on her face as sunlight filtered

through the window; a new day had dawned. As she opened her eyes, she was hit once again by the realisation of Jess's death. As she peered upwards she became aware of a warm presence beside her.

'My darlin', it feels so good to have you back in the land of the living.' Joy smiled compassionately. 'You have suffered so much but you are safe now.'

'I loved her, and she is gone forever. How can I live without her?' She buried her head deep in the pillow.

'When my husband was taken from me, my world was ripped apart, I couldn't imagine living a single day without him. Oh how I grieved for him Annie, my heart ached to have him back in my arms.' She paused, gazing at the small pale girl lying in the bed. 'But with every day that passed, I found the strength and the will to live my darlin'. Life is so very precious...'

'I feel empty and incomplete without Jess.'

'It is my belief that Jess will never leave your side, Annie. You may not be able to see her, but her spirit will always be with you. You have been parted by death,' she acknowledged, 'but one day, you will be reunited with Jess, and until that time comes, I believe that she would want you to lead a full and wonderful life. You will find the strength you need, I know you will.'

As Annie listened to Joy's wise and comforting words, she resolutely framed her thoughts:

I must face the new day with courage and conviction. I must stay awake to reality rather than escape from it. I feel angry that Jess has abandoned me in this way, but I am determined to survive: despite all the hurt; the abandonment; the betrayals.

I will make it, even if I have to make it alone.

CHAPTER 42

The Letter

The embers of an early autumnal bonfire smouldered red and grey in the garden by the old brick wall. Annie lay still and breathed in a hint of sweet applewood smoke drifting in through the open window; she felt strangely calm. The light was fading and Joy had fallen asleep in the chair next to her bed. There was a chill in the air and, as she pulled the bedclothes higher round her chin, she noticed something protruding from under the mattress. She reached over and pulled out a single folded sheet of paper. She unfolded it carefully and read the words on the page:

My darling Annie,

By now you will know that I am no longer with you on this earth. I am sorry my darling, I have let you down very badly. I hope that when you have read my letter, you will understand why it had to be this way. I am still very much with you in spirit.

I didn't want to leave you Annie. You are strong and courageous, you brought out the very best in me. With you I could be the wild artist; I felt truly inspired. With you I learned to love and accept love. With you I could be myself. Thank you Annie. You gave me laughter and joy, we were meant to be together.

I can almost hear you asking, so why leave me now? I was not strong like you. I could never accept help and always pushed people away who tried to get close to me. I have been in and out of hospital for most of my life and I feel certain that I could never survive in the real world; I was terrified of leaving Ashmeade. And what I am about to tell you might come as a shock Annie. I have taken drugs for years - hard drugs - to escape the harsh reality of my life, but in the end they didn't work, they just numbed and addled my brain. I didn't know what love was until I met you. But love terrified me. You are special, wise and strong, you deserve so much more than I could ever offer you. I guess Earth was always just a part of my tour, just like Jimi Hendrix. (Keep playing his music Annie, he is pure genius.) I am now free to explore the universe. I am no longer limited by my earthly body. "Dust to dust, ashes to ashes." I am truly sorry Annie.

Look into the sky and I will be there: I will be the brightest star shining down on the earth; I will be a grain of sand on the moon as it casts its light in the darkness. I will be the brightness of the sun shedding warmth on you; I will be the wind in your hair and the rain on your body. I will share every breath you take. We will walk through life together. Because you, Annie, are the love of my life.

Listen to me, I should be a poet as well as an artist! It sounds rather slushy but Annie, I mean every word.

Now I have a few things I would like you to do for me.

Confide in someone about your suffering and pain my darling Annie. Share with someone how your father made you suffer over the years, how he has abused you. Let the words out, don't hold the agony any longer. It will be then, and only then, that your healing can begin.

Learn to love yourself Annie. Your father has made you feel ashamed of who you are, and I believe this is why you loathe yourself and why you punish yourself by not eating. I see strength in you, and a rich and fulfilling life ahead. Believe in yourself, I have such hope for your future. Even though you feel self-conscious and ashamed of your body, you did agree to pose for the picture which showed great courage. Even though you feel despair, you have your music which brings you such joy and passion; it is this joy and passion that will get you through life. So Annie, eat good food and play beautiful music; they will nourish your body and soul and will give you the strength to lead a full and happy life, because you deserve it, Annie.

Accept the painting as a gift from me to you. I do hope you like it.

It was hard to do you justice; you really were the perfect model. As I painted you, I felt deep sadness that you were so thin, so frail, I wanted to help you to get better. But what struck me the most was just how much your extraordinary inner beauty shone through from deep within. I hope I have managed to capture this on the canvas. Do with it as you will, and think of me. The title of the painting is just right: The Unfinished Symphony of Love. I nearly finished it, Annie.

Now go and listen to the beautiful melody of "Little Wing." I believe that Jimi was thinking about an ideal woman (you) and a guardian angel (me) when he wrote it.

I can't deny that I am scared of dying my darling, but maybe, just maybe, I'll see some of my heroes amongst the stars for the wildest party! Jimi, the king of guitar, and Janis Joplin singing the heavenly blues; can you imagine the band? Perhaps Coco Chanel will be there to give me a few fashion tips. She once said, "Dress shabbily and they remember the dress; dress impeccably and they remember the woman." I wonder if she'll like my baseball boots? Please remember the strong women in history. Perhaps I'll meet Florence Nightingale, Emmeline Pankhurst, Jane Austen and so many more… What a party it will be!

Search for the biggest shiniest star, and I will be there waiting for you my darling.

Thank you for the memories.
Your friend forever,
Jess.

PS Just remember you are a strong woman, and a very foxy lady.

Annie read the words on the page over and over again:

Jess, you are the love of my life; my strong, crazy, creative friend. You had so much to offer, amazing talent, sensitivity, fun, incredible knowledge, and so much love to give. You are far too young to die. But life dealt you a poor hand my darling, you had too many struggles to face in your short life, too much hardship. You were damaged by life: damaged by circumstances, damaged by drugs; your thoughts were clouded, you just couldn't find a way to survive. I wish I could have saved you Jess, we would have found happiness together, but I understand. I'm heart-broken, but I now understand. Thank you my friend, I feel truly honoured to have known you.

She folded the precious letter and placed it carefully inside the front cover of her journal. She knew what she had to do.

CHAPTER 43

'Please can I see Patrice?'

'Of course Annie,' said Elizabeth, 'I'll go and ask her now.'

As she waited, Annie thought about Jess's wise words: she must tell the truth about Stan; it wouldn't be easy, but the time was right. Within minutes Elizabeth returned with the good news that Patrice was free to see her. She leant on Elizabeth's arm for support and, together, they slowly walked along the dimly-lit corridor.

Patrice welcomed her into the consultation room. 'Annie, I'm pleased to see you. Come and sit down. How are you feeling this morning?' she asked softly.

'I think I'm still in shock Patrice, I can't believe what's happened.' Annie rounded her shoulders, her eyes fixed on the sculpture standing in the centre of the room.

'Take as much time as you need, I'm here for you.' Patrice repositioned the tissues on the coffee table between them and put her head on one side. 'Tell me what's on your mind.'

Hush little baby don't say a word.

'There's something important I need to share with you.' Annie spoke her words with grim determination.

Sensing that Annie was on the verge of disclosing what was at the heart of her suffering, Patrice gently encouraged her to speak. 'I'm here for you Annie. I'm listening...'

'It will be painful for me to talk about this, but I must,' she said quietly.

Patrice sat calmly with her hands on her lap, giving Annie her full attention, conveying an air of patience and compassion for the deeply vulnerable woman in front of her. 'I wonder if this is about your father, Annie. Is it about Stan?'

'Yes, it is.' Sobs rose from deep within her and tears flowed freely down her cheeks.

As Annie told her story, her whole body and mind recoiled with deeply embedded pain and anguish. The horrific memories that she held in her head of that fateful Christmas day all those years ago, when she was a nine-year-old child, plagued her every day; every waking moment.

She recalled the single Christmas gift that Mutti had given her: a china doll called Greta that she had vowed to love. But Greta reminded her of Mutti; the cold fixed stare of an inanimate object; the lack of emotion and love. Detachment.

We are broken.

She recounted the story of the tiny homeless woman that she had met in a doorway on that freezing cold Christmas day. She described Nessy's pride and courage; her remarkable story of survival. Annie portrayed an image of a deserted town centre in winter; the single toll of the church bell; the solitude and desperation of homelessness, set against the cruel backdrop of a traditional family Christmas. Nessy was starving; she needed food and warmth; she wanted to give this strong woman comfort on a special day. But Annie knew she was dicing with danger when she invited Nessy to her home for some much needed nourishment.

Annie, now deeply immersed in her story, pulled her emaciated frame to full height as she recalled her joy of watching this proud lady eating simple fare - chicken and potatoes - with such relish; she savoured every morsel. But why should this only happen at Christmas? Life can be so cruel; so unfair. All Annie wanted to do was to make everything better. 'Was I so very wrong?' She described with wonder, the extraordinary bravery of Nessy: how she had confronted Stan; her tiny bent figure face-to-face with an overpowering brute. Her father. Stan.

Patrice remained still and silent, listening intently as the story unfolded.

Annie's face contorted with pain as she told of how Stan degraded Nessy, calling her, "a sorry excuse for a person." She flinched, as she recalled the terror of his outstretched hand sweeping down towards her face; of screwing up her eyes instinctively; of how the hot stinging pain overwhelmed her. She described the fearsome arguments that raged between her parents, as she lay upstairs in bed. As a young child, she truly believed that it was all her fault; the heavy burden of guilt gnawing away at her.

But the true horror was still to be told. The deafening silence; the creak on the fourth stair; his evil presence; she must dance with the devil. Her body braced for the inevitable, waiting for another crushing blow; she thought she deserved that; as a nine-year-old, she believed that she had done wrong.

Annie's breath became laboured; her chest concave, as she told of how she clung to Greta for meagre comfort, but the doll was hard. Cold. Unyielding.

But what happened next was unimaginable. Unthinkable.

'His body crushed me. I couldn't breathe. I tried to scream but I couldn't utter a sound. I thought I was going to die. The sudden pain was unbearable. He ripped my body apart.' Annie clenched her fists, her eyes boring into the eyes of her therapist. 'Make it stop, make it go away.' Annie let out a mournful wail of agony and grief. 'He took away my innocence. He robbed me of my childhood. He destroyed me.' She dug her nails deep into her flesh; the blood and tears mingled together to cut deep tracks down one side of her face.

'He raped me. I was only nine years old. Stan raped me.'
The damage is done.

The words hit her like a sharp blow to the stomach. She struggled to catch her breath. Her body stiffened with the stark realisation of what he had done. The tension in the room was palpable; neither person uttered a word. The true horror of what had happened to Annie confirmed Patrice's suspicions. Now she understood.

Her words tumbled out, as Annie described her feelings after that fateful Christmas day.

At first, she felt numb. She felt nothing; nothing at all. It felt safer that way. She constantly strived to block the horror from her mind, but the nightmare always returned to haunt her. Like a blood stain on a white sheet, it was impossible to erase.

She described her confusion and bewilderment; all the contradictions. He was her father. Wasn't he supposed to love and protect her? But instead, he violated her; he invaded her body. As a young child she questioned, 'Isn't that what daddy's do?' She feared him; she loathed him; and yet she craved his love. He told her that he loved her - she believed him - but then he hurt her. He damaged her.

As a nine-year-old, she had no words and nobody to talk to. She was silent.

But then the cumbersome burden of guilt started to gnaw at her, like a wasp on a rotten apple. She blamed herself for what her father had done. She turned her anger inwards, directing her hatred towards herself. She quickly discovered that she could control her own self-destruction, when everything else was out of control. She relentlessly punished herself for the sins of her father.

'But it didn't stop there, it wasn't just once. The agony continued for years.' Annie told of how she constantly scrubbed herself after every attack; over and over again until she bled. 'The filth never leaves my body. It will be with me forever.' She looked directly at Patrice through the mist of her tears. 'I thought I loved him. But I hate him. He has tainted me and damaged me forever. He has ruined my life.'

How could he have done this to me?

Annie shakily rose to her feet. Patrice gently held her hand. 'It's all right, there's no need to say another word.'

Annie felt a wave of relief wash over her body. She had at last shared her secret.

The silence is broken forever.

'You are very brave Annie,' said Patrice. She gazed at the exhausted figure in front of her: a fragile young woman who had finally found her courage, her strength and her voice. 'I need you to understand Annie, that I will have to report this to the Authorities. Your father sexually abused you, and he has to be held to account for his actions.'

She nodded meekly.

'What you have told me are some of the most courageous words you will ever utter.'

CHAPTER 44

The early morning sun streamed through the window and a slight breeze ruffled the curtains. Annie sat up in bed and looked round the empty dormitory. She had noticed that Elizabeth made less regular visits now that Annie was physically a little stronger, but this gave her longer periods to feel lonely and to think. Two days had passed since her last meeting with Patrice. She felt some relief having opened up to her, but she was fearful and anxious about the future. Her thoughts were interrupted by Joy who walked quietly towards her and leant over to give her a gentle peck on the cheek. 'My dear girl.' Annie was surprised by how different Joy looked. She wore a dark green and brown striped pinafore dress, no stockings and low-heeled shoes and there was deep sorrow in her eyes. 'You poor sweet girl, I know what that evil man did to you over the years. I can't even begin to tell you how sorry I am honey. What he did was unforgivable and you suffered in silence for so long, my poor lamb.'

Annie looked nervously at Joy, wondering what she would say next.

'Well, my darlin', two burly police officers came and they took him away. He said nothin', nothin' at all, he just walked meekly to the car. He didn't even look back. He knew he'd done wrong, Annie.'

Annie hung her head and listened in silence.

'He's in custody until he finds out his fate. He's lost his job at the school and people say he will be inside for a very long time. Word gets out quickly and he is hated in the town, I can tell you. He deserves it, he deserves to be punished.'

Annie had never seen Joy looking as serious and subdued.

'But Annie, I'm here for you,' she said softly.

Annie's stomach twisted into a tight knot. 'Everyone knows. I feel so ashamed...'

'But honey, you were the innocent victim. Stan abused you for years, he has to be punished. Darlin' I just wish I could have done more to help you.' She paused, looking intently at Annie. 'Did you ever worry that you might be pregnant?'

The horror of what might have been, suddenly dawned on Annie. 'It never even occurred to me. I've been very naïve.' She lapsed into silence as she thought about the enormity of Joy's question; her mind in turmoil. 'And what about Mutti? Where is she? Does she know about what has happened?' Annie asked nervously.

'Mutti is still in hospital. She is in good hands. I'm sure she'll be told what has happened in the fullness of time, but what matters now, Annie, is *you*.'

'But I have to see her now. I need to understand why she wasn't there for me. Why didn't she protect me?' Annie's anger welled in her throat as if it would choke her. 'She knew what Stan did to me. Why didn't she stop him years ago? She did nothing.' She put her head in her hands. 'I don't understand my own feelings, I feel angry and betrayed, and yet I love her. How will I ever make sense of it all?'

Joy paused, reflecting on the importance of Annie's words, and realised she must meet with Patrice urgently. But, for now, she needed to reassure Annie. 'It will take time, but I promise you my darlin' you will get through this, every day you will feel stronger.' She took a deep breath and smiled sympathetically. 'And in the meantime, I'll do everything I can to help you to get better, and I'll give you a few smiles along the way.' She paused, looking earnestly at the tiny damaged girl beside her. 'I can see those painful bruises and cuts on the side of your face, Dee really hurt you. She's obviously very ill, poor girl.'

'She attacked me,' Annie wailed.

'Hush my darlin',' Joy said gently, 'you are safe now.'

'Where is she now?'

'Dee is in a place of safety and I hope she's getting the help and support she needs to get better. I'm sure she didn't mean to hurt you, she has demons in her head. Find it in your heart to forgive her, Annie. It sounds like she had some kind of crisis; she didn't know what she was doing.'

Demons in her head. She is right, Dee is ill like me.

'I will try,' she muttered. 'It will take time, but I will forgive her. But it will take longer for me to forget.'

'Tell me about your friend Jess? I'm so sorry to hear what happened to her.'

'I can't Joy, it hurts too much.' Annie curled up into a tight ball.

'Don't worry my darlin', we'll have plenty of time together to remember your special friend,' she said, gently stroking Annie's rounded back. 'I've brought you something.' She rummaged in her bag and pulled out a generous bunch of pink and red tulips. 'We need to brighten up this dormitory. I thought these would look mighty pretty on the table. What do you think?'

Annie stared forlornly at the bed where Jess had lain. All her paintings and colourful possessions had been removed and the bed was stripped bare, leaving only the green plastic-covered mattress. It looked empty, cold and clinical. 'Thank you, I think they may help.'

'Do you remember when I told you about my early life in Jamaica? I was brought up to believe that I was a "somebody." I knew I was special and unique. You, Annie, are special and unique, too. I know you are capable of great things. Now all you have to do is believe it.' She spoke with passion and kindness. 'I must be going. I've got things to do. I need to catch Elizabeth and Joe to discuss one or two things. Bye-bye Annie, I'll be back soon.'

Annie was left wondering why Joy needed to speak with Elizabeth and Joe.

Joy's presence always lingered in the room long after she had left. Even in times of grief, she spread hope and optimism, and Annie couldn't help but love her.

Later that evening Annie was left with some dark thoughts. She had very mixed feelings about exposing Stan and she was worried about his welfare. She couldn't believe that after everything he had done, she still worried about him. Had she done the right thing? She read Jess's letter again and she knew.

Thank you my friend.

She felt a sudden and unexpected warm glow spread throughout her body and she smiled.

Jess, your body is no longer here but your spirit is deep within me.

***

'I ate a shortbread biscuit with my coffee today, Patrice. Okay, the coffee was black, but I ate a whole biscuit!'

Since Jess's death, Patrice had noticed that, although Annie was sad beyond measure, she seemed to be gaining strength and determination. 'Oh, I love shortbread biscuits, but ginger biscuits are better for dunking Annie!'

They both giggled.

'Okay, I'll try a ginger biscuit next time.' She licked her lips. 'Or maybe even a flapjack!'

'How are you feeling today, Annie?'

The atmosphere changed in an instant. 'Stan consumes my head every waking moment. I see him, I hear him, I feel him. I can smell the stench of his breath. He is always there.' She pulled loose strands of hair roughly away from her face.

'Annie, it will feel very raw at the moment, but you made a real breakthrough by sharing what has happened to you over the years, and now you are truly on the road to recovery.'

'I don't understand my own feelings. I hate him for what he has done.' She hesitated. 'But there is a small part of me that feels sorry for him. He's lost his teaching job and he's in a prison cell. Everyone knows. People where we live will hate him, and I feel ashamed. I was never the daughter that he wanted - I wonder if he even wanted me at all, he hated children. Perhaps if I'd been a boy he'd have loved me more?'

Patrice shook her head. 'Annie, it's abhorrent what he put you through over the years. There is no excuse for child abuse and incest, because that is what it was. He sexually abused his own daughter for years.' She looked searchingly into Annie's eyes. 'And Mutti? Was she aware of what was happening?'

Annie slumped in her chair and bowed her head. 'Yes, she was. She saw us, and she did nothing.' The silence of unsaid words hung in the air between them.

'I do understand the anger and hurt you must feel, knowing that Mutti witnessed everything, and yet she didn't protect you.' She stroked her chin, deep in thought. 'I can't imagine how any mother could stand back and let this happen. But she has been mentally ill for most of your childhood. Her brain has been damaged. I don't believe she was able to think rationally, otherwise she would have stepped in to help you.' She paused. 'Annie, from everything you've told me about Mutti, I feel sure that she loves you.'

' I do believe that, deep down, she loves me, and this brings me some comfort.'

'I'm glad to hear this. It is good to take something positive from this whole experience. We will be continuing our meetings for some time to come, to help you make some sense of everything that has happened to you, and to find some kind of peace and acceptance.'

'I understand, and I'm ready to accept help.' She set her chin determinedly. 'I want to get better.'

'And you will get better,' Patrice said reassuringly, 'but it will take time and patience.' She paused. 'I know that you must feel very shocked and saddened about the death of your friend.'

'I feel numb,' Annie replied, 'it feels like we have been torn apart. I don't understand why she did it, she had so much to live for.' The tears streamed down her face. 'I loved her Patrice, I truly loved her.'

Patrice leant forward. 'What I am going to say is going to be hard for you to hear, but it is important that I tell you that during the post-mortem, drugs were found in her system. Jess died from a drug overdose.'

'But how…?'

'There are many questions to be answered, but, for now, I would like us to focus on *you* and your feelings.'

'Jess was the most loving, amazing and talented person I've ever met. She had a hard upbringing and, in many ways, she was too good for this world. I'm absolutely bereft without her.' Annie took a deep breath. 'She thought that she hadn't been good for me and that she'd led me into the darkness of her life.'

'What did she mean by that?' Patrice probed gently.

Annie slowly pulled up both sleeves of her jumper to reveal the tight patchwork of scars on her emaciated arms. 'I promised Jess that I'd never do this again.'

Patrice leant forward to look at her arms, and Annie registered a flicker of shock in her eyes. 'You know Jess was right. This isn't the answer, Annie.'

'I know, and I'm ashamed, but it helped me at the time. The physical pain distracted me from everything else going on in my life. It was something that I could control.'

'It's important that we discuss this further, but I have faith that you'll keep the promise that you made to Jess.'

'I will.'

'What else did Jess say?'

'She thought that she'd let me down by not protecting me from Dee, but that was so far from the truth. Jess saved me from myself.' Annie reached for the tissues. 'I feel so lucky that Jess has been part of my life. She's taught me how to love. I can't believe I'll never see her again. I loved her deeply and I'll continue to love her for the rest of my life.'

'Grasp that wonderful feeling of being in love with both hands Annie…'

'But Patrice, I thought that I would love a boy, I still feel confused.' She paused. 'But I loved a girl, I still do. I love Jess with all my heart.'

'Annie, genuine love between two people is precious and priceless. My belief is that it really doesn't matter what sex you both are, it is the deep love and connection between you that is important. From what you tell me, you and Jess, in the short time you had known each other, had found that special and precious love. You are fortunate, because some people go through life and never experience true love. It probably won't be much comfort to you now, but in the wise words of a poet called Alfred Tennyson: "Tis better to have loved and lost than never to have loved at all." '

Annie considered the wise words as they sat in silence.

'And Annie, what are your feelings about Dee?' Patrice asked quietly.

'I have terrifying visions of Dee towering over me in a black intricate lace dress and torturing me with a whip. But when she took off her mask,' she said, putting a hand on her troubled brow, 'it was *him* Patrice, it was Stan. He is my true tormentor.'

Patrice shuffled uncomfortably in her chair. 'I'm sorry that Dee attacked you, it should not have happened to you here in Ashmeade. Questions will be raised about this in the investigation. Patients with schizophrenia sometimes direct aggression towards themselves, but Annie, they very rarely hurt other people.' She paused looking directly at Annie. 'But this is no excuse, staff should have been closely monitoring the situation.' Her face softened and she added reassuringly, 'Dee is no longer here, you are safe now.'

'Please don't let Claudia get into trouble. She worked so hard to look after us and she was called to an incident that was beyond her control. I'd hate her to be punished.'

'I hear what you say, Annie. You really are a kind and compassionate person.'

'Dee is ill, just like me. She needs help and support to get better, just like me. I'm sure she didn't mean to harm me. Joy helped me to understand this.'

'Ah yes, Joy, she seems to be a wonderful, lively person.' It had been a very intense session and Patrice added on a lighter note, 'And by the way, she has some great plans afoot!'

Oh no, what is she up to?

'Joy's unlike anyone I've ever met before. She manages to see the good in everyone, except Stan. She has no pity for him at all, she thinks he deserves to be punished. But she does care deeply about me and has offered to help me get better and find happiness in my life.'

***

As Annie lay on her bed the next morning, she heard something unusual coming from the sitting room. She opened her eyes and listened more intently. What was it? Still puzzled, she pulled on her jeans and went downstairs and stood just outside the sitting room. She listened to the beautiful lilting sound of Joy singing, and a multitude of people, both staff and patients, starting to join in, hesitantly at first, but then with increasing energy. Transfixed, Annie listened and then peered round the door. A large group of residents had gathered around Joy and, much to her surprise, Joe, the security guard, was sitting beside her, accompanying the tuneful singing on his guitar. Everyone joined in, swaying in time, as they sang a rousing and heart-warming Jamaican calypso.

Annie looked across at Elizabeth and Patrice standing shoulder to shoulder, singing their hearts out, and she beamed from ear to ear. Joy had spread her joy again and brought the heart of Jamaica into this place where so many had come for healing.

CHAPTER 45

'Elizabeth, I have a question for you. Would it be possible for me to keep Jess's artwork that she had on the wall by her bed?'

'Yes, Annie, I can quite understand why you would want to keep a few memento's of your time with Jess. In fact, I think there is quite a collection of Jess's drawings and paintings in the art room as well. I'll check with the next of kin today, but it should be okay. I'll go and collect them for you tomorrow.'

'Can I come with you when you go? I'd like to see the portrait that Jess painted of me. I know it'll be hard, but I feel that I need to see it urgently for some reason. She didn't quite finish it, but I know it will be very special.'

'Of course Annie, we'll go together tomorrow.'

It was early the next morning when Annie stepped out onto the garden. The rising sun cast a rosy hue over the immaculate lawns, and intricate cobwebs hung heavy with dew in the old gnarled apple tree. As she breathed in the fresh autumnal air, she was deep in thought. She longed to see the painting, and yet she felt nervous; she would have to come face-to-face with an image of herself. She reflected how skilfully Jess had encouraged and enabled her to expose her body for the painting by making her feel safe, accepted and loved, despite all her insecurities she had about herself.

She knew she must confront her fear and see the painting. As she wandered through the gardens, she paused at the old, weathered bench to read the inscription on the unpolished aluminium plaque:

"Cherished moments survive the ravages of time."

Now Annie understood. She would treasure her precious, timeless moments with her dear friend forever. Jess was unique and special: she was wild and impetuous, but she was also kind and compassionate. Annie smiled as she thought about their midnight dope-smoking rendezvous in the garden, within a whisker of being caught by old Joe the caretaker. The heartfelt moments when they shared their pain and mingled their blood together promising eternal friendship. With Jess, she had discovered her sensuality, the joy of touch, and the passion of love. In the studio, Jess had skilfully encouraged Annie to reveal her body and her mind by leading her towards acceptance and peace: wonder and enlightenment.

Her reverie was interrupted by Elizabeth waving from the front door. 'Annie, time to go.' They walked together in companionable silence to the art room. As Annie stepped into the studio, everything felt different. The fairy lights were now turned off and instead the sun streamed in through the open window. There was no music playing, instead everything was silent. Jess was not there to greet her with her smiling mischievous look and beguiling ways. But the chaise longue remained just where Jess had positioned it and the easel stood as a centrepiece in the room, covered in a white shroud. As she gazed around sadly at the studio, she slowly began to feel a warm comforting presence rise from deep within her. She felt strong.

Annie took a deep breath and turned to face Elizabeth. 'Could I have some time alone?'

'Of course,' Elizabeth replied. She squeezed Annie's hand gently. 'I'll be back soon.'

Annie walked slowly towards the easel and paused, just for a few seconds, before removing the shroud that protected the painting. She stood back and gasped: the artwork was truly breathtaking. Jess had captured the light in her eyes, the sensuality and fragility of her body, the sadness in her life. She had captured the intangible qualities of tenderness and the powerful and enduring love that they had shared together. She had reproduced every bone, every muscle and every hollow in minute and perfect detail. The dark, shadowy background accentuated the beauty and angelic qualities of the model, and yet she had also captured the vulnerabilities of a young woman suffering from anorexia nervosa. A few brush strokes were left unfinished on her right leg, but strangely it did not detract from the finished portrait. At that moment Annie knew she must get better, for Jess and for herself; she could clearly see the pathway ahead that would lead towards recovery, peace, happiness and fulfilment.

Jess, I thank you with all my heart.

Annie stepped forward to read the words that Jess had written:

The Unfinished Symphony of Love.
A special gift for my dearest Annie.
15 September 1974
Jess Waldron.

Jess knew in her heart that this was always going to be an unfinished symphony. She had always known that this would be a masterpiece.

.

EPILOGUE

19th December 1999

It is nearly Christmas and the building is bustling with busyness and excitement. I have taken a well-deserved break and I am now sitting in the cafe enjoying a steaming latte. I smile as I watch the huge meandering snowflakes drift past my window; it has been snowing for the best part of a week and the world outside is like a magical winter wonderland. Twenty-five years have passed since I was discharged from Ashmeade and two years ago I decided to write an account of my early experiences. I have finally completed all forty-five chapters, but just like my treasured painting, my story is also unfinished.

As I cradle my warm, comforting cup of coffee I catch myself thinking, O*h dear, over three hundred and fifty calories!* I find these thoughts still visit me, but I'm glad to say that my weight has been under control for years. I'm an anorexic in remission, and that's okay.

I sigh with satisfaction as I listen to the velvety voice of Bing Crosby singing "White Christmas." I listen to it every year. It transports me right back to my earliest memories of Christmas through the eyes of a young child, full of hope and anticipation.

But then everything changed. Stan has been at the heart of all my sadness and suffering. He was found in his prison cell, hanging from a beam, the day before he was due to appear in court. I still can't decide whether he was truly remorseful or simply a coward. He left me a short note which said:

"I'm sorry for everything. Love always, Stan."

It has taken years of therapy for me to even begin to understand or accept what happened to me. Stan has damaged me forever, but over the years, I have found the power and the strength to move forward, and to change the course of my life, and I now hold hope in my heart for a bright future.

As for Mutti, she was a beautiful woman and a loving mother in the first years of my life, but, after her brain surgery, she was never the same again. She was ill and vulnerable and suffered for years with depression, and prescription drug and alcohol dependency. It still torments me that, although she was ill, I believe she was aware of the atrocities that were happening at home and she did nothing. The bond between mother and child is strong and I did love her because she was my mother, but I strongly believe she could, and should, have protected me from years of abuse. She finally knew what she needed to do and she was to stand as a vital witness for the prosecution which would have proven Stan's guilt beyond doubt. After Stan's death, Mutti was deeply troubled; she knew she had failed me. She died of a heart attack a month after Stan died. While I was sorting out her possessions following her death, I found a poem which my mother had carefully copied in her spidery handwriting:

Prayer of an Unknown Confederate Soldier
"I asked for strength that I might achieve;
I was made weak that I might learn humbly to obey.
I asked for health that I might do greater things;
I was given infirmity that I might do better things.
I asked for riches that I might be happy;
I was given poverty that I might be wise.

I asked for power that I might have the praise of men;
I was given weakness that I might feel the need of God.
I asked for all things that I might enjoy life;
I was given life that I might enjoy all things.
I got nothing that I had asked for,
But everything that I had hoped for.
Almost despite myself my unspoken prayers were answered;
I am, among all people, most richly blessed."

Much of my mother's life was dominated by sadness and addiction, but the poignant words of the poem give me some comfort and peace.

My prize possession is the mourning brooch which I wear on the left lapel of my jacket. I didn't successfully keep the promises that I made to myself all those years ago, but I believe this was a good thing. Some of the promises I made were damaging for my health, but I have made the decision to wear it proudly in memory of Oma, my dear grandmother.

Harming ourselves did not provide any long-term relief or any solutions; it was a damaging and dangerous short-term distraction in an attempt to escape from the mental agony we were facing in our lives at that time. I have kept my promise to Jess to this day, but I still have the faint scars on my arms reminding me every day of the turmoil and sadness in my life.

Jess was extraordinary: Jess the artist, Jess the creator, Jess the enabler. Jess was the love of my life. A few years after her death, I took the collection of her paintings from the hospital, including *The Unfinished Symphony of Love*, to an established gallery in London. The director of the gallery was very impressed with the quality of her work and suggested that they should set up an art exhibition to celebrate the artwork created by this young artist. It was very popular and people flocked for miles to see the collection. I was the guest of honour at the preview of the exhibition and, as I was admiring the centrepiece, *The Unfinished*

Symphony of Love, holding my glass of champagne, I overheard the comments of a renowned art critic; 'Truly brilliant, this is indeed a masterpiece!'

Jess, I'm so proud of you, but I do feel sad that you are not standing here beside me. I can just picture you wowing the art critics with your cheeky lop-sided grin, and charming them with your beguiling ways, your modesty and your original thoughts. I know you would slip in some tantalising hints about your next art venture and they would be hanging on your every word. I don't know if there is some sort of afterlife, but if there is, I hope you are having a wild party with all your friends somewhere in the universe amongst the stars to celebrate the huge success of your art exhibition. Jimi will be setting fire to his guitar and you may even put a dress on for Coco; I somehow doubt it though!

The morning after the art exhibition in February 1982, I woke up feeling motivated and inspired; I had some exciting ideas running around in my head and I started to formulate a plan. I felt strongly that more funding and resources were needed to adequately support the needs of children and young people with mental health issues, and that I must work tirelessly towards that cause. My ambition was to set up a national academy to celebrate the Arts - music, art and dance - for children of all ages who have mental health challenges. It was an ambitious project and it took me many years to secure government and local funding. I had to fight for every penny and it was a long uphill struggle. But what made it all possible in the end was a generous donation made by an anonymous benefactor. I remember the day well:

One chilly morning in early March 1996, I received an unexpected telephone call from my accountant. Mr Michael Todds was usually a rather crusty and grumpy gentleman but today he seemed unusually cheery. 'Good morning Annie, I hope I find you well?'

'Hello Michael, I'm fine thanks, how are you?'

Michael had surprising news; a huge anonymous donation had been deposited into the project bank account. I listened to his words in amazement and disbelief.

'Did I hear you correctly?' I stammered.

'It's true, literally thousands of pounds have been donated towards setting up the academy.'

As I slowly assimilated the information, I glanced across at my desk over the mounds of never-ending paperwork and there, sitting proudly in the right-hand corner, was an elegant pink, white and fawn conch shell.

I'm sure that wasn't there yesterday.

Beside the shell there was a small, crumpled photo of two people on a beach: a girl and a boy, barefooted, arms interlocked and gazing out towards the horizon. On the back of the photo there was a simple message that read, "From me to you, my Skinny Minnie." Then I knew. Suddenly my dream had become a reality.

I wasted no time. I rented a splendid venue in Brixton and put my ambitious plan into action. I had heard Brixton described as "a backwater of opportunity," and this appealed to me. It was a part of London that wasn't trendy or expensive at the time, and yet could potentially offer exciting and creative possibilities. And of course, David Bowie, one of my favourite musicians, art enthusiasts, a true innovator, was born in Brixton.

***

I am full of anticipation and excitement! It has been three years since I received Tom's generous donation, and eighteen months have passed since the official opening of the Academy. Today I'm making one of my regular 'walk through' visits to see for myself how the centre is progressing. I start my tour outside on the street, reading the words written over the ornate Victorian wooden door:

The Jess Waldron Academy of the Arts.
The Joy of Learning through Music, Art and Dance.
Welcome!

I climb the well-trodden stone steps into the wide entrance hall. The walls are festooned with colourful pieces of art depicting people from all over the world: every race, every creed, every colour. Carefully crafted clay models are displayed on simple wooden benches, some recognisable as people or objects, and some more abstract shapes. Although the artwork and artefacts aren't immaculately arranged, they look alive and vibrant. The displays celebrate the process rather than a perfect end product and I love every single drawing, painting and model.

I quietly open the door of the first studio, which is enticingly named, "The Joy of Dance." The children are moving together rhythmically in time to a striking piece of African drumming music. They are perfectly in sync with each other, one child pushing his friend in a wheelchair and another sitting beside the dance teacher talking excitedly about the dance that the group had just created for themselves. I smile as I reflect on how powerful dance can be as a form of expression. The last time I watched the children dance, they were demonstrating how they were feeling through the movement of their bodies. I will never forget the deeply moving dance of a five-year-old boy, showing all the anguish and grief in his life through his expressive movement and gestures.

'Thank you children. What an amazing dance! Did you really make it up yourselves?' the teacher asks, smiling at the children in front of her. The children nod their heads and jump for joy. The dance teacher looks at the smiling sea of faces in front of her. 'Now then, let's do it again, and this time I'd like to see a few more arm movements. We're lucky to have our wonderful bodies, so let's enjoy them to the full.'

I quietly shut the door, feeling in awe of the children's sheer joy of movement.

I open the door of the adjacent studio, "Brilliant Brushes," and gasp with delight. The room is painted a deep blue and fairy lights are draped over a huge green rubber plant casting a golden glow over the room. Posters of famous artists are arranged thoughtfully around the studio to inspire creativity. I admire *Sunflowers* by Vincent van Gogh, and *The Water-Lily Pond* by Claude Monet, but the most striking picture of all is *Purple Haze* by Jess Waldron. The remaining wall has a colourful and diverse collection of artwork created by the children. As I enter the room, a teenage girl with autism holds my hand tightly and drags me across to the display.

'Look Miss, look up there.' She points to a small unframed pencil drawing of a father with his child. 'Can you see my dad? Can you see Aaron? That's my family and I drew it myself!' I put my hand lightly on her shoulder. 'What a wonderful family you must have, Lizzie. Aaron looks like a real bundle of fun!'

As I glance across the studio, the children are absorbed in their artwork, except one or two who are struggling. I remind myself that every single one of these children has challenges in their young lives and it is a miracle that the large majority of the children are motivated, absorbed and excited to learn. Jess would love it.

As I open the door to the music studio, "Shake, Rattle and Roll," I can hear the festive singing of the "Calypso Carol" being sung with infectious enthusiasm by the smiling group of children. Joy is standing at the front in her bright red and blue floral dress with matching sky-blue high heeled shoes, conducting the choir with energy and passion. Joe is strumming a lively calypso rhythm on his guitar, and a small group of children have gathered round him, enjoying a range of percussion instruments which they shake happily in time to the music. Little Beth on the front row of Joy's choir puffs out her chest and is singing louder and louder as the song progresses, and she helps to make the whole spectacle completely wondrous. Joy is sharing her joy once again.

Every Tuesday afternoon I facilitate "The Hub," in this studio; an informal weekly drop-in record club for teenagers, run by teenagers. The young people and staff bring in records from home and we drink squash, eat healthy nibbles, and listen and dance to a rich and diverse variety of music; from classical to rock, from Zydeco to Indian Sitar, from Schubert to Jemi Hendrix. The lively debate that follows is enjoyed by all and the session has become very popular. The other day I overheard one teenager saying to another, 'The Hub is so cool.' He nodded his head sagely. 'You have to be there, or be square!'

"The Magic of Maths" studio is my creation. This room is planned around the needs of the youngest children. There is a rich variety of open-ended practical and exciting activities laid out for them, sand and water, brick-building, imaginative role play, and games of bingo temptingly arranged for the children to enjoy. Every activity gives opportunities for them to explore the awe and wonder of maths. No one ever told me that maths can be fun! Today the room is a hive of activity. 'Come on, buy me 'nanas, a pound a pound the 'nanas!' I walk over to the young boy who stands behind the large till in the well-stocked role play shop set up in the corner of the studio. His eyes twinkle as I ask for two pounds of bananas. 'Ooooh,' he said without hesitation, 'that'll be two pounds please miss!' I push some imaginary coins into his out-stretched palm, and he throws open the till, hardly able to contain his excitement. I wish that I had been introduced to maths in this way, and I'm very tempted to stay just a little bit longer in this magical studio.

I pop in to see Patrice in her vibrant office, colourfully adorned with a striking collection of artwork reflecting her Ghanaian culture. A simple bronze sculpture entitled; "Together we are strong" is the centrepiece of the room. It depicts five young children, one child in a wheelchair, sitting together in a circle and holding hands. Two comfortable armchairs are placed around a low wooden coffee table. Patrice greets me with a wide smile and welcoming words. She provides an invaluable service for the children and their families.

I return to the refreshment area for a welcome cup of

tea. It has been an incredible tour of the Academy and I feel proud of the staff and the children. My aim is to place value and appropriate status on the Arts as a powerful vehicle for lifelong learning, and today, it feels like this has been achieved. Except I realise that I will have to throw open the doors to the garden for the children to have exciting opportunities to explore the outdoor environment, enjoy messy play and to make dens, but that is for another day. Perhaps I could enlist Claudia to help me.

As I close the old wooden door to the academy, I turn to stare in wonder at the snow-laden trees that majestically line the road that leads to my home. The snow has stopped now and everything is silent and still. I am looking forward to seeing my partner, Martha, who I know will be there to welcome me with open arms. Martha is a perfect match for me; she is a talented musician and plays cello in the local symphony orchestra. Jess was my first love, but Martha is my life partner and my soulmate. I quicken my steps now because it's Martha's birthday today and I plan to prepare a special meal for her.

Some way along the path, I pause to listen to a solitary robin singing tunefully as he perches precariously on the slippery metal bar of the dimly glowing street lamp. I love to hear the sound of a robin singing in winter because it means that he has built up enough fat reserves to survive the ravages of winter, and he has enough energy to defend his territory. As I continue to listen to the profound and hopeful song of the robin, I smile as he fluffs out his feathers proudly to reveal his deep red breast, and I marvel at the resilience of this tiny bird to survive the long winter months and live to see the warmth of a spring day.

I am reminded of how much I have learned in my life. I understand the importance of hope; of courage; of holding a belief that things can be better. Even if unimaginably awful things happen and life is full of despair, it is possible to steer life in another direction; towards peace, happiness and contentment. I have learned about the extraordinary healing power of love. The special love that Jess and I shared, and which I now have with Martha, has given me the strength to make peace with myself, and my body, and to live a happy and fulfilling life. The nurturing and enduring power of love can slowly and gently heal the pain and the suffering.

As I continue to walk along the snowy path, I think about the role that I value above everything else; my weekend night shifts, manning the telephone for an organisation which is there to support children who are suffering. I am proud to be part of a counselling service which can help children with a wide range of issues, such as physical, emotional or sexual abuse, mental illness, eating disorders, bullying, and self-harm. I can draw on my own personal experience in life to listen to and empathise with the agony of a troubled child at the end of the telephone line.

'Hello, my name is Annie. How can I help you?'

***

Mental Health Contact information

If you have been affected by issues raised in this book and need support:

Children and young people affected by mental health issues can find support, information and details about their local NHS mental health services at www.youngminds.org.uk/find-help or call Childline on 0800 1111.

For adults, whether you're concerned about yourself or a loved one, you can find local NHS urgent mental health helplines and a list of mental health charities, organisations and support groups offering expert advice on the NHS website at:

www.nhs.uk/conditions/stress-anxiety-depression/mental-health-helplines/

Or call Samaritans on 116 123.

ABOUT THE AUTHOR

Liz was born and brought up in Oxford. She started learning the violin aged seven, and discovered her love of music. She always enjoyed, and was a talented, acrobatic dancer, winning an All-England Creative Arts competition in her early teens.

She followed a rich and varied career in Education, culminating in an advisory role, working for Oxfordshire Education Authority. She is an advocate for young children, believing in the importance of fostering positive self-esteem in every child, from the earliest age.

During her time with the authority, Liz was a trainer for Early Years practitioners, specialising in the Expressive Arts - music, art and dance - always striving to raise the profile of the Arts as a valid and vital area of life-long learning.

Liz is a musician, and has played her violin and sung in local bands for many years, performing everything from classical to rock-and-roll and folk.

Since her retirement, Liz still enjoys practising her

acrobatic dancing, yoga, skiing and wild swimming. She and her partner spend a lot of time travelling. She finds the beaches of the Riviera, the pine forests of the Médoc, and the solitude of cruising under sail in the West Country, ideal for fostering her creative writing.

She likes nothing more than meeting up with her children and grandchildren, tramping through the forest, singing and dancing, and generally having a whole lot of fun.

Also from **Burton Mayers Books**

Post-pandemic dependence on tech is shattered by the glitch, a cyber-attack, which temporarily knocks out power and communication networks.

Hoping to escape society, securing a peaceful life off grid, Robin is thwarted, becoming stranded in Oxford when an unexpected second glitch strikes.

#Isolate and #FutureProof also out now

In 1977 a New York Cab driver Mike Redolfo is abducted by aliens after being mistaken for a renegade scientist. Meanwhile, back in 1944 a mysterious man and his Jewish fiancée are fleeing across Nazi-occupied Europe.

As the link between the timelines becomes clear, Redolfo must discover secrets from the past that may hold the key to saving the planet.

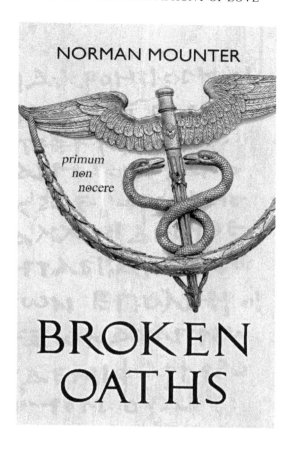

As Eichmann's Final Solution reaches its finale, Doctor Sárkány's attempts to save his career have failed.

On arriving at Auschwitz, can he break his Hippocratic Oath and betray his own people? Dr Mengele thinks that he can.

Available in hardback and paperback

Notes:

Milton Keynes UK
Ingram Content Group UK Ltd.
UKHW040614311023
431653UK00004B/69